To Aidan

Enjoy the adventure!

Lindsay
Schopfer

By Lindsay Schopfer

MAGIC, MYSTERY AND MIRTH

THE BEAST HUNTER

LOST UNDER TWO MOONS

Lost Under Two Moons

Lindsay Schopfer

to Mom and Dad
You were the first to believe in me

CONTENTS

ACKNOWLEDGMENTS

There are many people that I would like to formally thank for helping to make this book a reality.

My Papa Hutchins, for all those times fishing, camping, and just telling stories.

Sean Williams and Sara Huntington, for their edits of the early drafts of this novel and all of their encouragement, feedback, and suggestions.

Michael Thielen, president of Glacier Aviation, for his expert advice regarding small aircraft.

Randall Hodgson and his family, for their friendship and support.

My test readers, for their sacrifice of time and attention to detail.

All of my family and friends, for their faith and enthusiasm.

And finally my wife Elicia, for her unfailing love, support, and willingness to share in my dreams.

PROLOGUE - DOORWAYS

Fifth of Dula, in the second year of The Return
Yurril T'nak

    Today we begin our journey. While fear is never far from our hearts, we are all eager to set sail across the seas of all Creation. Brendell, our Divant and teacher, has told us the time of our departure from our world of Freiisian is near at hand. Soon we will be able to use the Divant's mysterious device to draw upon the powers of Shaelon, thus opening wide for a brief moment all portals that lead to one of the many worlds of the Ancestors. We have prepared ourselves as best we can, though I fear none of us are truly prepared to leave the boundaries of all we know.

    Brendell has explained that because we are as yet unskilled in the opening of the doorways, we will have to open every doorway leading to our destination, the world Alito. Every other world throughout Creation that ever had a passageway to that world will be opened for the moment we pass through. However, we have little worry for the inhabitants of any other worlds possessing these briefly open portals. Each doorway will be open for only a short time, and once we are through they will all shut safely again. Truly this is a blessing of Shaelon, for who could hope to live in such a dangerous world as that which we are about to enter without proper preparation?

    The time for departure has come. I must go.

    Grace be with you. Yurril T'nak

MR. SCREECH

August 25 – Day 1

I'm writing this as a record to anyone who may find this notebook. I don't know where we are or what has happened. It all feels like a dream. A terrible surreal nightmare. I keep trying to tell myself this isn't real. But it is. Everything is horribly real.

My name is Richard Parks. I've written my address and phone number in the front of this notebook so that my family can be contacted if this is ever found.

I don't know where I am. We were flying above the San Juan Islands in the Puget Sound, but I don't think I'm in Washington anymore. Everything's a blur…

I was on a sightseeing flight, writing a travel article for my summer journalism class. The plane took off at ten o'clock this morning. For the first half hour or so, everything was fine. I was talking with Dave, the pilot, when there was a flash of painfully bright light in front of us.

It was as if the gray sky was peeling open like the soft skin of a baked potato to reveal nothing but a searing brightness behind it. Dave swore as he tried to avoid the yawning emptiness, but we were too close. We flew straight on until the light grew so strong that I couldn't see anything else. Then the light disappeared.

I could barely see past the sunspots in my eyes. I heard Dave struggling with his seatbelt as he tried to look back at the tear in the sky through his side window. He got the belt off just as my eyes cleared enough to give me a brief image of strangely colored ground rushing towards us.

The impact was sudden and violent. My body was launched against the restraints of my seatbelt and then rebounded back to thud against my seat. I have no idea how long I sat there stunned. I couldn't believe what had just happened. My mind refused to admit that any of it was real. Eventually, the aching pain in my shoulders and neck roused me from my shock.

Dave doesn't look good at all. He's been out since we crashed. He never got his seat belt back on. He must have been thrown against the console. I'm not sure what I should do. He's got bruising under the eyes and there's a bloody liquid trickling from his nose. Maybe he broke it. I don't think I should move him, but beyond staunching the flow at his nose, I'm not sure what to do until he wakes up.

This landscape is strange… alien. Definitely nowhere near the Puget Sound. We're surrounded by what looks like a barren, desert wasteland. The ground is multi-hued, a wash of purple with swirls of crimson, cinnamon, and pale gold like a sand painting that's run together and lost its form. It's evening now, and the sky is deep purple, with two moons rising over the horizon. There's such an un-earthly beauty to this place that I keep wondering if I'm dead. Then my head starts throbbing again and I doubt it.

I don't know what to do. At first, I was sure that whoever (or whatever) was responsible for wrecking our plane and bringing us here would make themselves known, but it's been four hours since the crash now. It's not that I'm all that eager for anything to show up, but I'm worried for Dave. He needs help, alien or otherwise.

Night's falling. The sky is turning from purple to black, and unfamiliar stars are filling the sky. I'm so tired. I guess I'll try to get some sleep and try looking for help in the morning. Wherever we are, there might be someone who can help us. I just hope they get here in time. I'm worried Dave won't make it through the night.

August 26 – Day 2

Dave died last night. I was up most of the night with him. I kept checking his pulse, listening for his shallow breathing. It was a very long, cold, dark night. Eventually I felt for his pulse, and there was none.

I can't describe how I'm feeling. Detached, drained, nothing sinks in, like this is all happening to someone else. I've been eating the lunch I brought for the trip. Everything tastes like cardboard, but I eat and drink because I know I need to. I'm not sure what I'll do for food and water when my lunch is gone. I guess that doesn't matter if the aliens show up today. If there are any aliens. They're too late for Dave.

I'm alone now. I keep wishing Dave would wake up and somehow explain everything that has happened. I'm starting to wonder if there are even any aliens out there responsible for our… for my being here. I mean, maybe I passed through some kind of dimensional portal, like the one they say is responsible for the Bermuda Triangle. I never believed in those mysterious disappearance stories, but what else could this be?

The sun's starting to come up now. I have to bury Dave, but I don't want to. I wish I didn't have to touch him. I hate this.

* * *

It's done. I used a long paddle I found strapped to one of the plane's floats as a crude shovel. The black ground underneath the colored sand is hard-packed and dense. It took me most of the day to dig a grave deep enough to put Dave… Dave's body into. Carrying him out of the plane was terrible. I've never touched a dead person before. I had to drag him to the grave.

I didn't know what to do once he was in the grave. I'm not very religious. I think Dave may have been Catholic. He was wearing a crucifix under his shirt. Would God understand if he didn't get his last rites? I think so. I said a prayer, my first in a long time, and tried to explain to God about Dave and hoping He understood. I felt a little better after that.

I decided the least I could do was take Dave's personal effects to give to his family… if I ever get home. I took his wallet, watch, pocketknife, and then wondered if I should take his clothes. I wasn't going to -I didn't want to bury him that way- but in the end, I decided I would need them more than he would. I left his crucifix.

* * *

I've examined the damage to the plane. It doesn't look too bad. The floats must have acted like skis and allowed the plane to slide across the relatively flat ground until finally grinding to a halt. We must have come through that… portal a lot closer to the ground than we were on Earth to have made as good a landing as we did.

I can see for miles in each direction. Off to the south there's a line of small mountains or big hills, but I can't tell how far away they are. The desert around me is sprinkled with… things. Bushes? Rocks? I'm not sure. They look unnatural, like some sculptor's abstract art. I'll have to take a closer look at them when I get a chance. There's no sign of anyone else or any kind of building. It looks like I really am alone.

I'm going to have to start thinking about finding more food and water. I finished off my lunch from yesterday and I'm starving. I'll look in the plane. I think I saw a lunch sack next to Dave's seat. I'm not sure what I'll do after that.

* * *

Dave's lunch bag contained a ham, lettuce, and tomato sandwich, some potato chips, a banana, and a small can of (bleagh) Vienna sausage. There was also a bottle of water, which I've gratefully been nursing since my canteen ran out. I ate the banana since it was already turning mushy. I'll save the rest for later.

* * *

Nobody has come for me, and I don't think anyone will. I'm on my own, with no way to get home. I'll take a look at what's in the plane tomorrow to see what I have available to me. I guess I'll probably have to leave the plane when my food and water run out.

I'm scared. I wish Dave were still alive.

August 27 – Day 3

I couldn't sleep. I've been watching the sky as the sun rises. It's not a normal blue during the day but a deep, violet-blue spotted with white clouds ribbed with pink. I wonder what makes it do that.

I guess I should go through the plane now. I'll need to know what I've got to work with.

* * *

It's hot out here.

I think I have everything together now. It looks like I've got a better set-up here than I thought. I'll survive for at least another week. Let me write down everything I found to keep track of it easier.

First off, there's what was in my backpack. It's the one I use for day-hikes, so it's stocked-up fairly well. In it, I have my canteen, a large container of matches, a signaling mirror, a small package of iodine drops for purifying water, a rain poncho, toilet paper, and a space blanket. It also has a mess kit consisting of two shallow pans, two plastic cups, a small cutlery set, and a detachable handle that can convert one of the shallow pans into a frying pan. It's also got a small emergency pack containing a little more food. There's a bag of trail mix and ten smaller packages containing mixes for mashed potatoes, oatmeal, and something called "turkey blend". Everything's in really good condition. I've hardly used any of it before now.

I've also got the notebook I'm writing in, a few pens, and the plastic containers from my lunch. At least this is a big notebook, so I won't run out of paper any time soon.

For clothing, I have two pairs of pants, three shirts, two pairs of socks, my windbreaker jacket, Dave's coat, my hiking shoes and Dave's sneakers. All of Dave's clothes are a little too big for me, but I figure having two changes of clothing will come in very handy as the days go by.

Next are the contents of the plane itself. There's an odd, metal contraption that looks like a giant pair of pliers. It's about two feet long, and I think it has something to do with securing the plane to a trailer for transport. I'm not sure what good it'll be to me. There's also a new roll of duct tape, a large flashlight that already looks kinda dim, the first aid kit, a fire extinguisher, some kind of flare gun kit, a lot of old maps and charts, and the useless radio. I've also got Dave's pocketknife, which is one of those heavy-duty all-in-one tools. That'll probably come in handy.

Most importantly, I found a half-full, two-gallon water jug in the back. The water tastes a little stale, but at this point I'll take anything.

* * *

No one's coming. I know that now. I'm sure of it. Somehow, I've been dumped on this world and there's no way back. What am I going to do?

* * *

I've been crying. I want to go home. I'm trying to be brave and not get hysterical or panicked. That won't help me now. I'm trying to put on a brave face, but who am I trying to impress?

I can't stop thinking about home. I've tried not to think about Mom and Dad, or Bryant and Mark. Thinking about family hurts too much. I think about friends from school instead. Tyler, Aaron, Sarah, Tabitha, Curt. I imagine they're watching me, judging how well I'm doing. Would they be impressed with me?

I guess I won't be asking Sarah out later this week. I'd been meaning to, I was just busy. I was trying to meet a lot of deadlines and get ready for this trip. We'd left it kind of vague at the end of the spring quarter, and I wanted to celebrate her coming back to school. I wanted to start over and…

I'm crying again. Maybe I'm just tired. Goodnight.

August 28 – Day 4

I saw something weird this morning as I got up to answer nature's call. It's the first sign of animal life I've seen on this world. It looked like some kind of snake, with the head and forelimbs of a mouse. It slithered when it moved with the front legs just kind of cart wheeling around as the tail/body propelled it forward. I wonder what other kinds of strange things are out here.

* * *

I need to think. I've got to do something. It's been four days since the crash. I'm sure that no one's coming for me, so I need to start thinking about long-term survival.

I can't stay with the plane. It's hot, and I'll run out of water if I stay here. But I don't really want to leave the plane either. It's the only familiar thing on this weird world.

I need to leave. I guess the best I can do is to take as much as I can carry when I go. I could always come back later to get more. Or maybe I can figure out some way to carry everything at once.

I think it would be best to head south towards those hills. It doesn't look too far. Maybe a couple of miles.

They're pretty in the morning light, a kind of earthy red and purple, with a healthy sprinkling of what look like trees. Actually, they kind of look like a pile of dirty red potatoes piled up on the horizon.

Potatoes. I'm hungry. I'm gonna eat something.

* * *

Geez, it's hot! It's hard to think in all this heat. But I've figured something out. I could use the paddles strapped to the plane's floats to make a rough kind of sled. I could thread the giant pliers-thing (the one used for towing the plane) through the paddles as a body for the sled to attach my gear to. I think it would work well. But I'm so tired and it's so hot. I'm gonna take a long siesta and head out tonight after it cools down.

It's an oven inside the plane. I'm gonna try lying down in the shade of one of the wings. Hope the shadow doesn't move while I'm sleeping.

* * *

I just had a horrible nightmare. The images were terrible. I don't want to describe it. I just want to forget it. It was about Dave and having to bury him. I don't want to think about it. I'm so tired, but I don't want to sleep anymore. I better get to work.

* * *

Ok, I think I'm ready. The sled's all put together and loaded up. I figure I can pull during the night when it's cool and then use the sled's handles and my poncho for an awning to shield off the sun during the day. I plan on taking just about anything that isn't bolted down. You never know what may come in handy later.

I need some rest. It's gonna be a long night.

August 29 – Day 5

Oh my gosh I'm tired! My arms and back feel like they're on fire. I tried to pull until the sun had completely risen, but I had to stop just as it broke over the horizon. I barely got the sled turned away from the rising sun, planted the paddles in the hard ground, and stretched the poncho over them before collapsing underneath my makeshift shade. I have to sleep, I'll write more later.

* * *

It's the middle of the day and I can't sleep. Each time I try to my mind wanders to home and school. I guess I won't have to worry about that journalism paper that was due this week, or about getting my rent money paid on time. I also won't be taking Sarah out.

I keep thinking that I wouldn't be here at all if I hadn't tried writing that travel article about sightseeing on the San Juans. There's no way I could have known, but I still wish I'd never gone on the stupid trip now.

I wonder if any of my friends know about my disappearance yet. I bet Tyler would join the volunteers looking for my plane's crash site. That's just the kind of guy he is. He's always been a good friend. Sarah would look too if she knew. I hope she knows, and not just so that she'll forgive me for never calling her back. I hope she's not too worried. I wish I could get a message to everyone at home just to let them know I'm all right. I hope they don't give up on me.

I try not to think about finality, like I'll never see them again, but how can I think anything else? Am I going to die out here, alone and scared? I want to go home.

August 30 – Day 6

I just had another nightmare. It was about Dave. I was burying him again, only this time he was still alive. He kept trying to talk to me, but I kept shoveling dirt into his face. It didn't matter how much dirt I threw into the grave, I wasn't able to cover Dave's body. He kept trying to talk with me. He was so calm, as if he was just trying to help me. I woke up in a cold sweat. My stomach is all tangled together. I feel terrible.

* * *

My head aches and the rest of me feels about the same. I think I'm dehydrated. I've been trying to go easy on my water, but now I'm going to drink whenever I'm thirsty. I don't want to die of thirst when I still had some water.

I'm also gonna start using the soup mixes. I've been eating the trail mix, but it's gone now. All that's left are the mixes and the Vienna sausage. I was going to wait until I could make a fire to heat the soup, but now I'll just drink it cold, or rather lukewarm, since the water's not exactly chilly. Ok, I gotta stop writing and eat something.

August 31 – Day 7

Whew. Well, I'm still tired and sore, but at least my head feels better. I've got nice pink sunburns on my arms and hands where the sun had moved while I slept this morning. These are going to hurt later. I've already taken a nice long nap and had some cold oatmeal, so I feel I can write for a while now.

I never got to write about leaving the plane the other night. I used Dave's pocketknife to cut the seatbelts out of the plane to tie everything onto the sled. I didn't see much need in hanging around once the sled was done and loaded, but I thought I should visit Dave's grave before I left. It looked ok. Nothing had disturbed it yet. I wasn't there very long. I just couldn't think of much reason to stay. I thanked him for the help he gave me, wishing he was still alive.

I didn't get very far on the first night, though there was plenty of light since both the moons were full. By the time I stopped and the sun was up, I could still see the plane way off in the distance. The next night I did much better. I find that if I take frequent, short breaks that I actually make better time than when I try pulling straight through the night. Drinking the soup mixes helps too.

I guess I'll try to get a little more rest. Maybe I'll try some sketching. I could try drawing some of these stubby little plant/rock things. They don't resemble any kind of bush I've ever seen, and a few of them even look like stones with roots. Very strange.

* * *

The moons must be waning. The larger one is about three quarters full and the smaller one is shrinking even faster. Luckily, there's still plenty of light to see by as I travel at night. Also, the ground is very flat and even, so pulling is pretty easy. I try to aim myself for the middle of the hills to the south. Hopefully that'll put me there in a roughly straight line. Ok, I'm heading out again.

September 1 – Day 8

Happy September. It's hard to believe that it's already been a week since the plane crash. Seven long days since I disappeared off the face of the Earth. Six days since Dave was alive. I still have dreams about him. I don't know what's worse, having to pull the sled all night or having disturbing dreams all day.

Not much that's new to report. Had another good night of traveling. I'm tired.

* * *

I can't sleep, so I thought I'd describe a little of what's out here besides painted sand. I've managed to separate some of the objects out here into either plants or rocks, but some of them still defy classification. There's one that looks like the top half of a round rock, but when I pull it up it turns out to be a hollow shell, like a shield, with a root system underneath it. Another one looks like a new fern plant with curled up fronds that break like glass. How do these things live? Or are they alive at all?

I saw another animal yesterday I forgot to mention. I was sketching some kind of gigantic scraggly bush when I saw some movement inside it. I looked harder and found something that had been hiding right in front of me. It was a little monkey, or maybe more like a lemur.

It just sat inside the bush, watching me. He was about seven inches tall, with a tail about half that length. His coloring was splotched, ranging from pale white to black to orange, like a calico cat. Even after I found him,

I still had a hard time picking him out, as his short, colorful fur made a surprisingly good disguise against the multi-colored sand and the mixed light inside the bush.

The "painted monkey" didn't seem overly scared of me, just cautious and curious. He stayed still, watching me as I made several quick portraits of him before he climbed down to the roots of the bush and out of sight. For a second I considered trying to catch him. First because I thought he'd make a nice pet, and then because I was considering eating him. After all, if I'm going to survive out here I'll have to start replenishing my food somehow. I decided against it though. I've never been much of a hunter, and besides, I doubt I could bring myself to eat something so cute. I wonder if hunger will someday change that. I don't like to think about it.

September 2 – Day 9

Good morning. The southern hills are closer and the terrain is beginning to change. The plant-looking things are getting more plentiful, and there's even something that resembles a sparse, coarse grass growing in hardy little tufts. I can make out objects on the hillsides that I hope are something similar to trees. If they are trees then I'm almost sure that I'm looking at a long dead forest, as all the trunks are the same color as printer paper. I say almost, since I do see some green among the bleached white trunks. Maybe there's some life in those hills after all. I should know for sure in a few more days as long as traveling doesn't get any harder.

I'm worried. Even with a healthy food and water ration, I'm getting bone weary and aching all over. The ground is becoming slightly irregular, so now I have to deal with gradual rises and dips in the landscape. It gives variety, but it makes pulling the sled all that much harder.

At night, it seems the struggle of moving forward is only matched by how tedious and boring it is. Besides the hills in front of me, there are no landmarks, and there are times I feel I'm pulling on a gigantic treadmill. The silence in this desert is the worst part of traveling. There are no sounds out here except for my breathing and the sled sliding over the ground. Even the wind is silent, just a soft breeze to occasionally cool me down a little. It's soothing, but I wouldn't mind hearing something, anything, out here in this wasteland.

I try to keep my thoughts occupied as I pull mindlessly forward. Sometimes I like to imagine I'm pulling for a crowd of spectators made up of everyone I've ever known. All my friends are there, urging me on, especially Tyler and Sarah. I imagine all my teachers are there too, even Mr. Ruddel, my old high school P.E. teacher. Everyone's cheering, and they're all so amazed at how well I'm holding up. Maybe it's a silly daydream, but it gets me through the night. I miss…

Well, I'm gonna chug a little lukewarm turkey blend. Yum.

September 3 – Day 10

At least I've made some progress. The vegetation has become more substantial and I can see the slope of the nearest hill directly in front of me. I'm not among the trees yet, but I can see them. I could probably walk to them today if I didn't have the sled.

I can hear things other than myself now. I think that mostly what I'm hearing are bugs. There are little noises coming from the smaller plant life that's around me now, chirps and twitters and one in particular that I swear sounds like someone saying "sip sip sip sip" over and over again.

* * *

It's me again. Who else?

…why do I bother to keep writing in here? Am I lonely? Do I just need someone to talk to? I don't think I'm writing this for anyone else now. I'm just writing it for myself.

* * *

Sorry about earlier. I had meant to write about a flying animal I saw this afternoon. I tried sketching it, but it was pretty high up so I'm not sure how accurate I was. It was hard to try to get the double set of wings right. I wonder if it was big enough to have been a threat. It was too high to tell. Either way, I think I should look among the trees tomorrow for a good, sturdy spear. Now that I'm moving into territory that might have larger creatures in it, I want to be ready.

September 4 – Day 11

Not much time to talk. I need to get an early start. I'm going up into the woods to make a new spear. With any luck, I'll be sleeping under the trees tonight.

* * *

These are the first trees I've seen in over a week. They're not dead. At least, I don't think so. The trees are white, with strange shelf-like branches growing out in rings circling around each trunk and covered in wispy, pale green needles that almost look more like hair than true pine needles. Bizarre as they may look, these "ring pine" trees give off a very pleasant smell. All around me the scent of pine and sap is thicker and sweeter than I've ever smelled before. It's like wood smoke with all the acrid hardness purged from it, just bright and fresh.

It was nice at first to hear more sounds around me, though none of them were familiar and eventually I thought I'd rather have silence again. They sounded less like bird songs or bug noises and more like poorly tuned instruments being dropped repeatedly. It wasn't exactly a soothing noise to listen to all day.

I managed to make the spear I was planning on. Dave's pocketknife is definitely coming in handy. I'm really glad he had it. I just wish he were here to help me use it. It'd be nice.

I considered trying to make a new sled using the ring pines, but gave up on the idea. Crude as it is, my oars and plane-hook sled is working fine. If it comes apart I'll replace it, but until then I've got something more important to worry about… finding some fresh water.

I'll take a little time this evening and see how those iodine drops in my hiking kit actually work. I'm sure glad I've got them now.

September 5 – Day 12

I had a hard time sleeping last night. I stayed up worrying about what I may have left with the plane that I could have used. For one thing, I left the engine completely untouched. Maybe some of the belts and hoses would have been useful. I left all the plane's fuel too. If the seasons are the same here as they are on Earth it means that in another month or so, it's going to start getting colder. And even before then, I need to start thinking about making fires. That fuel would have come in handy, but I guess it's not that essential.

What is essential is finding water. The ground among the ring pines is hard-packed and dry, covered with dead needles and small branches. It makes for easy traveling, but it also means there probably isn't much rainfall here either. That's not surprising. I'm still close to the desert. My best bet is probably to head farther south, away from the dry plain where we crashed.

* * *

There was more new wildlife today. A small group of tiny, skittering creatures feeding and singing among the ring pines. They were muted orange, totally bald, and had long rat-tails. Each was just big enough to fit in my palm, and every one of them had a ridiculously elongated beak. I watched as the small group of three or four used their long, curved beaks to get at the seeds inside what I think are the trees' pinecones. They were fun to watch, but their "song" was a little hard on the ears. They made a long, drawn out note that almost sounded like someone whistling for their dog.

Not much else to write about. Didn't find any new water, and I'm running pretty low. Hope I find some soon. Guess I better turn in. I'll probably use Dave's coat for a blanket. It's been getting cooler at night.

September 6 – Day 13

Still no fresh water today. I'm really getting worried now.

I can't see the desert anymore. I've been traveling south all day and I know I've covered a lot of ground. I must be walking more than a few miles each day and yet no water. I keep wondering if there are certain signs I should be looking for. I've just been trying to find some actual water on the ground, or maybe a dried up creek bed that I can follow downstream. I don't know what else to look for.

My soreness isn't helping anything either. I've never felt this tired before. I have a dull pain that starts at my neck and goes all the way to the soles of my feet. I hate this. I want to go home.

Sorry to complain so much, but who else will listen?

* * *

I can't wait any longer. I've got to try to build a fire.

I don't know why I've avoided building a fire up until now. Maybe I felt finding water should be my top priority and everything else could wait. I still think that's true, but in the meantime I'm going to need some kind of warmth at night.

I'm worried that it always seems so hard to do it. In the few times I've been camping, it was always Dad's job to get the fire started. Mark always offered to help since he was an Eagle Scout and all, but I think it was a matter of pride for Dad. I remember him always struggling with matches, pitch squares, and wads of newspaper. Eventually Dad would make a show out of it by dousing the whole mess with lighter fluid and making a huge fireball to kick things off. Mom never liked that part.

* * *

So I tried making a fire this evening. I did my best to remember how Mark did it the few times Dad forgot the lighter fluid. I made a small tee-pee of sticks and kindling, then selected what I hoped would be the lucky match. It wasn't, but eventually I did get a fire that, while not very pretty, is at least doing more than just smoking.

Now I'm writing by firelight. This heat sure feels good. It's also good to finally have some properly cooked oatmeal. I know I still really need to find water, but at least I'll be warm tonight.

September 7 – Day 14

Still no water, and now I'm worrying about food too. After tonight, I'll have one package of mashed potatoes and the Vienna sausages left. I'm trying to save one meal each for the next two days, and then... and then I don't know.

I've been traveling in the same direction all this time, and the woods are starting to look different. The trees are growing closer together and there are hard, thick bushes growing between them. Traveling is much harder now. The bushes are more like tangles of unearthed roots than limp plants, with no foliage and no color on them besides slits of green running through each brown bough. The striped bushes make swell fuel for the fire but are a pain to go around.

There are whistlers everywhere in these woods. They were annoying before, but now they're really giving me a headache. I tried chucking rocks at them, but they're just too small and quick. Probably too many little bones to make a good meal anyway. I've tried looking for other animals to eat, but I'm no hunter. I need water right now more than food anyway.

* * *

I've been thinking a lot about Dave lately. I lit another fire tonight, and went through his belongings. I wonder what he was like. It's strange to think that although I was the last person to see him alive, I honestly hardly knew him. He didn't talk much, and his wallet is thin with few cards and no pictures except for a fuzzy driver's license photo. There were no rings on his hands, so I don't even know if he was married. His watch is old and beat up, with a thick, aged leather band. I wonder now if his family would even care to have it. He had just twenty dollars on him. Not much of an inheritance to whoever. Not much to give...

I'm going to put these things away and not look at them again. It only reminds me of burying Dave. I don't want the nightmares again.

I'm hungry. I haven't been really full for two weeks now. I hope tomorrow brings something better.

September 8 – Day 15

Finally some good news! It's the middle of the day right now. I've been moving roughly south, and the striped bushes and other plants have been getting denser and more frequent. I was frustrated at first about having to maneuver around all the undergrowth, but now I've found something wonderful. A bush, as tall as my chest, with purple berries all over it!

I'm so excited and grateful for this. There's got to be at least two buckets' worth of the little things. They look kind of like maroon blueberries all fused together in clumps of fours and fives. Of course, I have to be careful. I've eaten just one cluster of four to see if they're ok, but it's been a little while now and I still feel fine. The berries tasted really sour, but at least they're juicy.

At last, things are looking up.

* * *

I hate life. I hope I die soon. Those berries were poison. I got terrible cramps, and then I started to vomit purple. It just kept coming and coming. I only ate four. Just four! Even when there was nothing left I couldn't stop heaving, and then I was crying. I'm still crying.

I hate this. It isn't fair! Not only have I lost the rest of the day's traveling, but I'm probably dehydrated from being sick too. I can't take this. I'm gonna die here.

September 9 – Day 16

I feel weak. I didn't light a fire last night, so now I'm cold and sore too. I feel terrible.

Bad as I feel though, I can't stay here. Once I'm able to, I will have to head out again. Please, oh please let me find water today. I can worry about food later.

At the very least now I know what berries to avoid, I even have a name for them. After last night's agony, it seems appropriate: "hell berries."

* * *

I saw something new today, but I'm too tired to write much. It was a weird biped, very low to the ground with two short, stocky legs. It was about the size of a small dog, and was covered in brown and black fur. I didn't get that great a look at it because it ran off after only a moment of staring. Maybe I'll see it again. If I'm still here.

* * *

I can't pull the sled any farther. The water is all gone and I'm hungry. I just can't go any further.

I've found a beautiful meadow here. There's long, soft grass all over it. Strange flowers of white, purple, and reddish orange are here like I've never seen. The sky has opened up and I can see for miles. At last, I can see that this isn't just a string of hills. There are mountains up here. Real mountains. They tower up all around me except back to the north. It's a whole range of mountains.

I wish I had a camera. Evening has started to fall, and the sky is the same shade of violet-blue it was when I first arrived. The mountains are like great, dark sentinels standing guard around this pristine little meadow. A few of them even have little whitecaps that reflect the cooling blue of nightfall.

I'm so tired. I won't build a fire. There isn't any point.

I think I've done the best that I can do.

Goodnight.

September 10 – Day 17

Things are definitely looking up now, much better than they were last night. To think I was so close to giving up. I'm glad to be alive and making this entry.

This morning was like a dream. I'm not sure when I woke up, but I know it was in the pre-dawn light. It was cold and I was aching all over. I couldn't sleep but I didn't want to get up.

It took a moment to realize that I'd been woken by a strange sound. It was a low snuffling sound followed by the thudding of heavy footsteps. I opened my eyes and saw the largest creature I have seen yet on this world.

It was huge, standing at least six feet at the shoulder on four stocky legs. It was a grazing animal, with a large rounded snout and a massive single horn on top of its head. Its front shoulders met in an enormous hump before tapering down to its somewhat shorter back legs, its entire body covered with thick, bluish-brown hair. Perhaps most strangely of all, it seemed to have three nostrils along each side of its oversized snout. Why a creature would possibly need so many noses I have no idea.

I stayed totally still, not wanting to startle the beast standing just yards away. I tried to stand up slowly after a few seconds to get a better look without startling it, but it turned and saw me as I moved. I froze as the creature's large, dark eyes met mine and for a moment, I wondered how intelligent the creature was. What if it tried to communicate? How would I have a conversation with it? It turned out there wasn't anything I needed to worry about, since the great beast went back to feeding after only a brief pause.

I wasn't sure what I should do, so I stood there at the edge of the meadow and watched the peaceful beast continue eating. When the creature moved on I followed it. I trailed it for a while across the meadow and into the trees on the other side. Eventually I lost it among the ring pines and sat down on the ground, feeling tired and empty.

For a while, I wondered if I was going crazy chasing a "horn head" all over the forest. It certainly felt like I was going crazy with the incessant noise I kept hearing in the background. After a while, I finally focused on the sound and realized what it was… flowing water.

It took me a while to find the creek that made the sound. It isn't very big, just a few inches deep, but it stretches on forever in either direction and is clear as glass. I had to resist the urge to drop to my knees and start guzzling, but I did immediately start a fire to purify myself a drink.

Both banks of the creek are thick with berry bushes. These are definitely not hell berries. Each berry has two layers, one small, deep blue inner berry surrounded by a larger, bright orange enveloping berry. These "double-berries" seem safer since they have a sweet, fragrant smell while the hell berries had no smell at all. Still, I have no intentions on repeating my last mistake with strange food, so I ate only a single berry and gave myself plenty of time to digest it. The double berry was sweet, not sour, and gave me no problems, so I think I may have found my first real source of food on this world.

Evening is coming on now. I've brought my sled to the creek and built up my fire with enough fuel on hand to last me through the night. I still felt fine a couple hours after eating the double-berry, so I went ahead and had a small handful of them with my mashed potatoes. It tasted wonderful.

Tomorrow I'll figure out how to use the iodine drops, and then I can store some of this water. I can't get over how grateful I feel. I'm not out of the woods yet, but I have hope now. I've survived this long, and I'm gonna keep on surviving.

Expedition Log
Twenty Third of Dula, in the second year of The Return
Yurril T'nak, field scout

I despair that our Compass of Worlds is truly beyond our repairing. Brendell has declared the device unsalvageable and insists we must press on without it. This is truly a stumbling first step on our journey. Our single hope now is that we may find the Records and Artifacts for which we are seeking and thereby discover the pathway back to our homeland.

For this purpose we have divided our company and have each taken a role to serve within our camp. I will act as the group's field scout, while Brendell will continue as our Divant and inspired leader. Huntil will serve as camp director, while Flain will be responsible for the armaments and the protection of the company.

Our course has been outlined to us by Brendell. We shall travel along this isthmus to the eastern continent, then onward to the lost cities of Berrach and Sytol. Brendell will then give us further direction if we have not yet found that for which we seek.

I pray we will not long be on this inhospitable world. Already I ache for home.

Grace Be To You. Yurril T'nak

September 11 – Day 18

Well it's morning and I'm not dead. No cramps, no headaches, nothing. I feel great! Time for a breakfast of double-berries, and then I'll finally take a look at those iodine drops.

* * *

Huh. Well, this is kind of disappointing. The last time I looked at the iodine bottle I just saw the words "water purifying" and put it away. There's not much of anything to it though. One plastic jar of iodine pills, one plastic cup, and one small twenty-page survival guide wrapped around the bottle. The first half of the guide is an in-depth discussion on water purifying techniques, but the rest is a general discussion on things to do to survive in the wild. Of course, it assumes you'll only be lost a couple days. The first line under the heading FOOD says, "This shouldn't be a problem." Right.

Anyway, I looked at the iodine drops and saw that they were over a year past their expiration date, so I'm not going to risk it. I feel safer boiling it anyway. Speaking of which, my creek water is boiling right now.

* * *

Well I let the water bubble for a full minute just to make sure it was safe before letting it cool. I also drained it through one of my shirts before boiling, just so it would be clean. While I wait for the next batch to cool, I think I'll read the rest of the guide. Maybe I'll work on some sketches of all the things I've seen lately. For the first time since being here, I can finally relax a little.

* * *

I take back what I said about the guide. I read the rest of the section on food, and while it was short, it had at least one good idea. It suggested I try to drink something hot before going to sleep to retain some heat. It also said that pine needles could be used to make a basic, herbal tea. I wasn't sure if ring pine needles would work, but I tried it, and boy is it good. The flavor is a bit weird I admit. It tastes a little like a Christmas tree. At least it's hot and smells good. I bet I sleep good tonight. The manual had some other good things to say, but I'm feeling sleepy.

September 12 – Day 19

Good morning! I'm back in business. The last few days' rest along with waking up warm this morning has totally recharged me. That's good, because it's about time for me to move on.

When I got up this morning, I found that funny little furry biped thing in the double berries. I chased him away from my bushes but by that time, the berries were just about gone. No big deal, I'm sure there are probably plenty more bushes further downstream, which is the way I plan to head.

Maybe this creek feeds into an actual river or lake farther on. I hope so. I may not be much of a hunter, but I did like to fish now and then with Dad and Bryant. I could probably rig up something to catch whatever water creatures I may find. It's not that I don't enjoy an all double-berry diet, but I've been going without real protein for far too long. I'm worried I'll have to finally open that can of Vienna sausage. I'm trying to save it, not because I like it, but because it's the only food I still have that will keep more than just a few days.

Anyway, as far as protein goes, I may have a more immediate solution. The tiny survival guide suggests that bugs can make an excellent source of protein, provided that you always cook them first. I'm not very excited about the idea, but it's better than starving. At least that's what I'm telling myself.

Ok. After I make camp tonight I'll go on a little mini-monster safari for my dinner.

* * *

And the mighty hunter returns. I made a few discoveries to put in the pot tonight. Most of the bug-like creatures I found were too tiny to make even a small part of a meal, but there were a few that looked big enough to be a bite or more. One was under a large stone, with way more legs than it could ever need spreading in all directions like a shiny black sea anemone. A few more with longer but fewer legs were in the tall grass of a nearby meadow. Those ones were a little harder to catch since each one could jump away in the blink of an eye. Luckily, they make a very loud clicking noise almost constantly, so they were easy enough to find again.

The best thing I found were a bunch of big, lime green, fleshy grub-looking things in a dead log. Well, maybe saying "best" is a stretch, but they were easy to catch and nice and fleshy. Altogether, I've found almost a dozen or so creepy crawlies, so that should do for an average-sized meal tonight. I'll write again after dinner.

* * *

Well, the bugs aren't so bad. The trick is just not looking at them. Or thinking about them. Or breathing while you eat them. The grubs are the best. They don't give off much of an odor while they're cooking. The clickers on the other hand stink like burning plastic. I had to throw those away and clean the pan afterwards. I think I'll try boiling my bugs from now on.

Traveling is getting more and more difficult. I've been trying to move parallel to the stream, but it's getting harder as the foliage gets denser. I'm traveling west now. I'm not sure how close to the western mountains I am, but as long as I travel next to the creek I'll have water, and that's more important than anything else right now.

* * *

I can't sleep.

They've probably stopped searching for me by now. My family must think I'm dead. Bryant has his own family now. He could find comfort in Anne and little Jessica. Mark has his job to keep him busy. But Mom and Dad are all alone now. Maybe Dad can find some kind of project to keep himself busy. He's always loved doing projects.

…I should have helped him more. I should have been more willing.

Sometimes Mom said she had a sixth sense about her sons. She was convinced that she could always tell how they were doing, no matter where they might be. Maybe Mom knows that I'm all right.

Even if they think I'm dead, I hope they're all at peace with it.

I'm just glad I have this notebook to write in. It's nice to have someone to talk to.

September 13 – Day 20

I'm hungry. I want some fish. Mom baked the best fish, with garlic and butter and a little lemon…

The creek is getting bigger now and flowing slower as more and more other small waterways join it. Maybe I'll find something edible in the water soon. The easiest way for me to catch something would probably be by making a fish-spear. I don't have a hook or any string for a fishing line. Besides, I save anything bait-like for my dinner.

Speaking of which, I found a few new bugs today but nothing to add to my meals of boiled creepy crawlies. I tore open a rotting log and found a colony of tiny, squirming white things. I'm sure they would have been good, but they're small and hard to catch and besides, they bite. My hands are stinging horribly and I'm trying not to scratch them. I really wish the first aid kit had some insect repellant.

So hungry. I found some mushrooms at the base of a tree that looked pretty good, but I didn't try them. After the hell berries, I'm leery of anything I'm not familiar with. That doesn't leave many options. I only tried the double-berries out of desperation before, but how else would I know if something is edible or not?

* * *

Well, even if there's nothing to catch in the water right now, I figured I'd try making myself a fishing spear. I was hoping for a three-point spear, but I've settled on a sturdy Y-shaped branch. I also had a new idea. Tonight when I light my fire, I'll blacken the points of both my spears to harden the tips and keep them from splitting apart. I seem to remember learning that primitive men used to do that. Hope I don't set either of them on fire.

September 14 – Day 21

Things are starting to look different in the forest. There are a few new kinds of trees along with what resemble some moss and a variety of funguses. They all look unearthly, but the trees especially are like nothing I've ever heard of. One kind is almost totally black and is much bigger than the ring pines. Each of these trees has dull red needles, but unlike the ring pine's needles they're not small and hair-like. These needles are curved like fishhooks and are almost strong enough to be wood themselves. They make terrible tea.

Another new tree is a dark mud-brown with big, spade-shaped, silvery green leaves. Each mature tree is about as tall as a ring pine, but their crowns are more expansive than either the ring pines or the hook fir. These spade trees have the pleasant smell of fresh cut grass, and I have to admit that its leaves are definitely a relief in a very immediate sense… the toilet paper ran out last week and I've been using torn up maps. Thank goodness for little blessings.

September 15 – Day 22

I'm sorry I didn't write any more yesterday. I wanted to, but I was in too much pain and too frightened.

I was trying to find more bugs for lunch yesterday when I found this thing… I'm not sure if it was a huge bug or a small… something. It was totally different from anything else I've seen. It was all hard edges and sharp blades, with bands of yellow, black and brown. I was going to leave it alone, but it leapt out of the tall grass and bit my palm. Or stung it. Whatever it did, it hurt! It wouldn't let go. I couldn't shake it off. It felt like glass shards wedging into my hand. I hit my hand against a tree trunk to try to get it loose but that didn't work. I finally got a stick and pried it off of me. Then I killed it. I took a large rock and crushed it over and over.

I realized my hand was bleeding, so I cleaned it with pure water, then soaked some gauze with antiseptics and wrapped it with tape from the first aid kit.

Stupid thing. It still hurts. My hand is swollen now. I'm scared. What if it's infected? What if I'm poisoned? I took it easy the rest of yesterday and today. I hope I'm OK.

* * *

I've been resting most of today, and I feel a little better. My hand still hurts a lot, but the swelling has gone down. I took some painkillers and slept most of the morning. The bleeding's stopped, but I'll leave the bandages on for a while. At least it doesn't hurt as much to move it. I guess I wasn't poisoned by the blade bug after all. Lucky me.

I've made a decision. I'm going to set up a more substantial camp right here. It's not a bad spot for it. I'm at a bend in the creek that opens into a pool four or five feet deep, and I can sleep underneath a huge spade tree. I'll be staying here until I feel better. In the meanwhile, maybe I can find some real food.

* * *

Well this seems to be as good a place as any to make a more permanent camp. It's near a little meadow that stretches out for what must be several acres. I'm able to see the mountains again from the middle of the field and kinda gauge how far I've progressed. Judging from where the mountains are, I think I've been moving in a gradual southern direction.

I'm really starting to worry about my health now. I'm not sure when I last ate something really hearty. While I am eating, I have no idea what the nutrition-level of my food is. I could be malnourished in a variety of ways, and scurvy's just one of them. I keep craving foods I just can't have right now. Hamburgers, chicken, cheesy potatoes, mixed vegetables, ice cream… Maybe the cravings will go away with time. Maybe, but I doubt it.

At least my ring pine tea is fragrant and warm.

* * *

What a racket! I've been hearing noises from some kind of creatures around the bend in the creek. Warbles, twitters, something that sounds like gargling… a whole mishmash of not necessarily pleasant noises. To think I used to complain about how quiet this world was. I just want to sleep.

September 16 – Day 23

Well, I had a lot more excitement last night, but I was much too tired to write about it.

I had gone to the pool at the bend in the creek to try to find some of those creatures that were making so much noise. I crept to the edge of the water and peered through the tall plants. To my surprise, I found that the small pool was literally teeming with strange little creatures swimming around and warbling unpleasant songs into the night air.

Each of the creatures seemed to be all head and legs, with no body or forelimbs that I could see. They were just bulbous heads with a pair of long, muscular legs growing out of them. They were an odd collection of browns, yellows, and greens, and the smallest ones were barely the length of my thumb, while the largest were almost as long as my hand.

I tried catching one with my bare hands, but no luck. They're all too fast for me, and my hand was still hurting too much to really be all that accurate. Maybe I'll try again later.

I spent this morning setting up my camp, and I'm pretty happy with how it turned out. I used my sled and some dead branches to make a crude lean-to shelter against a big spade tree. I used the spade tree leafs and a bunch of hook fir limbs to make a bed inside it, which is the first bed I've had for a long time. The lean-to doesn't provide too much cover, but the skies have been mostly clear since I came to this world, so I'm not really worried about rain at this point.

Nearby the lean-to, I've set up the rest of my camp. I dug a fire pit and ringed it with stones, then piled the rest of my gear up against the spade tree with some branches thrown over it all to keep out any dampness.

Now that that's done, I think I'll take a bath in the bend in the creek. I just hope it isn't cold.

* * *

Well it wasn't too cold, but I'm not sure how effective it was. I have no soap out here. I do feel somewhat better though. After my bath, I took the opportunity to wash all the clothes that I have. They needed it. I've got just two changes of clothes: Dave's and mine. All of Dave's clothes are a little big on me, but I change between mine and his to try to save on wear and tear. The socks are already wearing pretty thin, but both pairs of shoes look to have plenty of miles left in them.

I made another little discovery while I was rinsing out my t-shirts. Down in the water, along the bottom of the pool I saw at least a dozen little creatures half-buried in the silt. They had burrowed in backwards so that all I could see were their slender necks and heads. I tried to grab some of them, but they disappeared into the creek bed. I quickly got an oar from my sled and dug furiously at the muddy ground below the pool's surface. It was hard work, but I was eventually rewarded with a handful of the pale, spineless things.

They're a little worm-like, but their heads are more defined and serpentine. They have one appendage, a flipper-like arm that they must use to push them through the soil. They're only about a couple inches long, but they're much easier to catch than the pond-hoppers. I'll write again and describe how they taste after dinner.

* * *

Well, the soilers aren't so bad. A little bland, but not bad. I figure they feed and live in the water, and just use the creek bed as a place for security. They have a soft exoskeleton kinda like a shrimp's shell, but just boil them, peel them, and they're pretty good.

I supplemented my soilers with a large, stick-like insect that was on the creek. It looked like an anorexic branch, with eight or nine limbs stretching almost a foot in total length. I added it to the pot, and ate the entire thing. About all I can say is it was crunchy. No taste. Just crunch.

You know, it's kind of funny how I've gotten used to everything I eat being bland. My food has no real taste. These days I'm just concerned with whether something is hot or not.

I wonder how those pond-hoppers taste. I mean, shrimp and other crustaceans are pretty tasteless on their own, so I wasn't surprised when the soilers didn't have any flavor. But chicken, beef, pork… they all have a kind of taste all their own, don't they? Maybe pond-hoppers have a good taste. They'd at least be a little more meat.

I can hear them now. I'm going to try to catch one. I'm not sure how, but I want one. I'm hungry.

September 17 – Day 24

Good morning. I have a lot to write about last night's hunt.

I figured my best bet would be to try for one of the bigger pond-hoppers just as it began to make its warbling call. My first idea was to throw a jacket over one and pound it with a rock, but I chickened out at the thought of crushing one of the things. Besides, I don't like the idea of wearing a coat with something's guts on it. Eventually I decided on my fishing spear, but I quickly learned that spearing something is not as easy as it looks. I spent a while just stabbing at thin air and almost wound up in the water twice. Luck favors the persistent though, and eventually I scored a solid hit. It was a big mottled brown one trying to hide in the shallows. I think I killed it instantly, although it occasionally twitched around.

I have to admit I was a little squeamish at first once I actually had the pond-hopper on the end of my spear. I know I've been killing and eating bugs for the last week or so, but they're just bugs. This is different. It was hard to not feel sorry for the little thing as it wriggled gently on the end of my sharpened stick. I'm sorry I had to kill it, but I have to eat, and I can't live on bugs forever.

Once the pond-hopper finally stopped moving, I brought it back to camp. I have to admit I wasn't too hungry just then, but I figured I still had to gut the thing right away. I used Dave's knife and just pretended I was dissecting a frog in Mr. Cutler's biology class again. After I gutted it, I hung the rest up overnight, since by then I really didn't feel like eating.

By the time I got up this morning I figured I should go ahead and eat the thing before it went bad. I thought about it for a while, and decided to just cook the legs. I know that some aquatic animals are poisonous and I don't want to take any chances. Of course, I suppose it could have poison glands in its legs, but I don't think so. Besides, I think most poisonous animals are brightly colored, whereas this hopper was just a dull brown. I think I'm ok.

Anyway, I cut off the legs, which were about the size of small drumsticks, and boiled them after skinning them and cutting off the feet. They were good. Kinda greasy. Tastes like chicken. Ha ha ha.

This is working out pretty well. I'll spend this afternoon doing a little more exploring. Maybe I'll go look at what's in the meadow and try to find some edible plants.

* * *

Well I didn't find anything edible in the meadow, just a bunch of grass and bushes. I'm almost tempted to try some of these lovely funguses around here. They look so good... but I know that mushrooms can definitely be poisonous. Even my little food and water safety book says "AVOID MUSHROOMS."

The only thing I did find were some hook fir pinecones lying on the forest floor. When I first saw the large, avocado-shaped cones, I started thinking. Pinecones are the nuts from pine trees, and just about all nuts are edible, right? But the cones have defeated me. Even a sturdy rock isn't strong enough to smash their tough, springy exteriors. I tried using the screwdriver from Dave's pocket knife as a chisel, but even then, I couldn't break it open. I even tried burning off the outer shells in the evening fire, but all I managed to do was to set the entire pinecone on fire. They don't even burn very well, so I can't use them as either food or fuel.

Oh well. I can always look for edible plants by the water tomorrow. At least I've found the hoppers, so I don't have to eat bugs again for a little while. I just wish I could have something other than meat and berries.

I can't believe I used to be one of those kids who refused to eat his vegetables. I'd do anything to have some of Mom's broccoli with cheese right now. Or her steamed carrots and peas. Or anything. I wish I could go home.

Sorry. Things are ok. I'll be all right. I have to go catch another pond-hopper for the morning. Goodnight.

September 18 – Day 25

Good morning. I'm just cooking my hopper breakfast. Gosh, what I wouldn't give for some bacon and eggs with hash browns this morning. Still, a breakfast of boiled pond-hopper meat is better than bug soup I guess.

I do have a little good news. I finally figured out the pinecones. Remember the ones I threw in the fire last night? This morning I noticed them again, cracked wide open. They must only open after being exposed to extreme heat. It makes sense. I remember trees on Earth whose pinecones would open only in a forest fire. It makes me wonder how often this place has forest fires. Should I be worried about that?

Either way, I've tried to find something like nuts inside the pinecones. I think I may have found something, little pale slivers that have a slightly oily texture. There's no way I could fill up on them, but they'll be a nice addition to my meals, especially now that I know how to get them.

I think I'll start the day with another bath just after breakfast. After that, I'll search the water's edge to try to find some edible plants. I really hope I find something.

* * *

I think I may have finally found something that's not only edible, but also better for me than anything I've been eating for the last few weeks.

I spent some time studying the plants growing in and around the water. Most of what is growing there is a chest-high variety of grass. The blades are very long, thin, and brownish in color except for a few strands on the tips and down at the stem near the root. I realized quickly that the blades themselves were inedible, and the stems are too fibrous to try chewing.

The other plant I found was definitely more promising. It's thicker than the water grass, with pale yellow stalks that resemble flimsy bamboo. The most interesting part of the plant is the bud-like protrusions along the stalk. Each one is about the size of a kiwi, dark brown and surprisingly light. When I broke one open I found it was full of tiny seeds. They may not look like much, but any seeds I can think of are edible, and I've never heard of a poisonous seed.

I've collected several pods and spilled their contents out into a cup. I've tried a few raw and they are definitely inedible. Next, I tried boiling them a while to soften them. I tried them again when they were soft, and you know what I realized? It's rice. Some kind of rice! A wild, impossible, amazing kind of rice! It's got to be. Granted I don't know much about plants. I mean, I don't know if Earth rice grows in pods. Probably not. But if this stuff is actually good, it means I've got a grain source again, not to mention something that will last longer in my supplies than berries and meat would.

I had a cup of pod rice with boiled soilers for dinner. It tasted bland, kinda like eating unseasoned noodles. Still, it was hot and filling, and we'll see how it affects me. Again, I don't think seeds can be toxic. I hope not, anyway.

* * *

Huzzah! Ha ha ha ha! Look out Psycho World, Richard Parks is here to survive! I have to tell you, this is great! What a wonderful feeling, to have had a balanced, large meal. It may not have been a turkey dinner, but it sure was nice to finally have something semi-healthy for me. I feel one hundred percent better. I am so glad I stopped here at this bend in the creek.

It feels good to be happy again. It's been a while. Looking up at the starry sky through the treetops, I can almost imagine getting to like living on this world. I suppose it goes without saying I've given up on anyone coming to look for me, whether of this world or another.

* * *

I just had a late night visitor. I was lying next to the fire when I saw a pair of large, glowing green eyes looking down at me from the tree's branches. After a moment of staring the creature climbed down into the light, obviously curious about my fire.

It was small, about the size of a large squirrel. Its fur was short and smooth, with a cat-like face and long whiskers. It had no visible tail, but its arms and legs were almost freakishly long, making up about three-quarters of its length. Like the painted monkey, it made no move to flee or attack. It just calmly observed me.

I tried to be quiet and still too, but a stick in the fire fell over, crashing in a shower of sparks and startling my observer. The spooked little creature squeaked and leapt out into the night air. I thought it would fall, but it spread open its long fingers and toes to reveal large, parachute-like webbing between its digits. It flew forward, gliding on the night air until it landed on an outstretched hook fir limb and disappeared.

Wow. What a night.

September 18 – Day 26

'Morning. I'm tired and a little stiff. Is it just me, or is it starting to get cooler at night? Usually I just sleep in my clothes, but early this morning I had to pull my rain slicker on to keep warm. Maybe it's because there are more trees around here and they're blocking the sunlight. I don't know.

I caught another pond-hopper last night for this morning's breakfast, and for the first time in a month ate something roasted. It was so much better! I know that boiling is still probably the best way to get nutrients, especially when I drink the broth, but that doesn't mean I can't enjoy a little variety now and again.

* * *

There's a new sound tonight that I can't identify. It's grating and harsh, like fingernails dragged across a wet chalkboard. I can't figure out what direction the noise is coming from. It seems to be everywhere and all around me. I'm too tired to try looking for whatever might be making all that racket, but in the morning I might take a look around. I just hope it's nothing dangerous, I've been lucky so far in avoiding any big predators, assuming this planet has any.

September 19 – Day 27

This is big. Really big! I think I may have found the dominant species of this world. I don't know who or what it was and I couldn't make contact, but I'll try again. I've got to keep trying.

* * *

No luck. I'm exhausted from running and searching, but I couldn't find a thing. I know I wasn't imagining it. There is someone out there.

I was walking through the woods this morning when I noticed a movement off to one side. Whatever it was moved too quickly for me to see any kind of detail, but I managed to see that it was human-shaped, though I can't be sure if it was a human being. It moved quickly, running off into the undergrowth before I could even say a word. I was scared out of my mind at first, but then I chased after it. I didn't see it again, but I'll look again tomorrow. I'll keep looking until I find whoever or whatever it is.

I've got to be careful, it could be dangerous. I'll keep my single-point spear close by until I find out just what I'm dealing with.

I need to make a fire, it's getting dark.

* * *

There's that noise again, just like last night. It's so grating, like it's grinding on my nerves. What could be making it? I wish whatever it is would shut up. I'll be trying to sleep soon.

Then again, could it be the mysterious figure I saw today making that noise? Could it be a vocal noise, or maybe the sound of some alien machinery? It could be a metallic noise. It's hard to be sure.

Part of me wants to run out into the woods and shout, "Here I am! Come find me!" But I'm not going to. I'm excited, but I'm scared. What are these people like? Are they people? Would they see me as a person? Could they get me home?

I just don't know what to expect. I'm frightened to go to sleep but I'm so tired. I suppose if they want to come for me in the night, they will. Staying up won't stop them. How do I communicate with them? How do I indicate friendship? Am I just jumping to conclusions? What should I do?

I'm not going to sleep.

September 20 – Day 28

I did get to sleep for a little while last night. Nothing happened. Nothing has been moved or changed since last night. Maybe I just imagined everything.

I really jumped the gun, didn't I? I mean, I see something that could have been a person and I go crazy. I have to think logically about this. If there were an advanced society on this planet, wouldn't I have found some evidence of it by now? No, I guess not. What if an alien was transported to the Amazon, or the Sahara, or somewhere out on the tundra? They could live their whole lives and never see a human.

So why give up hope? I know I saw something. I did. I'll find him, or he'll find me. If he's friendly then I won't be alone any more. If he's dangerous, well, I'll be ready for him.

* * *

It's funny, I just realized today would have been the first day of Fall semester for me. How far away that world seems now. It's almost been a month since I've spoken with another human being, almost a month since I enjoyed the comforts of being home on my own world. I wonder if I'm doing better than the average person would in this situation.

That makes me wonder, am I really the first Earthling to be on this planet? I mean, if the portal I went through was random, couldn't there be other people sucked through to other worlds? Could I find them? What if I already have? What if the mysterious figure I saw yesterday is really another human who fell through space to end up marooned on this world? Or it could be the descendant of someone else who was stranded here years ago. I've heard about mysterious disappearances, like the Bermuda Triangle and stuff. Could it have been something like that?

Sorry, I guess I'm just jumping to conclusions again. I have no idea how random that portal I went through was. It may have been the only one of its kind ever. I hope not.

* * *

Well, my noisy friend hasn't left me. I can hear him out there again tonight. Listening to the sound closely, I think I can finally be sure that it is a vocal noise. There are variations in the sound and frequency that convince me of it. I wonder if that noise is the way the mysterious figure tries to communicate. What if the calls that "Mr. Screech" has been making are an attempt to make contact from a safe distance before getting closer to me? If that's the case, I sure hope he knows more than just this one noise, or we'll have a very one-sided conversation. But either way, as long as he is friendly, we can work through any other communication issues.

I'll go out looking for him again in the morning. That is, if he shuts up long enough for me to get some sleep.

September 21 – Day 29

He was here. Mr. Screech was near the camp this morning, and I missed him. I was just waking up when I heard a rustling in the bushes. I wish I'd been awake enough to get up quietly to see him, but I stood up quickly and must have scared him off. I got a much better look at him this time though. His body has the basic shape of a human, though his arms are slightly longer than would be normal for an Earth person. His body was covered with dappled gray fur, and he didn't seem to be wearing any clothing. I didn't see his face as he ran away except for a pair of hairless, overlarge ears that stuck out like a fox's.

Of course, I tried to chase him, but he can move much faster than I ever could. I'm not sure if it's because he has superhuman speed or just seems to know where he's going better than I do. It's becoming pretty apparent that chasing after him isn't going to be much help in trying to make contact. Somehow, I'll have to draw him out, but how?

Well, I'm hungry. I'm off to forage.

* * *

Mr. Screech is calling again this evening. It's funny. At first, it was really annoying, but now it's kinda nice. At least it means I'm not alone. It's like Bryant's music playing in the next room when Mom and Dad were out for the night. It was annoying and kept me up a lot, but it was also kind of reassuring. I knew that Bryant was nearby, and I wasn't alone.

I just wish I could make contact with him. I know he might be primitive, but at least it'd be some social interaction. If he's patient, I could teach him some of my language. If he's really patient he could even teach me some of his. I'm not much of a linguist. I had a steady C+ through two years of French. But I could learn. For the chance to talk with someone again, I would definitely learn.

I'm trying to think of how I would teach someone English without any references. I guess a lot of it would be nouns, pointing at things and saying the word for them. I'm not sure how I'd teach him how to connect them into sentences. I'll have to think about that tonight. I'll be up anyway.

September 22 – Day 30

He was here again. I woke up slowly and heard movement. I tried getting up quietly but he saw me. I couldn't get a good look at him at all today, just the rustling of bushes as he ran off. I didn't try to chase him this time. I don't want him to think I'm overly aggressive.

Why does he keep coming back? Is it curiosity, as if he's just as confused by me as I am by him? I'm glad he hasn't left, but I'm worried he may lose interest. I may need him desperately, but what if he doesn't feel he needs me? If he stops coming around there'll be no way to find him. I can't even follow him when he's passed by just a moment before me.

Well, I'm going to do something about it this time. If I can't go to him, I'll try to make contact when I'm not nearby. I'm going to leave a message in the forest for him. I'm not sure what it will be, possibly some simple symbols that I hope will show I am peaceful and want to be friends. I haven't thought of what they would be yet. I'm also thinking of leaving some food along with the message as a kind of a peace offering.

Since Mr. Screech seems to prefer moving around at night, I'll set up the message this evening and check on it in the morning. That way I can sleep through most of the anxious waiting. I think it's a good idea, and I'm very excited to get started. I'll write again once I'm done.

* * *

So I've been trying to think of some good universal signs for peace and friendship, but it's a lot harder than I thought. I mean, all the symbols I can think of that indicate friendship and peace could mean anything to Mr. Screech. They could also mean nothing at all. I've decided my best bet is a "smiley" face. How could that be misunderstood? A simple face made with rocks would be best I think. I also plan to put a small pile of berries under the face. I don't want to offend him if he turns out to be vegetarian by leaving any meat.

I thought about making some kind of way for Mr. Screech to reply back, like a circle of rocks with the stones he'd need to make a second smiley face. But I'm just going with the one face and the berries for now. I can always get more complicated later.

* * *

I'm so excited. I don't think I'll be able to sleep. I've left my message for Mr. Screech out in the woods, a small distance from my camp. I can hear him out there, but I probably won't know anything more until morning. I hope he's friendly. I hope he can tell I'm friendly.

Even if he has no idea of how to get me back to Earth, it would still be wonderful to have someone else around. We could help each other. I could get firewood while he gets food, or he could work on a better structure to sleep in while I purify our water. It would be so nice to be able to split the work with someone else. I get tired of always doing everything, even if I know it's necessary. But with him around, we'll be able to get a lot more done. Of course, that's if he's alone. If he knows of others, if he can take me to his civilization… even if it is an alien society, I could learn their ways. I could grow to like it. I'm sure of it.

One thing at a time. I'm going to try to sleep. We'll see what happens in the morning.

September 23 – Day 31

I didn't bother writing a morning entry today. I just went to go check the message. He was there! He'd eaten the berries and left the smiley face alone. I'm not sure how to take that. Obviously he took the berries so that must be a good sign, but he seemed to ignore the face altogether. Maybe it's not his fault that he didn't leave any kind of reply. I didn't leave him the stones necessary to make a second face. Maybe he had the problem I did of not knowing what kind of symbol to leave to make his intentions known. Or maybe it was something else. What if he doesn't smile when he's happy? What if he can't smile? What if he doesn't know what a smile means? I never thought of that.

Well, either way, the message was a partial success. I'll try it again tonight, but I've got some ideas of how to improve it. I'll put the message a little closer to camp. Maybe I can use the peace offering of food to slowly bring him closer and eventually actually meet with me. I also want to make one smiley face and one partial one. Maybe that way he'll be able to tell that I want him to finish it for me. It makes sense to me.

OK, first I need to eat. I'm getting so excited lately it's hard to remember.

* * *

Everything's all set up. The message and the berries are close enough to camp that I should be able to get a good look at him if he's still near them in the morning.

I've been thinking of how to address him for the first time. I think food is still the safest bet I have. I've put a small amount of berries close at hand so that I can offer them to him when I meet him. I think a simple "hello" is best. We can go from there.

It's funny how food is the best way to make a connection with somebody. Maybe because everyone needs it, you can draw people in with it. I know the only time my family really spent time together was at dinner. All the dates I went on usually involved food too. Getting together with friends was about food and sharing, at least partially. I never thought of it like that before. I hope food brings Mr. Screech and I together. I hope food is the universal language.

September 24 – Day 32

It worked! He came closer to camp and ate the food, even though I didn't see him when I got up this morning. He also didn't make the other smiley face, but that doesn't matter. He probably doesn't realize what I want him to do. But I can show him. I can help him learn. But I need to make contact. He needs to realize I want to become friends.

I know what I'll do. I'll put the next message right in camp! Right by the fire. I'll make up a bed for him, along with the food and the smiley face. Wouldn't that be great? For me to wake up and there he is waiting for me? I mean, I know he'll be nervous about it, but so will I. I think I'm taking the bigger risk, inviting him into my camp while I'm asleep. But I think I can trust him. He doesn't want to hurt me or he would have done it already.

Finally, I won't be alone anymore.

* * *

I'm so excited. I don't know what to do with myself. I want it to be morning. I just can't handle the wait. I want to just yell out to Mr. Screech to come on down. Let's make contact.

It will be so nice to have a friend. Just having someone around will make this whole world more livable. I hope he finally makes friends with me tomorrow, because I've been kind of neglecting everything else. I'm almost out of fresh water. I guess I better boil some more for tomorrow. But maybe Mr. Screech has supplies of his own. I hope I can eat his food. I should be able to, since we're both able to eat the same berries.

Can you imagine what alien food might taste like? I hope he isn't into some weird alien version of blood sausage or sushi or whatever. Of course, anything would be better than bugs and pond-hoppers. I hope he understands that I'm hungry.

I can't wait to meet him.

* * *

I can't sleep. I'm too excited. Tomorrow's the day. It's like waiting for Christmas morning. I have to wait for him, but I'm so eager to finally meet him. I hope I can calm down enough to be able to talk with him tomorrow. I hope I can get some sleep, because I'll want to be awake to meet my new friend. I hope he's a friend. Please God, let him be a friend.

I'll try to sleep again. Tomorrow will be the start of something special. I can feel it.

September 25 – Day 33

I'm crying. I can't…
It's too hard. Why?!
I'll try again later.

* * *

I'm a little better. A little. Good enough to describe what happened this morning.

He came. Mr. Screech was here in the camp.

I didn't think I'd ever get to sleep last night, but somehow I slept through him coming into the camp. I woke up to hear him eating. I was so excited and scared I didn't move at first. When I finally did get up it was very slowly, trying not to startle him. He was crouching down in front of the smiley face and berries with his back to me.

He was around the size of a human, about seven feet tall or so when he stood up. He was naked and had short gray fur all over his body, with a short forked tail hanging between his legs. He had long ears that rotated around like a horse's. I couldn't see his face.

I was excited, but I was afraid too. Afraid that he would be hostile, or run away. But I didn't let myself wonder about why he was naked. I didn't let myself think he was anything less than a potential new friend.

I didn't dare stand, so I cleared my throat softly.

"Hello," I said in a voice that I tried to make confidant. "I'm Richard."

Instantly Mr. Screech whirled around and rose up to his full height, hissing like air brakes. I fell back and cried out in fear. I should have said something to calm him, but I couldn't stop staring at Mr. Screech's face. His features resembled a mix of lemur and rodent, with long whiskers and big, vacant eyes. I tried to see some kind of emotion behind his violet eyes, but there was nothing. His expression was completely animal. There was no spark of intelligence behind it. My blood ran cold as I realized I was looking into the eyes of a savage creature. He snarled at me, like a dog, and then galloped out of camp on all fours.

I was crushed. I am crushed. I was so excited not to be alone anymore. I guess I fooled myself into believing that if I could just find Mr. Screech everything would be ok. That face… it was not the face of a thinking animal. There's no way to communicate with that thing. I'm afraid I really am alone.

I want to go home. I want to see Sarah and Mom and Dad and Bryant and Mark. I want to go home. I don't want to be alone on this alien world. I don't want to be alone.

MISTY FALLS

Expedition Log
Third of Partok, in the Second year of The Return
Yurril T'nak, field scout

We have found nothing here at the ruins of Geldenfair. Our search goes on, and we struggle to keep faith in the divine assurance that our journey will not be fruitless. Since coming to this world, we have been disappointed twice already, yet we persevere. Our next destination is the lost village of Etol. We shall then brave the swamp to the south if we still have not found that for which we seek.

Our perishable provisions have run low, but our hunters have been most effective in supplementing our diet with the beasts of this land. Never before have we seen such creatures of bizarre and curious workmanship, though we have seen no species possessing either a culture or a recognizable language. Brendell tells us the Ancestors were not natives of this world, and that indeed their time spent on this plane was but a scant century. We know nothing of a native race, and have found little evidence of such. Perhaps we will find more as our journey continues.

Grace Be To You. Yurril T'nak

September 26 – Day 34

'Morning. Last night was… restless. There's something out there. It's not Mr. Screech. I can't tell what it is. It's something I haven't heard before, something that sounds… well, I don't know. It sounded like a low gargling, bubbling, rumbling noise throughout the night. It was so disturbing, I didn't even try to catch a pond-hopper last night for breakfast. Maybe I'll try to catch one this morning. The hoppers aren't calling right now so they'll be harder to find, but maybe I can find one that's hiding in the grass. You never know.

* * *

Well I did catch a pond-hopper this morning, though it took longer than it would have at night. I also found some kind of slimy, multi-limbed thing crawling around on the bottom of the pool. I've decided I'll stick to pod rice and pond-hoppers for now though. I'm not that hungry anymore.

* * *

I'm just cooking the evening meal of boiled soilers with hook fir pine nuts and pod rice. It's good, but I really wish I had a shaker of salt to add some flavor.

I didn't think I would have much to write about tonight, but I just saw a little creature I thought I'd describe. I was just starting to light my fire when I heard a splash in the pool over the usual noises of the pond-hoppers. For a while, the pool was still and I wondered if I had just heard a rock or stick fall in. After a moment though, I saw a small, beaked head rise up out of the water. I watched silently as the head disappeared and reappeared several times on the surface. Eventually the little creature lifted itself up onto the far bank and I was able to get a good look at it.

It was long and slender with powerful legs and blue-black scales. Its head and beak were both small and well proportioned, and it struck me how dignified the creature looked standing up on its sturdy back legs. It watched me for a moment, a soiler clenched tightly in its beak, before running off into the fading light, its every move full of grace and agility. What a lovely... thing.

Well dinner looks to be ready. I'll say goodnight, and see you in the morning.

September 27 – Day 35

Once again I didn't sleep very well. The strange low, gurgling, rumbling noise was back again. I wish whatever creature is making that sound would just migrate or something. Or else let a larger creature step on it.

I can't stop thinking about home this morning. Sometimes I try to keep thoughts of home and family out of my mind. Memories are painful and I can't afford to get depressed all the time when it's a daily struggle just to survive. I'd hate for it to seem like I don't think about my family any more though. I think about them all the time.

I wish I had listened to Dad more. I miss the little things he would try to teach me. The "how-to" kind of things. It wasn't that he didn't support my interests in English literature and writing, but I think he just wanted me to have a strong foundation of day-to-day, useful knowledge. Mom always encouraged me to write. Since Bryant, Mark, and I were little, she would tell us that we could be whatever we wanted to be. That's always meant a lot to me. I miss... I mean, sometimes I wish I had... never mind. This is still hard. I'm gonna go get some work done.

I'll try to find some more plants that might serve as food. My pod rice supply here at the pool is running low.

* * *

I've been throwing up. I just saw something horrible. It was so bad. My hands are shaking and I can barely write. This is very, very bad.

I was out and wandering, looking for edible plants like I said I would. I wasn't having any luck so I was on my way back to camp when I found a dead body. It was so mutilated that at first I couldn't even tell what it had been. The corpse was ripped in half, its insides and most of its flesh missing. It was really bad. I mean, I've seen cats and dogs run over by cars. I even saw my Uncle Henry slaughter a sheep once, though my eyes were closed for most of it. And then Dave... But this was worse. Dave died but was still in one piece. This thing had been completely torn apart.

I didn't want to look at it, but I kept staring. I couldn't help myself. It was revolting, but I couldn't look away. I used the point of my spear to turn part of it over and try to identify what kind of creature it was. At my touch, the head rolled over and two large eyes stared sightlessly up at me. It was Mr. Screech. I screamed. I threw up and screamed again, my throat hoarse and aching. Mr. Screech... He may not have been what I had hoped for, but he didn't deserve that. He'd been murdered horribly. I cried when I couldn't scream any more.

What could have done that? I saw bones bitten in two and the body ripped in half. I haven't seen anything on this world that could do that much damage. Not only that, but why didn't the killer finish eating Mr. Screech entirely? And why did it tear the body in half like that? Do you think that whatever it was might not have been just a predator? Could it have killed him for sport? Could it have killed for the pleasure of killing?

I'm sharpening up my spear tip and keeping it close tonight. I'll build up the fire extra high. It's going to be hard to sleep tonight.

* * *

I'm so scared. It's night. My heart is pounding. There's no way I can go back to sleep. That thing is close. I can still hear it. I'm trying to steady my nerves. Keep the fire up. Do some writing to stay awake. I have to stay awake. I have to stay alert.

I woke up because I was cold. The fire had died. I tried for a while to go back to sleep, but it was just too cold. I got up and fed the warm embers until the fire was up and going strong. It wasn't until then that I looked around at the surrounding forest. That was when I saw them.

Eyes. A pair of huge, glowing eyes. They were massive, each one the size of a baseball with V-shaped pupils dilated in the firelight.

I froze. I couldn't breathe. I stared at the shinning circles, like the lights of an oncoming car. I fumbled for my flashlight. It all felt like a surreal dream, as if I could look up and the unblinking eyes would be gone. I found my flashlight and looked up again. The eyes were closer. I aimed the flashlight and flipped it on. That's when the bulb burned out.

All I saw was a flash, one image of the thing, before it disappeared again except for its unblinking eyes. It had four legs and looked to be the size of a Saint Bernard, though it might have been much larger. Its fur looked dark grey in the dim light, and it had no tail, just a little stub. The thing's paws each held wicked looking claws, but it was the mouth that I think will haunt me the most. It was grotesque, a sick parody of nature. It didn't have teeth, just massive, deadly jaws. Its lips curled back from two sloping, serrated masses of bone, as if its individual teeth had all merged into two massive ridges. Its jaws were freakish, its gaping maw stretching above and below its enormous eyes, so that the thing's over-sized mouth dominated the rest of its face.

I've never been so glad that I keep my spear nearby. I grabbed it then and held onto it for dear life while watching the thing's eyes. It went on like that for a long time, just sitting and staring, with me only moving to put more sticks on the fire. After what seemed an eternity the creature turned and disappeared into the darkness. It was a long time before I relaxed enough to write some of this down. I still have the spear in my lap.

I won't be going back to sleep tonight. I can still see the thing in my mind. A big mouth… opening for me. A "bigamouth". I have to keep the fire up. I hope I have enough fuel. I don't know how long it will be before dawn.

September 28 – Day 36

I haven't slept. I couldn't have, even if I'd wanted to. I've managed to keep the fire going, although I couldn't leave camp to get more wood. I ended up using the sticks from my lean-to, so now all that's left is my sled and a few supporting limbs.

I really feel terrible. I have a nasty headache and my stomach is all twisted up. It must be the stress. Even after the bigamouth left, I could still hear it out there. So close. Always close.

I can't stay here. That guttural gurgling noise I've been hearing has to belong to the bigamouth. It must have been what killed Mr. Screech. I must be inside its territory. It makes sense that this pool is a gathering place for many animals, providing a good place for the bigamouth to focus its attentions. It could see me as a possible rival or even as potential prey. Either way, I know it's not safe to stay here anymore.

I guess my best option is to keep going downstream. I don't want to leave the water, and there's still a good chance this creek could run into a river or lake with plenty of food nearby. I can always find more pod rice plants and catch more pond-hoppers. Who knows? If I find a good enough spot I may be able to build a more permanent shelter. But first thing's first. I need to strike camp and put some distance between the bigamouth and me.

* * *

I'm tired, but I made some good distance today. Striking camp was simple, all I had to do was load up my sled. I took a little time to pick all the rice-pods I could find along with a few hook fir pinecones to take with me. I thought about catching a pond-hopper for the road, but I figured it would be better to concentrate on traveling as far as I could today.

I've taken out the flare gun kit I brought from the plane. I know it's not a proper gun, but it will definitely be a better weapon than a sharpened stick. I know it won't do any good for hunting, but I figure nothing could work better than this for a self-defense weapon. I've read the short operating instructions that came with it, and I feel confident I know how to use it. I'll have to be careful though. I only have two flares.

I've also made sure to gather enough wood and sticks to keep the fire going all night. I figure that if I build the flames up bigger than usual, I won't have to feed it as often. Speaking of feeding, I had to camp a little ways from the creek tonight, so I didn't try to catch anything for dinner. I'll have pod rice and hook fir pine nuts instead.

I suppose I'm a little disappointed to leave my camp by the pool, but I had no choice. I just hope I traveled far enough today. I do not want a repeat of last night.

September 29 – Day 37

Well last night was a little better than the night before, but not by much. That bigamouth is still out there. I didn't see it, but I heard it throughout the night. Sometimes it sounded way too close. I'll have to keep moving, but I hope I can get outside of the bigamouth's territory soon. I'm not sure how long I can keep this pace up without a good night's rest. My head is really hurting. I need a good night's sleep. Maybe tonight. Maybe.

* * *

The going has been slow, and I'm pretty tired. The trees and bushes around the creek are getting so dense I can't pull the sled along the banks anymore. Several times, I had to walk so far away from the creek that I was afraid I would lose it altogether.

I'm sure there's plenty of life around here, but either I'm making too much noise with the sled or else I'm too tired to pay attention to what's around me. I did see several hand-sized flying creatures from a distance, and there was a rustle in the bushes near last night's camp. Didn't see what it was though.

I'm tired. I hope I'm out of the bigamouth's territory by now. If I am, I'm planning to have a lazy morning to get some much-needed rest tomorrow.

September 30 – Day 38

No rest for me. It's still out there. Sounds a little farther off though. I suspect he's following me to make sure I'm leaving. At least he's not stalking me as prey. On the other hand, I wonder how large his territory is. What if it's hundreds of miles across? I guess it's best not to think about that. I'm tired and stressed enough as it is.

I have to try to make as much distance as possible today. I can't walk next to the creek anymore. The bushes and foliage are too dense. I'll just try to follow it as closely as possible.

* * *

I'm packing it in a little early this evening, just because I'm so tired. I really, really hope I'm out of the bigamouth's territory. I can't hear it right now, so maybe it will leave me alone. I hope so. I'm so sleepy. So tired. Please let me sleep. I'm so tired.

October 1 – Day 39

Well it was definitely nice to have a good, long rest after all the excitement. I slept straight through last night and never heard the bigamouth. I think he's finally gone. Thank goodness.

Maybe now I can start looking for a permanent campsite. The area around here won't work. The undergrowth is too dense. I can't even see the creek. I'll have to keep moving downstream until it opens up again. At least the sound of the water has been getting louder over the last few days, so it's very easy to follow, even if I can't see it right now.

I just realized that it's now October. I have to admit that I'm proud of the fact that I've survived this long on an alien world. Speaking of which, I still don't know what to call this place. I've been giving things nicknames, but I guess I should try to come up with a good name for this world. I'll have to think about that.

* * *

I can definitely hear the water now! It's roaring! Like ocean waves, or a waterfall.

I haven't seen my creek since yesterday. The undergrowth is just too dense. I'll spend tomorrow trying to find some kind of trail to the sound of the water. I need to. My supplies are running low.

For the time being, I've made another small culinary discovery. I was trying to find something to add to my pod rice for tonight. Since I'm not near any water, I couldn't find any pond-hoppers or soilers, so I went bug hunting instead. I hit the jackpot when I cracked open a rotting log and found a bunch of black beetle-like bugs squirming around. Each is about half the length of my thumb, with large protrusions that extend from their back-ends and arch over their heads and bodies. I tried to pick one up by its "umbrella", but the squishy appendage came off in my hand and the beetle scurried off. It must be some kind of defense mechanism. I used my baseball cap (the one from Dave) and was able to brush the entire group of beetles into a waiting jacket, then onward to the pot. The umbrella beetles wouldn't have filled me on their own, but when mixed in with the pod rice they made a satisfying, if bland stew. What I wouldn't give for some crackers to go with it. Or salt. Or potatoes. Or beef chunks.

Now I'm hungry again.

October 2 – Day 40

I've just found something amazing! I got up early to try to find some water since I was nearly out. It wasn't hard to hear where the water was, but finding a trail through the thick underbrush took forever. As I got closer, the noise of the water kept growing until it became a thunderous, constant roar. The noise was almost deafening. When I finally broke out of the dense trees, I realized what was making all the racket. I was standing at the top of a huge waterfall!

My little creek must have been just one of many estuaries that fed into this single location. I followed the main waterway backwards, and it looks like the top of the falls is the culmination of at least four connecting creeks and rivers. These waterways meet and immediately plunge down at least a hundred feet to a massive pool or grotto. From up here on the cliff side I can just see the beginnings of an impressive river spurring off from the far end of the grotto below me.

I've never seen or heard anything as awe-inspiring as these falls. It's like a thunderous army of great white beasts shrouded in mist, roaring and leaping down to the deep mirror-surface below. It's an overcast day, so the grotto itself glimmers and shivers like a living cloud, fed and bled by the constant inward and outward flow of water and vapor. I bet when the sun is out there are rainbows everywhere in all this mist. I think that's what I'll call this place: Misty Falls.

* * *

Well, as lovely as the Misty Falls are, I can't stay up here looking at them all day. It's windy and all the moisture in the air makes it kinda cold. I think the best place to make camp is down by the grotto. It's almost the size of a small lake, and the surrounding forest looks healthy and full of life. A prime location for a secure, long-term camp.

The problem is how to get down there. Like I said before, it has to be at least a hundred feet down from where I am at the top of the cliff. While I might be able to climb down the rock face below me, I think I'll go with the pit in my stomach and take the long way around. I'm on the south side of the Falls, so I'll continue south until the ground levels out, and then double back this way again. Everything in that direction is so densely forested I'm not sure how far I'll have to go before I can come back. I'll make sure to refill my water supplies up here for the trip. There's enough pod rice by the water for me to pack a good three-day's supply. I should be at the grotto well before then.

Ok, better get started. The sooner I head out the sooner I can get to the grotto, and the sooner I can see the Falls from below.

* * *

I'm in the forest somewhere south of the Misty Falls and it's starting to rain. It's not a heavy rain. It's more like a good Washington rain, constant and gentle. I've made tonight's camp in the shelter of a large tree with yellow leafs the size and shape of half-dollars covering almost every square inch of its branches and trunk. I'm eating a bowl of pod rice soup without a garnish since I didn't feel like looking for bugs in the rain.

* * *

Sarah must be well into her fall semester by now. She was studying fashion, did I mention that? I never understood what she saw in it. It was just something she loved. But she didn't mind that I disagreed with her. We would talk about it a lot. I was always saying how I thought models were all just a bunch of anorexics in scraps of material. Sarah would always try to explain to me why she thought I was wrong. We never did agree about it, but I loved talking with her anyway. Sometimes when we talked, she'd start musing about all kinds of random things. She called it her mental screensaver. I wonder if I'm her mental screensaver now. Does she muse about me while her instructor drones on about the difference between satin and silk? Does she draw portraits of me from memory in her sketchbook? I tried drawing her tonight. I threw the page in the fire. It didn't do her justice.

Anyway, I'll probably reach the grotto tomorrow or the next day. Maybe I'll finally get a chance to use my fishing spear for what I actually made it for... fishing. I'd love some roasted fish.

October 3 – Day 41

It's another rainy morning. It's no big deal. I've got the poncho from my survival kit, my trusty windbreaker jacket, and Dave's cap to keep me nice and dry.

I better get going.

* * *

Well I'm finally at the foot of Misty Falls. I got a little lost for a while, but I'm finally here. You know, I think the Falls may be even more beautiful down at ground level. I never thought anything could look so crystalline and delicate while thundering and crashing with such raw power. The grotto is also a contradiction, violent and frothy at the cliff side and calm as a swimming pool at its center. When it warms up and stops raining I'd like to go for a swim. I'm due for a bath.

I need to find a good spot to set up a permanent camp. I've ruled out the boulders all around the banks of the grotto. While they would make great support structures for a sturdy hut, they're just too close to the Falls to keep me dry. I think I'll be happier making camp in the shelter of some of these big trees. Maybe this time I'll try to make a freestanding hut. I'd like to have a place where I can stand up and walk around inside without getting wet. In the meantime, I'll make due with another lean-to using the sled for the main construction.

I've already gotten the lean-to set up and I've set aside enough semi-dry wood for tonight's fire. I think I'll use the remaining daylight to look for dinner down by the water. I'm not sure if I'll see any pond-hoppers or other edible creatures, but I'm hopeful.

* * *

Well I didn't catch anything, but the grotto looks promising as a good source of food. I saw dark shapes in the water that may have been something fish-like, and there's plenty of tall grass for pond-hoppers. I saw a ton of pod rice stalks among the tall grass, so I won't go hungry while waiting to catch something.

That's about everything I guess. If the rain's gone in the morning, I'll have a proper look around my new home. I definitely think I'm going to like it here.

October 4 – Day 42

Good morning. Well the rain has stopped and the air is bright and fresh, if a little on the cool side. There's a slight mist trailing from the Falls that adds luster to the vivid colors all around me. What a beautiful place this is.

I guess today I'll go out and explore the area surrounding the grotto. I wonder what I'll find.

* * *

This place is going to make a great camp. I spent the rest of the morning picking pod rice. I noticed today that some of the pods had split open and the rice inside had dried and hardened. I wonder how long the shelf life of the rice is while it's still in the pods. Either way, I left all the unripe pods on their stalks to mature in the next few weeks, so food shouldn't be a problem until after that.

Speaking of food, there's a healthy stock of swimming creatures in the pond. There's a peaceful rock pool where several types seem to like to rest during the day. I think that definitely would be the best place to try out some fishing. I'm excited to try to catch something new to eat, but I think there are some other things I need to think through first. With all the pod rice I've collected, I'm not going to starve to death any time soon, so my next priority should be making a real shelter for myself.

I've been struggling to think of a workable design. I'm no architect. I don't know the first thing about building a freestanding structure. I've never even set up a tent by myself. I keep trying to think of stories I've read or movies I've seen with simple buildings, but I just can't come up with any that I'd be able to make.

The big issue I'm trying to figure out right now is building supplies. There's plenty of small logs and tree limbs lying around, but how do I connect them together? I could make a cabin by notching and stacking the logs, but I'm guessing that that would take at least a month. If I want the structure sooner than that, I'll have to secure the timbers some other way. I guess my only option would be tying it all together, but there's three problems with that: one, I've got no rope; two, I don't know how to make rope; and three, I only remember two knots from Boy Scouts. I wish I had paid better attention to Mark when he tried to get me past Tenderfoot rank. He's the big Eagle Scout, not me. I don't know how I'm going to get this together.

I've got a headache. This building thing is going to be a lot harder than I thought. Oh well, I'm going to try to plan a little longer. Maybe a good first step would be to invent some kind of rope. Luckily, I do have plenty of one luxury right now… time.

* * *

'Evening. Since it's not raining, I can really hear the pond-hoppers' song mixed with the crashing of the Falls. The sky is bright and clear, with stars like diamonds scattered among the treetops. I wish someone were here to share this with. I mean, I know I've only got pod rice for tonight's dinner, but at least it's hot and filling, and the fire is pleasant. All in all, this place wouldn't make for that bad of a date.

Speaking of which, tomorrow I'm definitely due for a bath. Maybe I'll catch something for dinner too. You never know.

October 5 – Day 43

I woke up this morning kinda damp. I really need a structure that's more closed in than a lean-to to keep out some of the dew and mist from the Falls. At least the morning is fresh and bright. I'm making some hook fir tea. It's gross, but I'm out of ring pine needles and there aren't any of those trees around here. Maybe it's too wet for them. At least my tea's warm. I think when I finish my brew I'll go for a swim. I'll let you know how the water is.

* * *

The water is COLD! Brr! It was like taking a bath in a refrigerator! Of course, now that I've thought about it, it makes sense. Tributaries from the mountains flow directly into these Falls. Still, I guess I can't complain too much. The water is fresh and clear, and I feel better after having done it, but it will take a lot of willpower to jump in there again!

Since I didn't realize how cold the water was going to be I hadn't bothered to keep the fire going, so I had to sun myself on the boulders to get dry. Actually, that part wasn't so bad, especially when the day warmed up a little. It gave me a chance to admire the Falls for a while. I really wish I were a real artist so I could capture what they look like.

The Falls weren't the only thing I had a chance to study closely. Looking into the clear water backlit by the cloudy sky, I found that the grotto's surface made for a surprisingly good mirror. I didn't even realize that I hadn't seen myself in over a month. I mean, I know I have the signaling mirror, but I've never used it to just look at myself.

I think I look pretty good, all things considered. I'm skinnier, but I guess that's to be expected. My hair is all dark and greasy. It's clumped together around my face and ears, and while I normally wouldn't bother cutting it, my bangs are growing over my eyes and it's getting harder to see. I'll have to take care of that. Other than those things, not much else has changed besides my fledgling beard. There is one other thing that is different, but less obvious. I look older.

Well anyway, enough time wasting. I'm going to hack off some hair with my knife and then do some fishing while I still have light.

* * *

I had no luck fishing but I did catch a fat pond-hopper around twilight. I also gave myself a little touchup on my hair. It doesn't look very good, but it's out of my eyes and that's all that matters. I'll need to be able to see to get started on the plans I came up with for tomorrow.

Today I had plenty of time to think, and I've thought a lot on the problem of building a structure. I think I've got something that will work. Since my main problem is a way to fasten it all together, I figured that my best bet would be some kind of structure that required as few connections as possible. I came up with the idea of a teepee. Of course, it would have to be a little unorthodox. I don't have any animal hides to stretch between the supporting poles, but if I used sticks and branches to build up the walls, and then use mud to fill in the cracks, it could work out nicely. I think at that point it wouldn't technically be a teepee anymore. Maybe something more like a wigwam. I don't really remember what a wigwam is, but I seem it to remember it being mostly sticks and mud. Good enough for me.

It's getting late and I'm tired. I'll try to get some rest and tackle this project in the morning. I'm kind of excited. This will definitely be my most ambitious project yet!

October 6 – Day 44

Good morning world, whatever you're called. I guess I still have to work on that one.

I woke up this morning with the worst craving. More than anything, I got up wanting something sweet. I've never had what I thought was much of a sweet tooth, but man was I hurting for a candy bar, some ice cream, even some fruit juice. I hope that this craving is just a mental thing and not a physical need for natural sugars or anything. Either way, I know I need more balance in my diet. I'll keep it in mind.

I've come up with a solution to the rope issue for building the wigwam. I still have the seatbelts from the plane with me, and I think that's my answer. The ends are a little frayed where I cut them out of the plane, but I think the weave of the belts is too thick to just fall apart when cut. I hope so, because I plan on using at least one of the belts to secure the tops of the poles together.

Before I do that, I'll have to cut and prepare the support poles. I plan on finding some saplings as close to my target length as possible and then using my utility knife to take off their branches. It'll take a while, but it's my best idea and I want to get started. I don't want to spend any more nights in the lean-to than I have to.

First though, I'm going to do some fishing. Wish me luck.

* * *

Ha! Add fish to the menu tonight! Or... something fish-like. I'll call it a fish, just because I don't know how else to categorize it. It doesn't have scales, just a tough grayish brown skin. It was resting on the bottom of the rock pool when I speared it, so I think it's probably a bottom feeder. It has a long, rounded tail that's flattened out like a whale or a dolphin's. The fins along its sides are elongated so they stretch along the length of its body. The whalefish was stationary when I speared it, so I'm unsure exactly what it looks like in motion. Now I just have to figure out how to prepare this thing.

Of all outdoor activities, I always liked fishing the best, but I never cleaned the fish. Dad always did that, and I only watched him do it a couple times. I know I'm supposed to cut the head off, scale it (or peel off the skin in this case), and take the guts out. Beyond that, I'm kinda at a loss. I guess I'll cut the fins and tail off, and then try to get the bones out. I already decided to try boiling it. I would have liked to fry it, but I don't have any cooking oil. If it's good to eat I'll try roasting it next time. I'll write again and tell how the whalefish turns out.

* * *

Yum. Despite the funky tail and weird fins, this fish is still fish when it counts. Really good. I only wish there was more. The one I caught was about a foot long, but I did such a terrible job cleaning it that there wasn't much useable meat left. I'll have to try to either catch more fish at a time or get more effective at cleaning them. Probably both. At least it was something relatively familiar, which is a welcome change.

By the way, I finally came up with a name for this planet: Other World. It just seems to fit. Everything here is just a bit off, as if the Earth had been slightly altered. There are even times when I almost forget I'm not on Earth, but then I look around at the red and black hook firs or the two moons in the night sky and I remember. I'm on another world. Other World. I think it's appropriate.

October 7 – Day 45

I'm not going to write much this morning. I wanted to try some more fishing. I'd like to catch enough for multiple meals so I can concentrate on building the wigwam. I'll write again after I catch something.

* * *

Once again, fishing was successful, and I did a much better job of cleaning them this time.

I've been toying with the idea of making a more complicated fishing rig. I mean, the spear works ok, but what if I had an actual line and hook? It would probably work much better in the long run, but I really don't have anything to use for the line. All I can think of using is the threads from my clothes or grass. I'm not ready to destroy my clothes yet, and I doubt the grass would be strong enough. It's something to think about though.

The big project for tomorrow is getting started on my wigwam. I'm excited to sleep under a real roof again, especially since the weather has been so cloudy lately. Oops, the fish is burning!

October 8 – Day 46

I'm gonna keep this morning's entry short. I really want to get to work on the wigwam. Wish me luck.

* * *

This is taking too long. It took forever to find four coin-leaf tree saplings that were the right size and cut them down with the little saw on my utility knife. By the time I managed to bring down the four trees and drag them back to camp it was time for lunch. Good thing I already had the fish I caught yesterday.

I've got to finish this hut. The nights are getting colder and I'm not sleeping very well. I don't feel so great. Kinda funny in my stomach and just... weird.

Great, now it's raining.

I'm just going to get back to work. Maybe I'll have this finished by tomorrow night.

* * *

Gosh, my arms and back ache. The pain starts at my wrists and moves all the way to the base of my spine. It doesn't help that I also have a headache and my stomach hurts.

Anyway, I got all the limbs off the saplings. Right now, I'm just trying to figure out how to attach the ends together to form the top joint. I've tried several made-up knots with the seatbelts, but I've decided on what I hope is the simplest option. I'll just wrap a belt around the poles several times then do the one knot I remember, the clove hitch, to finish it off. We'll find out tomorrow whether it works or not.

If it does work, all I'll have to do is fill in the walls using a bunch of branches and leafs. I'm not going to worry about filling the cracks in with mud right now. I just don't have the energy for that.

October 9 – Day 47

Oh my head. My stomach is all twisted up. It's hard to stand up straight. I didn't sleep so well. I sure hope I get my hut up tonight. I'm sure I'll sleep better once I'm inside.

Ok, I've got to get to work.

* * *

It's up. I crisscrossed the tops of the poles together and tied a belt around the top. Gravity keeps the base of the poles spread apart and the belt keeps the levered posts together. Finally. I'm gonna rest a while, and then I'll fill it in with branches and then... then I'll have an early dinner.

* * *

Well the hut's not done completely, but it's good enough for now. I feel so bad. I think I'm really sick. I feel terrible. It's my stomach and head. I think that maybe I ate something bad. Maybe I didn't cook my fish enough the other night. You can die from food poisoning, right? Oh, it's so hard to write. I'm getting spasms of pain all through my body. I'm not sure if it is food poisoning. Maybe it's something else?

I'm going to try to sleep. I really hope I feel better tomorrow.

October 10 – Day 48

It's starting to rain. I don't feel any better. I'm just lying here in the hut, finding where my filled in walls have holes. There are lots of places where the water gets in. At least I was able to finish it. It just needs more branches in the walls and maybe some mud to make it waterproof. I'll do that when I'm feeling better. Right now though, I just want to rest.

* * *

It's evening and still raining. I haven't eaten much, just one pot of pod rice. I want to sleep. I'm so tired.

October 11 – Day 49

I feel a little better today, but I'm still really tired. I'm just going to rest. I'm sure I'll be all right. Those cramps are gone now. I think I just needed to get whatever that was out of my system. Ok, I'm going to get some more sleep.

* * *

Still a little tired, but I wanted to describe something I saw this evening. It was around dusk and the light was getting blue and dim. I was just staring up at the sky when I saw something fly over. It was large, with big black wings and an oversize mouth. It was hard to see much definition, but it definitely appeared to be some kind of nocturnal creature, flying through the air with its mouth open like a fisherman's net. I think it may have been trolling for bugs.

OK, I'm going to try to get some more sleep. Have a good night, and don't worry, I'm sure I am on the mend.

October 12 – Day 50

Well I may be feeling much better this morning, but I'm absolutely starving. I'm probably a little malnourished and underfed. I haven't been eating enough since I've been sick. One meal a day just won't cut it. I'm going to collect more pod rice, throw some hook fir pinecones in the fire, dig up some soilers, and try to catch another whalefish in the rock pool. I'm gonna have a feast tonight!

* * *

What a meal! I haven't eaten this well for weeks. I caught a new fish today and ate the whole thing with a healthy helping of pod rice. The fish was long, with a chubby belly and a bone-plated head that looks like a garden trowel. It was covered with sliver-shaped scales that came away like dried candle wax. The meat was pretty good. I can't help but think that fishing would be much easier with an actual fishing line, but whatever.

Now that I'm feeling better, I have to say I'm very happy with my set-up here at Misty Falls. I have a new place to live in, plenty of food, and a gorgeous view. What could be better? It could be a little warmer, but you can't have everything. I'll just have to wear two layers of clothes until it warms up again.

* * *

I just saw another night creature a minute ago. I suspect that many of them are attracted to my fire, since I'm sure none of them has ever seen a light at night other than the moons. This one was another flying creature, though it didn't have feathers, at least I don't think so. It looked fuzzy, like a Valentine's Day teddy bear. It did have wings and a beak, with two enormous eyes and a low, lilting song like someone blowing into a conch shell. Its big eyes reminded me of an owl, and I have to admit that its fuzzy coat reminded me of my friend Amy's big fur coat she always wore. An "Amy owl". How funny.

Well, goodnight.

October 13 – Day 51

Well it's morning and I've already gone down to the water to pick some pod rice for breakfast. I've been thinking that now that I have the wigwam up I should shift my top priority from shelter to food. That good meal I had last night has convinced me that I'll be much happier as long as I keep myself well fed. With that in mind, I now have several methods I can use to get food. There is the pod rice of course, which has been a lifesaver as a continuous staple. Other options are fishing and catching pond-hoppers, bugs, and soilers. I'll see what else I can come up with.

The rice is ready. I better go.

* * *

Scrounging for food hasn't gone very well so far. I picked all the pod rice I could find without going too far from camp. I'm keeping the rice in the pod until I eat them, hoping that it will keep them somewhat preserved. I managed to gather a good amount of rice, but everything else is slim pickings. I couldn't find any pond-hoppers, and the ground around the grotto is devoid of soilers.

This afternoon I'll try doing some fishing, and if that doesn't work, I'll do some evening bug hunting.

Well lunch is ready. I guess it goes without saying that I'm really tired of pod rice by now.

* * *

At least I'm eating something in addition to the pod rice tonight. I managed to spear a whalefish even though this one is smaller than the ones I had before. I know there are probably other, bigger fish in the river that the grotto feeds into, but for the time being I have no way to get them. I really should invest some time into trying to rig up some kind of fishing pole.

Before that though, I want to try my hand at some hunting. I still have that single-point spear that I made a while ago, but I've never tried using it. I'll bet if I head away from the Falls and into the forest, I could probably find a variety of birds and small creatures. Actually, I think it'd be kind of fun.

Fun. I guess I haven't had much fun lately.

Anyway, hunting should be exciting. Tomorrow after breakfast, I'll practice throwing my spear, since I doubt I'll be able to get close enough to stab anything.

October 14 – Day 52

Well, throwing practice was disappointing. I've got no skill. I couldn't throw my spear more than ten paces away, and even then, it wouldn't stick into anything. When it comes to accuracy I'm even worse. Three feet is my maximum range for an accurate throw. Wonderful.

Still, it's better than nothing, and no one is saying I can't improve. In the meantime, who knows? Maybe I'll get lucky and some dumb creature will wander within three feet of me.

* * *

I didn't catch anything today, but at least I know that there is plenty of wildlife around here. It only took a few minutes before I found some whistlers flying around a hell berry bush. They're welcome to them.

I also saw two new species during my foray. The first one remained up in the treetops and was about the size of a cat with long dark fur. There seemed to be something odd about the way he moved through the upper branches above me, but after observing him for a while, I realized what it was. Instead of having normally shaped limbs, this creature had an arm and a leg that didn't terminate into paws or feet. Instead, they connected together into one looped limb! The creature used this natural, bizarre loop to catch, climb, and hold onto branches with amazing agility. There's no way I could get my spear all the way up to the treetops, so the 'tree-hugger' is definitely safe from my stew pot.

The other creature I saw may not be so lucky. As I was coming back to camp, I heard a rustling in a nearby bush and a pudgy, furry little creature skittered away from me. He was about the size of the tree-hugger, but lacked the other creature's grace and dexterity. He waddled at high speed away from me, looking like an overfed guinea pig. Unfortunately, I wasn't ready for him and I never even tried throwing my spear, but it definitely looked like a promising quarry for the future. I suppose the moral of the story is that I'll have to try being a lot stealthier next time, along with being a better shot.

I realized just now that it's almost been a week since I last wrote about home. I wonder why. Maybe it's just a survival technique. I almost feel guilty saying it, but it's a lot easier to get through a day when I don't think about home. Aside from starvation and deadly creatures, I think my biggest enemy right now is depression. I'm my only chance for survival. I can't afford to give up. That's why I think projects like the wigwam and going hunting are so important. They give me immediate goals that directly affect my lifestyle for the better.

I think I'm going to practice my spear throwing a little more before I go to sleep.

October 15 – Day 53

You'll never believe what I just saw! I'm having a hard time believing it myself! It was just incredible!

I was up this morning practicing my spear throwing when I heard a deep, thunder-like rumbling. I stopped and listened to the sound, but it didn't fade away like thunder. It just kept coming. Then I started to feel tremors in the ground. It felt like the start of an earthquake. My first thought was to jump back into the hut, but then I realized how stupid that was. Here I am in the wide open during an earthquake and I wanted to go INTO the only rickety structure on the planet!

Anyway, the shuddering tremors didn't increase to a full-on

earthquake, but they didn't disappear either. I really got my hopes up then. I got these ideas of a large vehicle of some kind rumbling through the forest. I ran into the woods trying to find the source of the sound.

I finally stopped in a thicket of trees. The shuddering had also stopped, but I still heard odd sounds nearby that I couldn't identify. I started to walk slowly forward, but then one of the trees moved. It lifted up, bent sideways, and then came down again several yards away. I looked up at the tree and screamed. I tried to back away but I tripped and landed on my back. A head, massive and ponderous, turned and looked down at me. I screamed again.

The thing was huge! At least three-stories tall at the shoulder. Its legs were long and thick, with circular feet like an elephant's. The creature had four massive legs and a tail that looked proportionately small compared to the rest of its gray and brown streaked body. For some reason it looked like the only hair it had was a long, dark mane all along its neck. The rangy looking hair was at least fifteen feet long, though it still had no chance of touching the ground.

Of course, all of this was stuff I noticed later. My first thought, staring up at that big head, was whether or not I was about to be eaten. The head was so big it wouldn't have taken much to make me a bite-sized meal. Luckily, it didn't eat me. Actually, I think it's strictly a vegetarian.

I guess I startled it when I yelled like I did. It watched me for a moment as I kept completely still. Eventually it lost interest and went back to eating. I started breathing again and got a chance to study the great behemoth as it ate. It ate the treetops. Not the greenery, not the leafs, not the branches. It ate the tree tops! Spade-leaf trees, hook firs, coin-leaf trees, it chomped all of them.

At one point, the behemoth was trying to reach the top of a particularly tall hook fir. The creature chewed at the middle point of the trunk, looking like an enormously oversized beaver. Then, once the middle was more than half-chewed through, the behemoth took a step back, shifted its massive bulk onto its back legs and tail, and then lifted its forelimbs and head up into the air. It placed its huge, round feet against the tree trunk, gave a guttural grunt, and began pushing. Immediately the formerly solid tree began to bend and creak frighteningly. I watched the hook fir's crown reel back and forth wildly with each heave of the behemoth's powerful muscles.

Soon there was a snap and with a terrible groaning, the tree began to fall, broken at the chewed middle point. I jumped out of the way, thinking the tree's crown was about to come crashing down on top of me. Luckily, the tree only partially came down. The upper half is now hanging off to the side and probably won't take much to eventually come down completely. I guess the behemoth chewed the trunk just to break the tree in half and get to the softer top branches. It's clever, but it doesn't do the tree much good.

Eventually the big lug ate his fill and moved on. The tree he brought partially down won't survive with a large section of its remaining trunk suspended by a portion of frayed wood fiber.

Amazing.

* * *

I've been thinking about the forest behemoth I saw today and about that incredible mane it had. It could be really handy to have some of that hair. I could use single strands for thread and mend my clothes. I could wind a dozen strands together and make twine and fishing line. I could even make rope, possibly, if I managed to wind some lengths of twine together. Most importantly, I'm sure that it would be sturdier and longer-lived than anything I would make out of dried water grass. But am I too late?

I saw the behemoth late this morning. It could be miles away by now. Then again, it wasn't moving very fast when I saw it. And its trail would be pretty easy to follow.

Either way, it's too dark and late for me to start after it now. But I could head out in the morning. Once I find it, I think my best bet would be to sneak up to it and cut as much of the hair as I can without the thing noticing me. I'll have to be careful. As docile as it is, it probably won't appreciate an unsolicited haircut. I might be able to pull it off if the behemoth were asleep. But if I wanted to catch it while it was sleeping, now is the time I should be trying to catch up to it.

Come to think of it, maybe I should get going right now. It's not really all that dark. The moons are out, and I should have enough light to follow the thing's fairly obvious trail. Ok, I better get going. Wish me luck!

October 16 – Day 54

Ugh, what a night. I can't sleep, so I guess I better write about what happened.

I set out right away after finishing last night's entry, taking my backpack, spear, and trusty utility knife. I made my way back to where I'd last seen the behemoth by the light of Mike and Ike. That's what I've decided to call the two Moons. The big one's Mike and the little one's Ike. Both of them are around half-full, although I think Mike is waxing while Ike is waning.

Anyway, back to last night. I quickly found the broken tree trunk where I'd last seen the behemoth. I followed its trail, weaving through the forest somewhat before settling on a course parallel with the river flowing from Misty Falls.

I found the behemoth with its head held suspended over the gently flowing water. At first, I was worried it was still awake, but when I got closer, I realized it was actually asleep on its feet. It was breathing slowly and deeply, its knees locked so that its legs again resembled four sturdy tree trunks.

I wasn't sure how to proceed. With its head held out over the water, I had no way to reach it. I must have sat in the dark for ten minutes trying to figure out what I would do. Eventually, I realized that if I seriously wanted the behemoth's hair I'd have to actually climb up on top of the thing, but back home I would get nervous just being up on a horse.

I decided to try climbing up its tail, which was lying flat on the ground. It wasn't that bad once I got started. It was like climbing a thick, warm tree trunk… except that it was moving slowly… and it smelled. It really smelled. Not really a bad smell, just a very strong, musky scent.

Once I got up on its hindquarters I paused, hoping I hadn't been noticed. The behemoth remained quiet and still, breathing like a massive bellows. I didn't dare get overconfident and try to walk upright along its back. Even if it was as broad as a driveway I was still very aware that I was at least fifteen feet in the air. I moved on my hands and knees, following the gentle rise of its spine.

The mane itself began at the base of its long neck. I didn't want to push my luck so I decided to take the strands closest to my reach. I'm not sure if cutting hair right next to the skin hurts, but I gave myself a foot's length of slack just to be safe. I started out just cutting one or two strands at a time, coiling each one into the bottom of my backpack. Eventually I realized that the behemoth wasn't waking up and started cutting big handfuls of hair at a time.

It couldn't have gone better. The behemoth stayed quiet, even when I had to reach out onto its neck to get to additional strands. I kept cutting and stuffing until my bag was completely full of coiled hair. I sealed it up, put away my knife, and began to make my way back to its tail. By that time, I was definitely feeling the effects of hard exercise and tension, especially with it being so late at night. All my muscles were aching. I guess that's why I fell.

I didn't fall completely off, just part way. My leg slipped and I kinda tumbled to the side before I could get a grip on the behemoth's backbone. I'm not sure if it was the fall or my cry of surprise that woke the thing up. It stirred, and then gave a shuddering groan. The behemoth turned, swinging its massive head around to me. I screamed. So did the behemoth. It shuffled away to the side and I lost my grip. Luckily, I kinda slid down the side of the creature instead of falling straight down. I landed with a thump and lay there stunned for a second, just barely aware of being nearly crushed by a massive foot.

At last, I had the presence of mind to roll over and crawl away. I tried to stand a couple of times, but for some reason my legs wouldn't work, so I just kept crawling. Eventually I managed to get on my feet and somehow found the energy to run the rest of the way home. I don't know what happened to the behemoth.

So that's how it all happened. It was way more excitement than I want to have again anytime soon, but I've got my prize. A whole bag full of coiled behemoth's hair to use any way I can think of.

And now… I will take a nap.

* * *

Mmm, not a whole lot happened today, just being kind of lazy and tired. I did mess with the behemoth hair some and I think I'll be able to figure out some way to make twine as well as a rope. I'll tie several strands to two sticks then twist the sticks until the hair is wound tight, then tie off the ends. It's fairly simple and probably the crudest way I could do it, but it's the best I could think of.

I was thinking about hunting again today. I really don't have the time or skill to wander through the forest with a spear trying to find something for dinner. I was wondering… now that I have a way to make rope, how about trying my hand at making some traps? They could be fairly simple ones, like maybe a loop tied with a slipknot to try and catch something walking by. Or maybe I could try digging a pit trap. Anyway, it's something to think about. I'll wrap my brain around it tonight while I'm twisting behemoth hair.

October 17 – Day 55

I just got done doing my morning throwing practice with my spear. I was disappointed that my throwing arm hasn't improved, but I guess I can't expect amazing success with just a few days' practice. It just means I'm going to have to work harder on making my traps effective. I finished a length of rope this morning. It looks pretty pathetic, but it's strong and it should work as an effective snare. My best idea is to tie it in a slipknot and leave it open on the forest floor. I'd bait it if I had anything to bait it with, but I haven't seen any berries for a while, so it will just have to sit there. Maybe I'll get lucky. I'll set it up this morning, and we'll see what I get by the evening.

I hope I catch something. A nice warm meal would really do me good right now. The temperature has stayed fairly brisk for a while now and I haven't gone without my windbreaker jacket for the last three days. I'm worried that this turn of the temperature is more than just a cold snap. What if the season is changing? Since I started this journal, I've been recording the dates as if I were still on Earth. It just seemed easiest to keep track of time that way. Now it looks like it's getting cooler here, while at the same time autumn is coming to Earth, at least in the Northern Hemisphere. Could it be that the seasons of this world are somehow linked to what they are back home? How could that be possible?

I guess the only way I'll know for sure is if the leafs start changing color, that is, if they even do that on Other World. Until then I still have to eat. I'll go set up that trap now. I really hope I catch something today. I also hope it doesn't rain. It looks pretty overcast.

* * *

Well it's raining. Not a hard rain, just a drizzle that doesn't look to let up anytime soon. When I got back to my hut after setting up the snare trap in the forest I found that the interior of my little home was a little dryer than outside. I've put more branches and leafs in the roof so now it's much more comfortable. I'm sitting in here now, looking out at the rainfall and listening to the Misty Falls and the pond-hoppers. You'd think the hoppers would really like this rain, but they seem quieter than usual. After lunch I'm gonna try to catch a few for dinner.

Incidentally, I'm glad I had the presence of mind to keep my firewood inside the hut, but I'm not too sure how well the fire will work out. There's a little gap in the very top of the wigwam since there's no way to seal the tied-off tops of the support poles. I just hope that the hole will be enough to let the smoke out. I guess we'll see.

* * *

Well I didn't catch anything today. The snare trap looked just the same as it did when I laid it this morning. Oh well. I'll try again tomorrow. At least I'm not wasting time wandering around the forest 'hunting.' I was actually thinking that tomorrow I'll also try my idea of a pit trap. I'll just use one of the oars from the plane as a shovel and dig a nice big hole in the forest floor, put some sharpened sticks in the bottom, and cover it up. A nice little spike trap. It should work well as long as I don't forget where I made it.

I couldn't find any pond-hoppers tonight so it's pod rice soup again. I've put the fire out, but even with a small fire, I know everything in here is going to smell like smoke now. I guess that from now on I should try to cook enough food to leave some over in case I can't have a fire. Of course, that would require me to catch enough food to have leftovers. Oh well. Maybe I'll have more luck tomorrow.

October 18 – Day 56

What a nice day to stay in bed. The rain's falling softly, pattering on leafs and tree trunks. Everything looks more vibrant and full of life. It's so pretty, and so warm and cozy here in the hut.

I wish I had someone here to share all of this with. Do you realize how much easier this would be with two people? Someone could cook the food and boil the drinking water while the other person checked the traps and got firewood. If I had another person here, I could take the time to enjoy a morning like this.

All right, I guess I better get up and get started.

* * *

Well, today was fairly uneventful. The snare trap didn't catch anything, and the newly made pit trap was just as useless. After I set them up this morning, I did my throwing practice in the rain and fixed up the roof of the hut again. I thought I'd try to mix things up by doing a little fishing, but I had no luck. I tried to switch to pond-hopper hunting, but there weren't any of them to be found again.

In the end, I went back to the old standby: bugs. It actually wasn't too hard to find the little critters. I think the rain draws them out. I found a bunch of umbrella beetles to add to tonight's rice. I also found something new, some kind of undulating slug-like creature with two heads. At least, I think they're heads since each one has a set of antenna. I decided the beetles would be enough of a supplement for tonight. I may be hungry, but I'm not starving.

* * *

Yuck! How did I ever eat these things?! Blegh! I guess the fish and pond-hoppers have got me spoiled. Well, it's better than starving. I think. I hope I catch something a little more substantial tomorrow.

October 19 – Day 57

It's raining again this morning. It was pretty yesterday, but now it's gotten a little monotonous. Anyway, I'm going to go check the traps, see if I caught anything last night. I'm sure I'll get lucky at some point. I mean, the animals can't just disappear when it's wet. Even if they were holed up somewhere, they'd have to come out to eat. If nothing else, I hope I catch something just to avoid eating more bugs. It's bad enough being cold and wet. Wish me luck.

* * *

Well, I have a whole lot to write about tonight. I guess I'd better start at the beginning. After doing my throwing practice and having a breakfast of pod rice, I set out to the south to check my traps. It rained continually all day, with large raindrops beating a steady pattern on the spade leafs. Walking through the woods, listening to the rain and looking at the drooping foliage I got to thinking about home a little. I thought about Sarah too. You know, it's already been two months. I wonder if she even thinks of me anymore. School's probably taking up a lot of her time. Maybe she's met someone. Maybe it's for the best.

Anyway, I was thinking so much about her that I almost passed my snare trap. It was empty. I just don't think the design works. Anything could step in it without getting caught. Some creature would have to step in it and then drag its foot to get caught. I may just have to give up on the design. But when I went to check the pit trap, I was amazed to find I'd actually caught something!

Inside the hole lay a pitiful creature, stiff and unmoving. It was a fat, furry creature about the size of a large cat with a body that looked like a guinea pig with only two legs. It had fallen into the trap and impaled its chubby body in three places on the sharpened spikes inside. A perfect catch. I wanted to be happy, but I felt more sad than anything.

I know I've caught fish and pond-hoppers and bugs before, but this is different. This creature just looked so harmless and... cute. I know that shouldn't make any difference, but it did. I can't help it. I think I understand now a little better why primitive hunters would give thanks and praise to an animal's spirit after killing it. When you live so close to the natural world, you would have to develop some kind of philosophy to keep from feeling guilty for just staying alive. That's why I had to kill the creature. I'm not a pleasure killer. I'm just another predator out here, trying to survive. I just hope it didn't suffer for too long.

After bringing it back to camp to prepare for dinner I realized I had another problem. I've never skinned and cleaned something with fur. From my experience with the pond-hoppers, I knew how to get the skin off and the guts out, but beyond that… Well, I just had to learn as I went. I used my knife blade to take off the head and appendages, then cut and peeled the fur off with my knife's set of pliers. At first, I considered keeping the fur and trying to make something out of it. But I botched the job so badly that all that's left are random bits and pieces of the pelt. I threw it away.

I decided the best way to prepare the meat was to cut it away from the bones and boil it. That seemed safest. That's where I am now, just waiting for the meat to finish cooking. Actually, it looks pretty done. I'll write again to report how it is.

* * *

It's good. The meat is tender and juicy and it's far more filling than anything I've eaten in a month. I think I'm actually full. There's probably enough meat here to make another healthy meal tomorrow. I think I've come up with an appropriate name for this creature: the meal pig. I'm really grateful to have caught it, and even more grateful that I actually have some leftovers. I'll put it in the plastic containers I kept my lunch in on that fateful day of the plane crash.

I'm looking forward to a good night's rest. It's chilly and a cold breeze has replaced the rain. Better bundle up.

October 20 – Day 58

Good morning. I've got bad news. Fall is definitely here. At first I wasn't sure. I mean, the leafs were all changing colors, but how am I supposed to know what it means when a silver spade tree leaf turns burgundy, or a golden coin leaf turns paper white? But now they're all falling. There's a stiff breeze, and the first spade and coin leafs are spreading themselves on the ground. It's no use trying to deny it anymore. The seasons are changing, and if I'm right, it's only going to get colder around here.

What am I supposed to do? I've got to think. I'll write again after my morning chores.

* * *

Well it's lunchtime. The pit trap didn't have anything new in it this morning, but at least I still have last night's meat. It's good to have something hearty to eat. The breeze from this morning is still blowing the leafs around and the sky is filled with a dull overcast.

I've come to a decision. I'm not happy with it, but I don't think I have much choice. I have to leave Misty Falls. It's been so nice to have some level of stability, a place I can come home to. But if I'm right, and the seasons are changing, then I can't stay. Once the leafs are all down it will only get colder, maybe even snow. I don't have clothes for winter weather. I'm wearing all my layers as it is, and I have no confidence in my ability to either skin some furred animal or turn its pelt into some kind of garment.

So I'll have to leave. My first thought was to go south. Dad always joked that if he ever got the money that he'd get a condo down in Florida to hide from winter weather. But how do I know the weather south will be any warmer? I don't even know if I'm in Other World's northern hemisphere. I don't know what to do. If I make the wrong choice and go the wrong direction I could freeze.

Well, the meal pig meat is all gone so I better find some dinner. Maybe I'll come up with a plan for travelling as I do some fishing.

* * *

Things are worse than I thought. Much worse. On my way down to the grotto, I saw that the pod rice plants are changing. The pods are all splitting open and spilling rice everywhere. They must be reaching fruition. Perfect. Now my only stable source of food is disappearing. I went back to camp and got some plastic containers to put the rice in. I broke open and emptied all the unbroken pods I could find, and came up with about two small boxes worth. That's all the food I've got left now. I have to get out of here… go someplace with more food and preferably a warmer climate. But where should I go? I've got to figure it out one way or the other. I'll decide in the morning.

October 21 – Day 59

I've made my decision. It's kind of crazy, but it makes the most sense. If I can't decide which direction on the compass to go, I'll follow the river.

I've thought it through. By staying close to the river, I'll have plenty of water, which could be hard to find if I went wandering in some random direction through the forest. I'll also be able to continue fishing, and I may even find rice pods that haven't broken open yet further downstream. The best part of my idea is that I can make some kind of boat and cruise down the river. Wouldn't that be great? I wouldn't be tiring myself out each day dragging a sled around, and if I can get that fishing pole figured out, I could fish for lunch and dinner while I cruised along. It'd be a welcome change of pace from what I've been doing lately.

The biggest challenge will be designing and building my boat. The way I see it I've got two options. Either tie a dozen logs together to make a raft or carve a canoe out of a single large log. The canoe would be compact and solid, so I wouldn't have to worry about it breaking apart on a rock or something. On the other hand, I have no idea how to correctly carve and shape a canoe. I could end up making a pretty design but have it constantly rolling over on me. Besides, cutting down and carving a tree thick enough to serve my needs would take a very long time. I'm not sure I'd be able to finish it before I freeze or starve.

I think the raft is my best option. I know it'd be flimsier than the canoe and harder to steer and control. But it'd be faster to make and probably more stable. I'll probably need ten to fifteen logs tied together to support my gear and me. It should work.

I'm feeling a lot better now that I have a project again. There's just something about having an activity to focus your energies on. I better get started.

* * *

Huh. Well… huh. Today didn't go exactly as planned. I was all set and ready to start looking for suitable trees for my raft when the weather turned sour. It started out as a light drizzle with the occasional healthy breeze, but now the wind is gusty and it's not letting up. Between the steady rain and blustery wind chill, it's just not a good day to be outside. I've decided instead to stay in the wigwam and work on my fishing pole.

* * *

I've managed to make a fishhook, and I hope it works. I had to sacrifice some of the wire holding together this notebook, using the pliers in my utility knife to shape it. We'll see how it holds up. I hope it's sturdy enough to keep something hooked. I've made the fishing line out of twine woven from the behemoth hair. It's strong and should do the job nicely.

In the meantime, wind or no wind, I still need to check the traps. I'll be right back.

* * *

The storm hasn't lightened up. This is really bad. The wind's not just blustery any more, now it's hammering! I'm sitting here in the wigwam listening to the trees creaking and moaning. Every now and then I hear a snap, and then a crash. I hope nothing comes down on the wigwam. I was almost tempted to try to spend the night down by the grotto away from the trees. But I'd rather stay here than go out into the wind and rain. It's terrible out there.

Of course, it's not much better in here. I never really did finish the walls for the wigwam, and I'm paying for it now. The branches and leafs between the support poles can't block out all the rain. It's especially bad up towards the joining point of the support poles and the wind keeps opening up new holes in the walls. Worst of all, every now and then a gust comes so hard I think the whole shoddy thing will flip over.

It goes without saying that keeping a fire going is impossible. No fire means no dinner tonight. I'm hungry.

* * *

Oh man. Ok, that was a massive crash. Sounded kinda close too, like the sound of a car wreck. I hope I'm all right tonight.

I'm losing my light. I can barely see what I'm writing. Cross your fingers, tonight's going to be bad.

October 22 – Day 60

Ugh. Well, I'm alive. I'm tired and I'm sore, but I'm alive. The wind's still blowing, but it's not as fierce as it was last night. The ground around the wigwam is covered with broken branches and torn leafs. I'm gonna go take a look around. Maybe the wind blew over some trees that I could use for my raft. I'll try looking down by the river.

* * *

Nice to say I've got some good news. I caught another meal pig in the pit trap last night. Can you believe it was out in the storm? No wonder it ran into the pit. Lucky I had my hunting spear with me, because I had to finish the thing off before I could take it back to camp. I'm glad to have some meat again. I should be able to make it last for today and tomorrow if I eat sparingly.

I also found a few trees that had blown over in the storm, but none of them were straight enough to serve as logs for the raft. I'll go look in the forest one more time before tonight. At least I have some food again.

* * *

I've got it! I know what to do about the boat. Remember the forest behemoth I saw a week or so ago that broke that big tree in half? Well it looks like the broken-off top finally tore away from the rest of the tree in the windstorm. It'd be perfect for a canoe! It might be a little longer and heavier than what I had imagined, but it'll still work much better than any raft. All I have to do is hollow out the interior, bring the slender end of the log to a point, and flatten the bottom so it won't roll so easily. It won't be pretty, but it should work. I'm excited to get started.

I'll make myself a big celebration dinner and get started on the log in the morning. This is gonna be great!

October 23 – Day 61

Mmm… what a morning. There's nothing like waking up with a full stomach and a brand new plan of action. Even the autumn chill can't affect my good mood. Why should it? The spade and coin leafs are falling like white and burgundy snow. It's a lovely fall day. Of course, I don't want to be around when the real snow starts falling. Speaking of which, I better go and get to work on that log.

* * *

Well, the canoe idea definitely looks like it'll work. My first job will be cutting all the limbs off the trunk. Most of them have been gnawed to stubs by the forest behemoth already, so that shouldn't be too difficult. I'm still trying to figure out what I'll do after that. I'm not sure if I should start by carving out the middle or by flattening the bottom. I don't even know if I should strip all the bark off or just leave it on.

Maybe I'll figure it out while I'm working. I'll get started on these limbs.

* * *

'Evening. Well, I set to work getting all the limbs off with my trusty little saw blade. I hadn't worked more than an hour before I glanced up and noticed I had a spectator. A furry red creature with a tall plume of black and yellow feathers was watching me from the branches of a partially eaten hook fir. I'm not sure if he was more monkey or bird. His body looked kinda like an orangutan but he had a distinct parrot-like beak in the middle of his dark face.

He also had a low, piercing voice and cawed angrily at me the whole time I was working. Maybe he was mad about the racket I was making. I wonder what he's doing around here at this time in the season. I assume his diet would mainly consist of nuts and pinecones because of that large beak. But I think all the pinecones are gone by now. Why doesn't he move on to warmer climates with more and better food? Odd.

This fellow was really talkative. "Awrk! Awrk! Awrk!" is nice for the first ten seconds, but gets awful old after the first half hour. It's just lucky for him that he's staying up in his tree and well out of my reach. He'll be going straight to my dinner pot if I ever catch him, even if he wasn't annoying.

Despite my noisy neighbor, I was able to get all the tree limbs off today except for two long ones on opposite sides that I hope will serve as an extra form of balance while the canoe is in the water to keep it from rolling. I've decided to start carving out the inside tomorrow. That should make the log much lighter and easier to work with. I've also decided to take the bark off, since a lot of it has already broken away. The bark is hard, with deep treads like a car tire, and prying it off is pretty easy.

It's a beautiful night. The stars are lovely. It feels good to be alive and to be working hard. Hopefully I can stay warm tonight.

October 24 – Day 62

I'm worried. I'm running low on pod rice and I'm out of meal pig meat. There are no pond-hoppers in the grotto anymore and bugs are getting harder to find. I think it's just getting too cold. I've still got the Vienna sausage of course, but I really don't want to open my only nonperishable food item until I run out of all other options. Maybe I can try a little fishing at some point again. I finished the fishing rod, and that seems to be my best bet for finding more food besides the pit trap. Hunting would be even more useless than before, what with all the fallen leafs getting hard and crunchy on the forest floor.

Speaking of which, I think there's more leafs on the ground now than in the branches. I hope I get my canoe done before winter really hits. I'd rather not see what snow looks like on Other World.

* * *

Well, I got a fair amount of work done on the canoe today. I used two shards of rock broken off the boulders at the base of Misty Falls as a hammer and chisel to start digging out an interior. It was hard work, but I managed to make a two-inch-deep hollow in the top of the log. It's a good start, but this may take a lot longer than I thought.

My noisy friend was still around today. You'd think that he would eventually find something more interesting to do besides harassing me. He only took a break every now and then to peel the bark off his tree and gnaw the soft underside. But he always started his cawing again when he was done, and it's driving me nuts. I finally got so frustrated I started yelling back at him for the first "conversation" I've had since coming to Other World.

"Arwk! Arwk!"

"Shut up!"

"Arwk! Arwk! Arwk!"

"I said shut up!"

"Arwk!"

"Ahhhhh!"

 "Arwk! Arwk!"

"Stupid monkey!"

"Arwk! Arwk! Arwk! Arwk!"

"Shut up!"

It got repetitive after that. Hopefully he'll leave as it gets a little colder. Hopefully.

October 25 – Day 63

Good morning. I just had an idea as I was clearing the ashes out of my fire pit. I was considering using a charred stick to outline where I'd make my cuts in the canoe when I realized something. The blackened parts of the stick came away with just the pressure from my fingers. The burnt wood simply brook off.

That got me thinking. What if I could somehow burn the places in the canoe that I wanted to hollow out? That would make chiseling with a couple of rock shards much easier. It makes sense, but I need to figure out a way to make it work.

* * *

Ok, I think I have it figured out. My first idea was to start a very small fire on the log itself, but I decided against that. The risk of seeing the whole thing go up in flames was too scary. I've got a better idea anyway. It's based on a "minor" accident involving a hot skillet that I put on Mom's kitchen counter. The counter didn't actually go up in smoke, but the pan did leave a large black circle that Dad eventually covered up with the microwave.

While I'd rather not use my one and only skillet, I think rocks could potentially work just as well. I'll definitely have to build a larger fire than I'm used to, but that shouldn't be a problem. The only other trick will be moving the hot rocks from the fire to the log, but I think I can use that old plane-hitch hook for that. I knew holding onto that stupid thing would eventually come in handy! I'll give it a try and let you know how it works.

* * *

Ok, good news, bad news time.

The good news is that the heated rocks technique actually works! I made a large fire and let it burn a while before carefully putting several fist-sized rocks among the glowing embers. After that, I placed them in the hollow trench I chipped out yesterday while putting more rocks in the fire to heat up.

Through the course of the day, I learned that it works much better to leave the rocks in the fire longer than I thought necessary at first. I was worried when I first saw smoke coming off the trunk, but it turned out to be just what I wanted. The wood burns but doesn't burst into flame. I bet I got twice as much work done on the canoe today compared to yesterday.

So that was the good news. The bad news is that stupid beak monkey is still around. And now he has friends! Three more adults and one baby now share the same tree. They're all just as loud as the first one, except the baby who still seems to be learning the finer points of aggravated annoyance. I've never really hated an innocent animal, but I'm definitely getting there.

Anyway, at least I can eat the small fish I caught today and work on my canoe. Now if I could just get this ringing out of my ears.

October 26 – Day 64

Brrr… it's cold. Looks like most of the leafs are down now. I hope I can pick up the pace on the canoe. Maybe if I can get more stones going I can speed up the work. I can also make use of the time the rocks are smoldering by carving out the front of the canoe. I don't need a fancy front end, but I do want it to be at least vaguely wedge-shaped. I'm afraid I won't be able to use hot rocks for that. I'll just have to make do with my chiseling rocks.

That's my battle plan for today. Let's hope it all goes well.

* * *

Ahhhhh! Why?! Why now?! Why so many stupid monkeys?! Oh no, one wasn't enough. Five wasn't enough. Now I've got a whole dumb tree full. Cawing and squawking all day long! My head feels like it's splitting in half!

I wish, I really wish, that one or two of them would climb down far enough for me to get a chance to lob my spear at them. Of course, what I really wish I had is a gun, even if I weren't starving. Anything to shut them up.

I'm sorry. I really shouldn't get so upset. Sure, the beak monkeys are obnoxious, but at least I'm not lonely. That's something. And the canoe is starting to actually look like a boat. I'm making great progress with carving out the interior. The prow will still take some time to get to a point, but I'm getting there.

At least I've been able to catch a little bit of fish. But I'm still hungry. I'll try again in the morning.

October 27 – Day 65

No luck fishing this morning, but I like starting the day that way anyway. It's peaceful.

* * *

I got a lot of work done on the canoe today. And before you ask... yes, the beak monkeys are still there, and yes, there are even more of them now.

You know, by now, I'm not as annoyed at the beak monkeys as I am intrigued. I counted between fifty and sixty beak monkeys around my work site, and even more throughout the rest of the forest. What in the world are they all doing here? Mating? Doesn't look like it. Most of them seem to be keeping to themselves, except for the mothers with their babies. What are they all doing here?

Well, we'll see if there are any more of them in the morning. I just hope they stay away from the trees near my wigwam. As it is, I can already hear them faintly at night as I try to sleep.

October 28 – Day 66

Morning. I've already been up for a while. Tried my luck fishing again and was happily successful. It wasn't the biggest fish in the world, but it did make for a hearty breakfast anyway. Definitely enough to give me some needed energy for the canoe. Two more solid days of work and I should have the interior completely done. After that, there's really not much left but finishing the point at the front and getting the heavy monster to the water. I wonder how I'm gonna manage that little trick. I'll think about it.

* * *

The beak monkeys are everywhere. I'm not exaggerating. They're in the tops of almost every tree. I suppose I should be grateful that they're not all squawking their crested heads off, but seem to instead be intent on taking a day-long siesta. For every beak monkey that's chattering there are five or more sleeping, blissfully unaware of their noisy neighbors. I envy them.

The canoe really looks to be coming together nicely. While I've built some stuff before, I think this is the first time I can say that I've actually crafted something. It may even be nice to look at when it's done in a simple, functional kind of way. I'm actually kind of amazed by it. I know I never could have done something like this before coming to Other World.

Then again, maybe I could have. I don't know. Trying to compare myself now with who I was then is almost impossible. So much has happened, and I'm so far away from where I was and who I was just two months ago. Lying here tonight in my handmade wigwam, listening to the stereo song of the cawing beak monkeys, I know I'm not the same person I was. I'm not even sure if I'd want to be.

October 29 – Day 67

Last night was incredible. I saw one of the most amazing spectacles I've seen since coming to Other World. I'd finished last night's entry and was watching the fire burn itself out. I was feeling particularly thoughtful, just kind of ruminating on everything that's happened lately. After a while, I noticed that the constant cries of the beak monkeys had changed. An excited chatter mixed with other new sounds that I didn't recognize had replaced their endless cawing.

I got up and moved outside into the chilly night air. It was late, but I could see the Misty Falls clearly from the combined light of Mike and Ike. It was by that light that I saw the tiny, fluttering creatures. There were hundreds of them! I'd never seen these creatures before. Each of their pale gray bodies was about the size and shape of a radish with wingspans nearly a foot across and bright red eyes that looked like small raspberries. I realized then why the beak monkeys had quieted down. They were busy eating the "flutterbys". All around me, the beak monkeys were plucking up the docile creatures and stuffing them into their beaks. The flutterbys didn't seem overly concerned about their predators. They barely even attempted to avoid them.

This must have been why the beak monkeys had been gathering here. Somehow, they knew the flutterbys would come. Perhaps the flutterbys only come out at a certain time each year. There must be a reason, because they seemed to be emerging in unison from everything around me. Trees, rocks, the ground, everything just kept pouring more and more flutterbys into the night. I watched the beak monkeys stuffing themselves and realized what an opportunity this was for me.

I hurried back into the hut, grabbed my backpack and started catching flutterbys in midflight and stuffing them in the bag. It was so easy, like picking flying fruit from the air. After a couple of minutes, I had another idea. Acting on a hunch, I quickly made my way to the worksite where I'd seen the greatest concentration of beak monkeys.

When I got there, I was rewarded with a spectacular sight. Flutterbys were everywhere! Millions more than back at the hut. The night air was thick with their little bodies made silver by the moons' light. The air itself seemed alive with the sparkling dust from their wings, giving shape to every breath of wind through the amazing scene. The beak monkeys were there too, gorging themselves on this incredible bonanza and almost completely silent for the first time in days.

I immediately set to filling my bag with the fluttering morsels. As I worked, I noticed that other creatures from the forest were also taking advantage of this feast. Wide-mouth bats and Amy owls shared their dinner in the night air. Several tree-huggers and a small glider ate in the treetops with the beak monkeys as the occasional ground hawk dashed through the behemoth-made clearing next to my canoe.

It didn't take long for me to fill my backpack and I hurried back to the wigwam to find any more containers for my captured flutterbys. By the end of the night, I had filled my backpack, shoulder bag, and even my empty plastic containers with the writhing insects. I'm so happy to have so much food again. This will last me for at least several days… more than that if they can be used as fish bait.

Well, the morning is getting on and I still need to eat. I think I'll try some cooked flutterbys for breakfast. I can't help smiling to myself. Sure, things were really tough when I first got to Other World, but I'm surviving. Harsh as this world may be, I've managed to use all my resources to support me and keep me alive for over two months now. Things are definitely looking up.

* * *

I already did a lot of writing this morning so I'll try to keep this second entry brief. I spent what was left of the day working on the canoe. The ground was littered with millions of the dead bodies of the flutterbys from last night. What a short time to live.

The beak monkeys were quiet. I suppose they were trying to sleep off their massive gorging last night. Various other creatures moved among the carpet of flutterbys, feeding as they went. I even saw a giant slug-like creature slowly crawling between the trees. He was about the size of my arm, with nine stalks protruding from his orange and black body. I don't think he moved more than ten feet all day while I was working.

I've eaten a couple meals consisting almost entirely of flutterbys today, and I'm relieved to say that they're pretty easy to get down, though I find I prefer them roasted instead of boiled. They're fatty, and have good meat on them. The only annoying thing is all the iridescent dust that comes off when I touch them. After a while, it kind of covers everything like silver party glitter. It's pretty, but hard to remove.

Well I'm gonna catch some Z's. Night.

October 30 – Day 68

Morning. I don't want to waste too much time chatting. I'm gonna try to get the interior of the canoe finished today before it's too cold to do anything else. Just give me a couple more days or so and I should have it finished. The only thing to do then will be to name it.

* * *

The canoe is finished! Well, near enough anyway. I spent all day working as hard as I could and it's just about done. I just have to clean up the front end a bit, but that shouldn't take more than an hour tomorrow. I probably would have finished it completely today, but I had to do some… unexpected restoration. Remember the giant slug I mentioned yesterday? Well, he uh, slimed my boat last night. Do you have any idea what it's like to clear off the mucus trail left by a slug the size of a bloodhound? Well it's gross, let's leave it at that.

Most of the flutterby bodies are gone now. So are the beak monkeys. They must have finally moved on to warmer climes. Funny, I kind of miss them now. No, never mind… I take that back. Silence is definitely golden. The worst part of them being gone though is that it means my time is running out. It just keeps getting colder. Good thing I got the canoe finished in time. Now all I have to do is somehow get it down to the river and get out of here before I freeze.

I've thought it through one more time, and I still think this my best bet for survival. Following the river to escape the cold is a matter of simple logic. Regardless of which hemisphere I'm in, rivers always flow downhill. At least, I hope they do. Anyway, as long as Other World continues to play by Newton's rules it'll head towards the lowest point that it can. Lower elevation means warmer temperatures and that what's I want. Besides, I might end up somewhere a little easier to find food. A lake maybe, or even an ocean. A body of water that big could sustain me indefinitely.

Anyway, that's my ultimate goal. My immediate goal is getting the canoe to the river. I'll think about it as I go to sleep tonight. Heaven forbid that I should go to sleep without anything to worry about.

October 31 – Day 69

I've run a few ideas through my head about how to make canoe and river meet. First off, here are the logistics as I see them.

The canoe weighs more than I can push over uneven ground. The trees growing around the worksite are fairly far apart, which is good, but there are plenty of bushes between them, which is bad. I suppose the best I can do is clear the bushes away, and maybe use small logs or large tree limbs as rollers underneath it.

I guess I've got my plan then. I better get started. With any luck, I'll be able to test the canoe in actual water tomorrow morning.

* * *

'Evening. Well, tonight I'm spending the night inside the canoe. My wigwam, my little home away from home, is no more. I had to dismantle it to make the rollers to move the canoe over the forest floor. I'm a little sad to say goodbye to the old wigwam. It was drafty, leaky, and flimsy, but it was all I had. Then again, maybe the next one I build won't be such a wreck.

As far as moving the canoe is concerned everything is going fairly well. I'm having a little more trouble getting through the undergrowth than I had anticipated, but I should be to the lagoon by tomorrow afternoon, and not a moment too soon either. It's so cold out here in the open. I really can't wait to be off and away downstream.

November 1 – Day 70

Brrrr! It's cold! I'm freezing, and no wonder. I woke up today to find a layer of frost on the ground, the canoe, and me. I'm really worried now about frostbite, or hypothermia, or worse. I'm wearing all the clothes that I have. I really hope I can get the canoe to the water today. I've got to try to get to some place warmer.

* * *

I can only think of two other times since coming to Other World when I was as terrified as I was today as I launched my canoe... when I first appeared in the purple desert, and the night I was visited by the bigamouth. But despite all that, my fears today proved to be unfounded. It floats! It really works! I almost can't believe it.

After I was fairly confident it wouldn't sink out from under me, I took my new transport of choice for a little spin around the lagoon. All in all, I'm very pleased with how it handles. It turns really slowly, but I can handle that. I can finally use the paddles from the plane for their original function, and the pointed front of the canoe cuts the water like a fish's nose. By the way, I also finally named the canoe today. I'm calling it the Miss Sarah. It just seems appropriate that a watercraft should have a feminine name. I hope the real Sarah wouldn't be too insulted to see her namesake.

It was already early evening by the time I got the Miss Sarah to the lagoon, so I'll head out first thing in the morning. I guess I'm setting off once again. Part of me wishes I didn't have to keep moving so far from the original crash site. But it can't be helped. If I want to survive on Other World, I have to keep on the move. Maybe one day I'll find somewhere that I can settle down and begin to build a new life. But for now, I'm nothing more than a refugee still fleeing through hostile country.

Well, I better get some rest. Tomorrow I'll say goodbye to Misty Falls, and once again jump blindly into the unknown.

November 2 – Day 71

Wow. This has been a good, good day. After a week of desperate boat building it was wonderful to serenely float along with the current. It was so nice. Nothing to do but keep the Miss Sarah pointed downriver as I cast out a line to catch dinner. Even my catch today was amazing. It's the biggest fish I've caught on Other World and probably my biggest fish ever. The thing is huge with six sets of fins and two tails. I thought for sure it would break my line and I had to wrestle the thing into the boat since I don't have a net. I'll have to work on that. For now though, I'm happy, and the bi-tail is sizzling in my frying pan as I write this.

I just had a random thought. If I follow this river all the way to its end and it leads to an ocean, I may just get an unexpected perk. If Other World's oceans are salty, I could figure out a way to make my own course sea salt. Not only would my food have more flavor, but I could use the salt to store meat and keep it from going bad right away. Then I could catch fish or meat for several days all at once and not have to worry about it spoiling overnight.

Well, it's a nice daydream at least, but for now I'm very content with how things are going. I'll ponder the net problem tonight over dinner.

Things are sure looking up these days.

November 3 – Day 72

Morning! Well, breakfast is leftover bi-tail fish from last night. In case you're wondering, it's still very cold. There was frost everywhere this morning, and yesterday I had to keep blowing on my frozen fingers so I could keep a firm grip on my fishing pole. At least I have something to eat.

I figured out a makeshift net. It's not perfect, but it should work. Basically, I found a forked branch and loosely tied several lengths of twine across the two prongs. It won't catch much on its own but it should work as a lifting support when I hook something on the line.

Other than that, not much more to report. Just looking forward to another relaxing day of floating down the river.

* * *

You know, I've been sitting here floating for a while and I just kinda felt like singing a little while ago. I don't know why. I've never been much of a singer, unless you count shower serenading. It just seemed to fit as I cruise along. I'm happy.

It didn't really matter what I sang. There's only me and the fish that have to hear it. I sang until I couldn't think of any more songs. It was fun. I should probably cut it out fairly soon though, or I'll never catch tonight's dinner.

* * *

What a catch today! Good thing I made that new net this morning. I hope I can eat this all before it goes bad. Three fish, and big ones too! Ok, can't write much, gotta get cooking.

November 4 – Day 73

Oh man. Ok. Gotta get it together. Just let my hands stop shaking so I can write.

Ok. Sorry. I'll try to calm down and write what's just happened this morning. Last night was great. I cooked all the fish and ate my fill and there was still more than half of it left over for breakfast. That was the plan anyway.

I woke up cold and stiff, with the pale light of dawn around me. At first I tried closing my eyes and going back to sleep, at least until the sun warmed me a little. But in a moment, I realized I'd been woken up by an unfamiliar sound. It was a guttural, mewling sound, like a cat being sick or something. I slowly looked around and found a new creature trying to steal my breakfast.

It was about the size of a large dog with matted red fur and an oddly over-shaped head. The thing had been sniffing my cooked fish from last night and had already started to quickly gulp them down whole. I should have been afraid, but I was more angry about the thing's theft of my hard-earned food.

Acting quickly, I grabbed my hunting spear and charged at the thing, yelling and screaming as loud as I could. The creature looked up and watched me with large dark eyes. It made a kind of mewling bark in the back of its throat and at first I thought it was going to put up a fight. But I was feeling full of courage and righteous fury and swung my spear like a baseball bat to smack the think hard on its rear end. The creature yelped and bolted for the forest. I should have left it alone, but I was too caught up in the moment and chased after it screaming like a madman as it caterwauled pitifully. Suddenly the creature stopped and spun around to meet me. I tried to stop but lost my balance and fell forward, landing on my hands and knees and dropping my spear. I shook my head to clear it and heard a terrible crashing sound in the forest. I looked to see what it was and saw another, much larger creature rushing towards me. It was the size of a shuttle bus and seemed to be an uneven blend of grizzly bear and ground sloth, with oversized front limbs that ended in huge claws as if it were a giant mole. I realize that the awkward creature I had been chasing before was actually the young offspring of this beast.

As it charged, the massive adult made a hissing sound like a slit tire, opening wide its great maw and revealing that what I had thought to be an oversized head was actually a series of frill-like fans surrounding its face. As it roared, huge fleshy flaps of skin pulled back from around its head and opened out into a stunning crest all shot-through with vivid reds and golds. It looked like pictures I remember seeing of some frilled lizard in Australia. If I'd been somewhere else I might have laughed as the extended, petal-like frills around beast's fearsome jaws made it look like nothing so much as a big, angry flower.

But as the thing charged me, I forgot all about how funny it looked. I stumbled backward, rolling to my feet and began running back to camp. I left my spear on the ground behind me. My first instinct was to make for my canoe and flee downstream but I quickly gave up that idea. I'd tied the canoe to a coin leaf sapling to keep it from drifting and had no time to untie or cut the line. My second idea wasn't much better but I didn't have time to come up with anything else. As fast as I could I ran to a large hook fir tree with some low branches and began furiously climbing for my life.

I don't know how high I was when the beast reached the base of my tree. I was too busy trying not to fall. It's amazing how hard it is to climb when your whole body is shaking. But I knew when the beast reached my tree because suddenly I wasn't the only thing shaking. I had to stop climbing and cling to the trunk as the whole world spun around me. A stolen glance told me the thing was trying to climb up after me, and I struggled to scramble even farther up my perch. The shaking finally stopped as I arrived as high in the tree as I could safely climb and looked down again at my pursuer. It stood below me, surrounded by the torn off branches it had ripped down in its attempt to get to me. Its large, black eyes met mine as it hissed and spat furiously.

"Go away!" I wanted to shout, and at first, it seemed it would do just that. It left my tree and plodded a few yards away towards its young, which was now contentedly entertaining itself by eating the rest of my breakfast. I was about to start breathing again, wondering how I'd eventually get down with all those limbs broken off below me, when the thing turned. With a burst of speed, it charged the tree, smashing into it with the force of an out-of-control truck. The tree groaned and shook horribly, then tilted severely to the side. I clung desperately to the trunk as the creature backed up for another run. I knew the tree wouldn't remain standing after another hit, and I looked desperately for some kind of escape. I found it in a branch extending from a much larger tree hanging just out of reach. I knew I would have one chance, and as the creature hit the tree a second time, I grabbed the branch as I fell past it, leaving my tree to smash into the ground below me. For an agonizing eternity, I hung well above the beast until it finally gave up and left me alone. I managed to pull myself to a more comfortable position and sat in the new tree for half an hour before getting down to my canoe and getting myself out of there.

Well, if you couldn't tell, I spent the rest of the day writing about this morning. Now it's night and I've having a sparse dinner since I only caught one fish for supper. Oh well. I guess I'll make a night of it. I'm so tired and not feeling well at all. I hope I'm not coming down with something.

ON THE WATER

Expedition Log
16th of Klune, in the 2nd year of The Return
Yurril T'nak, field scout

Blasted bugs. There is nothing in this swamp but muck and bugs. This ruin is empty as well. I think Brendell has given up finding what we seek here, and I do not blame him, though it worries me that he seems disheartened. Where are the rest of us if the Divant loses his faith in himself? Perhaps I am overreacting. I am sure I would not be so downtrodden if it were not for this infernal rain.

Brendell says we have three more possible locations to search. I worry that a few members of the group are muttering that Brendell ought to know which one we should go to without all this tiresome searching. Why are they so prideful? Do they not understand how incredible it is to even be here on this world? We know the few places where we may find the Records and Tokens. If not for Brendell's leadership, we could be searching for decades instead of months.

I would worry for Brendell's safety, except we have our doggedly loyal Flain. No one has yet gotten the courage to challenge Brendell and his eight-foot tall bodyguard. Still, I fear that I and Sasha are the only others who truly believe in Brendell's directions anymore. May it change soon.

We have yet to find any other intelligent creatures on this world. It seems completely uninhabited by any sentient species. It's no wonder. This world seems too hostile to have had a native race. I am surprised the Ancestors were able to have a presence here, even with their great powers. At least we came prepared and with a group. I would hate to think about being lost out there all alone.

Grace be with you. Yurril T'nak

November 5 – Day 74

I don't feel so good. I woke up cold this morning with a stuffed up nose and sore throat. I thought I was getting a cold, but I've also got this terrible aching in all my joints, which I don't ever remember getting when I've had colds before. Could this be a condition exclusive to Other World? Come to think of it, it's a wonder I haven't gotten sick more often up to this point. I mean, my Earth immune system could be totally useless against Other World viruses and such. What if I catch something bad?

One thing's for sure. It's a real chore to write when I'm feeling this scummy. And drowsy. So tired… I'll write again tomorrow, hopefully I'll feel better by then.

November 6 – Day 75

I don't feel better. I feel horrible. I almost didn't want to make camp tonight. I'm really worried. I just don't feel good. It hurts to swallow, that's the worst. That and the soreness all over. The drowsiness is still terrible as well. I just hope I get to warmer climes. Good thing I have the canoe. I doubt I could travel any other way right now.

I just took some cold medicine that was in the first aid kit. Hope it works.

Well, as long as I can't sleep, I might as well boil and prepare a new batch of fresh water. I wish I was home.

November 7 – Day 76

I feel terrible. I don't have the strength to pull to the shore and make camp. So woozy, I'm really sick. I wish someone was here. Anyone.

I'm lucky the boat hasn't wrecked, but the river's getting bigger all the time so I'm safe for now. I'm hurting so much everywhere! At least it's not as cold as it was. I guess I'll go to sleep.

November 8 – Day 77

It's a storm. I can't write.

November 9 – Day 78

I can't believe this. I'm on the ocean. I can't see land. I don't know how this happened. There was a storm. It rained all night. I must have passed out. I woke up, and I'm out to sea. Land must be back to the east. But I can't get there. I can't paddle. My hand's shaking from the pain of just writing. I gotta rest.

* * *

Don't feel any better. I don't know what to say. I guess I'm gonna die out here. Feels like soon. Sorry, there's just not much more I can do. I just can't.

November 10 – Day 79

[unreadable] …my head. Pain. Water. Can't keep [unreadable] loose in my [unreadable]. At least have water. I… [unreadable] …die slowly. Pour out water. Faster. [unreadable] …just drown. Easier. My head. [unreadable] …Mom… [unreadable]

* * *

[unreadable] Pretty stars. [unreadable] …fly. Fly away. So hard. I wish [unreadable].

November 11 – Day 80

[unreadable]

November 12 – Day 81

[unreadable]

November 13 – Day 82

Starving. Dead soon. [unreadable]

* * *

I REFUSE TO DIE.

November 14 – Day 83

Alive. Find food. Raw fish. [unreadable] Need bait.

* * *

Vienna sausage. Thank you God.

* * *

Caught fish. Don't eat. More bait. Next fish. Food will stop the pain. [unreadable]

November 15 – Day 84

I have eaten. Raw fish so good. Sushi. Doing a little better now. Head hurts less. Not gone, just less. Still hard to write. Hard to write clearly. But maybe getting better. Pray so.

* * *

Stars so bright. The sky is so big. Both moons full, see so much. Must sleep though.

November 16 – Day 85

Good morning. I feel a lot better. Still very weak, but at least I can think straight again. The headache is just a dull throb now. I can handle it. Hope I can catch another fish or something.

* * *

Caught something, it's not a fish. I can't find its head. It's hot pink with two foot-like tentacles coming out of it. It keeps squirming and coiling, knotting itself into a rolling ball in the bottom of the boat. I'm not sure if I should eat it. I'm thinking not. I can cut up the feet/tentacles for bait though.

I just realized I haven't really had a chance to explain my current situation. First off, I'm adrift at sea. Obviously. It's kind of ridiculous really… in a heartbreaking way. I still can't see land, though I'm pretty sure that it's still off in the east somewhere.

Ok, I'll have to write more later. I'm still hungry and I have to concentrate on fishing. One thing more though. I notice each time I cast out my line that it drifts back to the back of the boat. I must be moving roughly south. It's definitely warmer than it was last week. How about that? If I survive this, my original idiot plan might actually work.

November 17 – Day 86

It took a long time but I finally did catch something with a piece of the Pink Lady. I split the catch in half, part for bait and part for me. You know, I always thought sushi was gross, but I'm definitely a fan now. I'll always prefer it cooked, but for now, I couldn't be happier to eat fish any way I can.

Now that I'm feeling a little better, I need to start thinking about what I'm going to do. I can't stay out here much longer. Thank goodness I made a new batch of water before I got really sick, but it's almost all gone now. I've been drinking my fill each day, so I'm pretty hydrated. I can last probably another two, three days once it runs out. After that, I don't know. I'm trying to keep myself covered from the sun, which is becoming increasingly uncomfortable as it gets hotter. Luckily, the poncho seems to work really well for that. I keep wishing for rain but the sky's clear, remaining that fantastic shade of powder blue and violet.

* * *

I was really mad for a while there but there's nothing for it. Something broke my fishing line and stole my hook. Must have been something really big. There was just a violent yank on the line and when I tried to hold it steady it just snapped. Luckily, I still have the rest of the forest behemoth's hair in my bag for a new line, and I've got some more wire in this notebook that I can make into a new hook.

The sun is setting now. It's so pretty. The sky is spliced with bands of yellow, orange, purple and blue. The sun looks so massive and majestic as it is slowly swallowed into the sea. I just wish I had someone to share this with. Or I wish I had a set of watercolors and that I was an actual artist. I can sketch some of what I see, but I really wish I could do this justice. Even if I'm never found, I wish I could give this picture to the people of Earth. What a gift that would be.

Well, this new fishing line isn't going to make itself. I better get to work.

November 18 – Day 87

Wow. It's the pale light of dawn now, but I couldn't wait to write.

I wasn't really all that tired last night, so I worked in the semi-darkness on the new fishing line. There was a cool, steady breeze and I worked by the light of Ike and Mike.

I had been trying to bend the new hook into shape when I heard a strange, rumbling noise. At first, I couldn't identify what the sound was or even where it was coming from. It was so low I could barely hear it, but I could definitely feel it. When it came again everything in the canoe began to vibrate. I looked around but I was alone on the water as far as I could tell. Once again, I heard the sound and this time the canoe shook so violently I worried that whatever the mysterious noise was would end up sinking me. I desperately tried to find what was causing it and finally thought to look over the edge of the canoe into the deep, dark water. That's when I saw it.

The creature was immense. Bigger than the petal bear, bigger even than the forest behemoth, it seemed to stretch on forever in the water below me. But it wasn't the creature's size that captivated me. From its spade shaped head to its triple-fluked tail, the massive animal's body glowed with a green-tinged white light. That bioluminescence made it possible for me to see the creature's entire body structure. It had two pairs of flippers along its sides with the wingspan of the forward pair equaling the creature's total length. It used its flippers and tails to move through the water with a docile grace, slowly barrel rolling through the inky blackness. If it was a mammal, it must have amazing lung capacity because it never came up for air. The creature continued its rumbling song as it swam below me, and even after it disappeared, the sound lingered.

It was an awesome experience. I wish I could breathe underwater and follow the glowing creature. With all the incredible diversity on land, just think what the oceans of Other World must be like! I'd love to see what it's like down there. I can only imagine.

Well, I've hardly gotten any sleep so I'll try and take a little nap now. I can try out my new fishing line this afternoon. Sweet dreams.

* * *

Land! I see land! I'm heading in! See you on the shore.

* * *

Well, that was disappointing. Of course, I suppose trying to paddle all that way was a little impulsive. The good news at least is that there is visible land to the east. The bad news is I can't figure out how to get there. I tried to paddle towards it but I didn't seem to make any headway all day. I don't know if it's just an optical illusion, but I don't think I'm any closer now than I was when I first saw it. I just don't think paddling is an option… maybe I could figure something else out.

I'm sure if I were in a movie I could just sew together a makeshift sail and cruise on in. After all, there has been a steady breeze for the last hour or so. Unfortunately, I don't know the first thing about sailing. What would I do if the wind didn't blow towards the shore? What if it didn't blow at all? Still, I think it's worth trying. I'll wrap my head around the problem tonight and see what I can come up with. 'K. Goodnight.

November 19 – Day 88

Ugh. I am so sick of raw fish right now. At least it's better than nothing at all.

Good news today. I think the land is closer. I can make out the shore a little. Looks mostly rocky… no sandy beaches around here. Can't see much beyond the shore.

I've thought about the whole propulsion problem, and I think I've got an even better idea than the sail. I brainstormed as many ways of moving a boat as I could and I think the most effective method I could use would be a kind of double-paddle like the kind kayakers use. I could duct-tape the two paddles together pretty easily. I'm hoping that by combining the paddles I can increase the strength, control, and rhythm of each stroke. I think that's my best bet. I'm gonna go ahead and try it. Wish me luck.

* * *

Well, I think it worked. I mean, it's still hard to discern distances on the water. But I can see the shore more distinctly, so I think I'm closer. I just hope the current doesn't carry me back out to where I was while I sleep tonight. Either way I've got to stop for today and try to catch something to eat.

* * *

Holy cow! I'm gonna eat good tonight! I've caught five… things…. in just half an hour or so. They're smaller than the pink lady I caught earlier or anything else I've been eating lately. They look like feathery combs with pale green and blue bodies. Normally I'd be cautious to eat things like these, but I just can't do without the energy. Hopefully I don't get sick, but I need some food if I'm gonna try for land again tomorrow. We'll just have to see how they agree with me in the morning.

November 20 – Day 89

I've got good news today. I woke up early this morning to a noise I couldn't identify. It was a rolling, pounding sound and my first thought was a thunderstorm. But as it got light, I realized it was something much better. I'm drifting almost right below a massive sea cliff. The roaring I heard was the waves crashing against the wall of black rock. I had to use my double-paddle to keep myself far enough back and avoid getting smashed against it.

I'm at a safe distance now though, and the current continues to carry me along the shoreline to the south. Unfortunately, it's nothing but cliffs right now, but I'm close enough to land that once I see something like a beach I'll make a break for it.

* * *

I've found my beach. I was watching some slender flying creatures (I'll call them silver swifts) flying around the sea cliffs when I saw the gap in the rock walls a little to the south. The beach isn't terribly long and there are rocks all along the length of it, but it's the best place I can see to make landfall. Even as close as I am to the shore it will probably be difficult. I'll have to work pretty hard to maneuver and deal with all those big waves. I'm just waiting until I clear the last of the cliffs before I start moving in.

The weather looks pretty gray and nasty. The wind is coming in sharply from the west and there's a misty rain that will probably only increase throughout the day. I'm wishing now I had made that sail but I guess a tail wind should still be helpful. Of course the problem now isn't just making it in... it's making it in without getting smashed against all those rocks. Ok... looks like my window's coming up. Wish me luck. Here we go!

* * *

I'm on land. Thank you God. I'm on land.

November 21 – Day 90

Good morning. Well, I'm on land. I can barely stand up but I am on land, which is enough of a miracle for me. There were a couple of times yesterday when I really wondered if I was going to make it.

After yesterday morning's entry, I started to make my way towards the shore. It was hard going. The wind had picked up and the rain started falling in large, cold drops. I was quickly cold and soaked from the rain and the spray from the rocks scattered along the beach. It took all my energy and remaining strength to avoid running aground or wrecking my canoe on any of the jagged outcroppings. Several times throughout the day I hit a large rock that bounced me like a crash test dummy before the waves pulled me back away from it. I was never so glad as I was yesterday that I had chosen a solidly constructed boat. A raft would have been reduced to splinters in the first hour.

After I got past the last of the rocks, the rest of the way in was pretty smooth. The sky was darkening when I finally made landfall. I pulled the canoe up onto the beach and fell asleep under the cover of some driftwood. I'm not sure how long I was out but when I finally woke up today it was already pretty late.

I'm sitting on the beach now, watching the waves that I struggled through yesterday. Off to the west the sky is dominated by a low, deep blue cloud cover. It's very pretty in a stormy way, but I wish the sun was out.

Anyway, I should probably make camp. The rain's stopped for now, so I think the first thing I'm gonna do is start a fire to finish drying myself out. It's funny, but despite the danger I was in yesterday, what worried me the most was getting my journal wet. (It's fine by the way, I wrapped it in my spare clothes and the space blanket then put it in my backpack.) OK, I've got to get to work.

* * *

Well, my camp is made and I've got my fire going, although it's kind of a sad one. The driftwood I found makes great fuel, but it's all pretty wet and the wind is not helping. I was glad to have the wind yesterday to help get me to shore but now it keeps trying to put my fire out. I'll have to bundle up again tonight.

I wonder where I am. I spent some time calculating tonight and I have a rough estimate of my position. I was on the water for at least eleven full days. For the majority of that time I think I was in that southbound current. While I don't know how fast ocean currents can travel (especially Other World currents) if I assume that the current I was in was moving at a steady speed of just four miles an hour, I could be over a thousand miles from where I started. That could explain the warmer temperatures over the last few days, though it may also be some quirk of the weather.

My point is that I may be in a completely new ecosystem with completely different plant and animal life from what I've encountered so far. It may sound odd, but in a way, I'm kind of excited. Who knows what I might find here? Maybe this area will be easier to survive in than Misty Falls and the Purple Desert. I hope so, because I'm tired of this aimless wandering. As soon as I can, I plan on moving inland and looking for a permanent residence. If Other World's going to be my home for the rest of my life, I'm going to make the best of it. I'm determined to do more than survive. I'm determined to thrive.

November 22 – Day 91

Looks like a storm's coming in. The wind's really picking up. The waves are large and ugly, filled with dark silt and sand from the churned-up bottom. Off in the distance a great, dark, green-tinged thunderhead is on its way in. Sitting here on the beach, I can see far-off flashes of lightening and the dull haze of heavy rain. I really need to find some shelter.

I won't find any place to weather out the storm here on the beach. There's a big pile of rocks on top of the sea cliff that I passed the day I landed the canoe. Maybe I can find a large hole or crevice to wedge myself into until the storm passes.

Ok, the wind's picking up. I better start climbing.

* * *

I… I don't believe it. You… hold on a second.

* * *

Yes. I'm not just imagining this. It's real.

I'm here at the top of the sea cliff and I'm looking at the large pile of rocks I saw before. But these aren't just rocks. They're ruins! There used to be a stone structure of some kind up here.

Do you realize what this means? It means I'm not the only person on Other World… or at least that I wasn't always the only person. I don't think anyone's been here for centuries. It looks like most of the structure fell down years ago. Rectangular rocks, worn smooth by water and wind, are scattered everywhere. The timeworn stones that aren't lying around are stacked tightly together to form a circular base without any kind of mortar between them. The seaside wall is the most intact remnant of the ancient structure and should make a good shelter from the storm.

I really wish I could spend more time studying all of this but the wind's picking up and it's full of cold rain. I've got to get all my stuff up here before the full brunt of the storm hits.

* * *

Well, I'm hunkered down and listening to the storm raging around me. Luckily, there's a portion of the stone wall that's collapsed against the seaside wall and makes a good cover from the wind and the rain.

The wind is blowing horribly. I could barely keep my feet when I came back up the sea cliff with all my gear. I got everything I could lay my hands on tucked away with me up here in the ruins, but I had to leave my canoe down on the beach. I pulled it up on shore as much as I could before I finally had to make a run for cover. I hope I pulled it up far enough to avoid those terrible waves. I'd hate to lose that boat.

It's like a screaming banshee out there. I can feel the wind as it strikes the other side of the wall that I'm leaning against. I hope these old rocks can stay together one more night. I'm glad I found this place. I never knew the wind could blow so hard.

One bright spot is that if I live through the night, I'll have plenty of drinking water again. I've set out all my watertight containers to gather some of this rain. Scared as I am, I can't afford to lose this chance for clean water. I just hope these walls can keep the wind from blowing all my containers over.

* * *

What was that?! There was a huge crash, thunderously loud even with the roaring wind. The whole ruins shook and I thought I'd plummet down to the ocean inside these dead stones. I still may. I'm so scared. God help me, I'm scared.

November 23 – Day 92

Well, I'm alive. Exhausted, but alive. I think I got about one hour of sleep. All night long, it was like trying to sleep inside a vacuum cleaner. Ugh. It's clearing up now though. The wind is still pretty brisk but the rain's gone and the sky is a brighter shade of gray.

* * *

At least all that rainwater was good for something. I managed to fill almost every container I have with clean rainwater. Best of all is that I don't have to boil it before drinking. Then again… maybe I should boil the water just to be safe. Probably.

Luckily, the ruins managed to stay together throughout the night, but I guess that shouldn't be too much of a surprise. After all, what's left standing here has stood for a long, long time already. I'll have to take some time and check it all out once the wind up here on the sea cliff dies off.

But first, I want get down to the beach. I have to know if my canoe is still there. Maybe I'll also see what that massive crash was I heard last night.

* * *

I found out what that terrible crash was last night. It was a giant wave, maybe more than one. The extent of the destruction is tremendous. There's driftwood, sea plants, and even marine life spread all over the sand and a long distance inland as well. You know, as horrible as the storm was, maybe it was a blessing in disguise. I can pick up all the fish and other ocean creatures I could ever want to eat, although quite a bit of it looks questionable.

There's a whole menagerie of weird sea life lying dead on the ground. I wish I had the time to sketch some of them. One creature looks like some kind of softball-sized crustacean with five feet long hair sprouting out all over it. Another creature has three pointed "swords" surrounding its round jaws that I guess it uses to spear dinner for itself. There's a different thing that doesn't seem to have a head. It's a fleshy, gelatinous mass about the size and weight of a large pig with five limbs that resemble the pseudopods of an amoeba. It makes me think of a great, bloated fetus of some shapeless monster. But even the giant amoeba is no comparison to what I found when I went looking for my canoe.

First, I have to sadly say that the Miss Sarah is lost and totally gone. I guess I shouldn't be surprised, and I'm not… I'm just disappointed. It may have been crude and a little rough around the edges, but I put a lot of work and effort into that little boat. It was probably the best thing I've ever built. Well, at any rate, it looks like I'm land bound again. I'll miss that boat.

Anyway, I was out on the beach looking for fish and things that I already know are edible when I came across a gigantic, dead sea creature washed up on the shore. It was the size of a city bus, all bloated and dark. Four tentacles extended from powerful shoulders near a head filled with needle-sharp teeth, each one nearly three feet long. Its flesh was so porous that when I pressed a stick into the fatty folds of its black skin a small trickle of water flowed out of it. Most disturbing were the leviathan's eyes, which were open and glassy and stared at me with the sleeping menace of a stuffed alligator. I felt them watching me as I walked from its gaping jaws all the way to the sharp point of its tail.

My immediate thought -once I had finished studying the thing- was how I could make use of it. I quickly decided that I would not try eating any part of it. The leviathan's spongy flesh was just as black and full of water under its skin as it was on the surface, and the wreaking stench of it almost turned my stomach.

I then considered the thing's teeth. I had the idea that just one tooth would make an impressive weapon, and I decided I would try to get as many of the teeth as I could. Removing them from the leviathan's gaping mouth turned into quite the long, messy project. After spending half the day and using my utility knife, spear, rocks, random pieces of wood, and even other dead creatures, I finally got four teeth free. I hope it was worth it.

Anyway, time for lunch. I've cooked up a seafood buffet. Luckily, there's enough edible stuff lying on the beach that I don't have to experiment with any new creatures.

* * *

Mmm… very satisfying. It's nice to be able to eat until I'm full again. I just wish I had some kind of vegetable or fruit to eat along with all this meat. It's funny… as soon as starvation isn't a concern anymore, I immediately start thinking about nutritional content. Mom would be proud.

It's a beautiful evening. I can barely see the leftovers of last night's storm now that it's moved inland. I'm sitting on an old rock wall watching the sunset. Maybe it's because of the storm, but the sky seems so much more vibrant tonight. Hues of red, gold, and violet stretch out across the vault of the heavens as the shimmering turquoise green of the sea collides with the horizon. It's breathtaking.

It's dark now. Tomorrow I plan on studying this old pile of ruins from top to bottom. Maybe I can find some clue about the people who built it. I might even find something I could use to survive. We'll see what the morning brings.

November 24 – Day 93

Good morning. I've already spent some time studying the ruins and there's definitely more to this place than first meets the eye. For one thing, whoever built this went to a lot of trouble to cart the building materials from somewhere else. I figured that out as I examined the stones in the remaining walls and compared them with the natural rocks around the area. Whoever built this thing didn't use the naturally occurring black rock to make their structure, but a light grey rock that is much denser and heavier.

After I realized the differences in the rock, I started looking for the grey stones elsewhere on the sea cliff. They were scattered all around the ruins' circular base, giving some hint to the scale of this building when it was first constructed. Eventually I thought to look over the edge of the cliff at the rocks below. Although it was difficult to tell with the large waves crashing in and out, I'm sure I saw several more of the grey stones down among the towers of natural rock carved by the sea. There's no way of knowing exactly how tall the building was at one time, but judging from the relatively small circular base I'd guess that this was originally a tower. Perhaps a lighthouse. That would certainly explain its location. From up here I have a good view of the nasty rocks and cliffs all along the shoreline. It appears that the small stretch of sandy beach that I pulled my canoe onto is the only safe place to lay anchor in the area.

When I realized that these ruins were most likely a lighthouse, I immediately made several educated guesses about the ruin's constructors. Not only did they have knowledge of stone masonry and architecture, but they also had a working knowledge of ship building and sailing. That suggests a well-developed society. I hope I'm not jumping to too many conclusions but I think my logic is sound. Besides, what else can I do but guess and hypothesize? There's no one around to ask about all this.

Well, the day is getting on. I'll write more after I've fixed and eaten something.

* * *

I've been thinking about the lighthouse again. Why build it here? Obviously, this was an important location to shipping if somebody went to all the trouble of building it, to say nothing of carting all the necessary stone up here. What was it about this spot that was so important? Perhaps there was a town or village nearby at one time. Since there's nothing visible from the beach or the cliff, I'll have to look inland if I want to find what the lighthouse was a signal for. It's just as well. It's about time I moved on anyway.

It'd be nice to stay here at the lighthouse a little longer, but I can't afford to. There's no source of fresh water besides rain. Besides, the washed up marine life is already starting to stink and the noise of the birds and other creatures feeding on them is keeping me up at night. Still, it's hard to leave when I'm not sure which way to go.

Well, I don't have to decide this very instant. I'll sleep on it. Maybe I'll come up with something in the morning.

November 25 – Day 94

I woke up early to the horrendous racket coming from the beach. The sound of the seabirds and other scavengers are different from the beak monkeys, but no less annoying. I'm definitely leaving today.

As I stepped out of the ruins this morning I saw a new kind of bird watching me nearby. It had the strange three-jointed wings common to most birds on Other World and the metallic sheen of its plumage was a kind of muted teal. Oddly, while it had one head it actually had three wings spaced around its body, so that when it flew it kind of spun slowly in the air like a corkscrew. I tried to catch it, but I have no net and my aim with rock throwing never has been all that good.

Since I'm heading out today, I might as well go down to the beach one more time to see if there's anything more I can scavenge. Most of the sea life is rotting, but I might as well try. Maybe I'll find something that's still fresh and hasn't been eaten yet. Maybe I'll be able to catch a bird or something while it's eating. Maybe I can hold my breath the whole time I'm there.

* * *

My ears hurt. Squawking, trilling, barking... yes, barking. I can't describe it any other way.

There were all kinds of flying scavengers down at the beach. One of them was huge and grotesquely fat. Like a farm-bred thanksgiving turkey, it seemed to have never been intended to fly. Its featherless, bulbous body and warted, bald head stood in sharp contrast to the graceful silver swifts flashing in the noontime sun.

The flying creatures weren't the only ones that were enjoying the decaying buffet. When I walked past the dead leviathan, I stopped and watched as its muscles and skin seemed to twitch and spasm. It took a moment to realize that the massive body was actually filled with small creatures burrowing and devouring its putrid flesh from the inside out. Sick.

Most of the land-bound scavengers I saw were small, though I did spot one who looked like it may usually be carnivorous. It was a muted green, with six skinny legs and a broad flat snout that looked like a fox that had been hit in the face with a shovel. It was only about the size of a raccoon so I didn't worry too much as I watched it eat. I was surprised when it picked up a shelled crustacean of some kind and crunched the entire thing down, carapace and all. The thing must have an iron stomach. I envy it.

In the end, I didn't get anything new to eat. The rotting smell and ear-splitting noise ruined my appetite. I guess there's nothing left to do but make a new sled out of my oars and plane hook and pack up once again.

* * *

I'm all packed and ready to go. I guess there's nothing left to do.

In a way, I wish I didn't have to go. I'd like to spend more time studying the lighthouse and maybe even search for lost artifacts. But I can't stay here with all this rotting flesh and risk getting sick again, not to mention running out of water and food. Besides, maybe by traveling inland I'll find more evidence of the people who built the lighthouse. I might even find their descendants.

It's time to go. Good luck Richard... I feel I may need it.

SEA OF GRASS

Expedition Log
11th of Spurr, in the 2nd year of The Return
Yurril T'nak, field scout

The fighting was much worse today. Huntil still insists that he should be the new Divant. He says that Brendell has led us out here into the wilderness so that those who don't support him will die. What a fool he is! Why do so many listen to him? What can he promise but lies and falsehoods? He has no favor with Shaelon, he receives no divine guidance. He keeps his counsel only with himself and his followers, preying upon their fears while he feeds the doubts of men far from home and safety.

Few remain faithful to the Divant. Only myself, Sasha, Treiipe, and Flain are still bold in our support of Shaelon's Chosen. I am especially grateful for the stalwart heart of Flain. He alone now commands respect from the doubters by his mighty strength and fearsome countenance. For days, he has stood like a sole bulwark against open rebellion, but even he may not stem the tide of anger and resentment after the events of today.

It was while hunting this afternoon that three of the disbelievers attacked Sasha when he spoke out against Huntil. I dare not think what might have happened had not Flain arrived in time to administer his own form of abrupt discipline. Pieorch still hasn't woken up from the blow to the head that Flain gave him. While I am glad Sasha is safe I fear the incident has only made matters worse.

Huntil now refuses to go any further under Brendell's leadership. He has declared himself and his followers apart from us and demands to be made the new

Divant by right of majority decision. It is a fool's demand, for a Divant of Shaelon is not selected by vote.

Brendell has valiantly tried to convince the others of the importance of finding the Records and Tokens. I know that without them there is no way the Order can be re-established. We are so close to the next of their possible locations. If we could continue, it would be just two more days of traveling through the jungle according to the Divant. I wonder if we will all survive to arrive there.

I fear the beasts less than the terrors around our own campfires. Flain has suggested to Brendell that we should take the weapons away from the others, but the Divant refuses. He insists that the men will revolt as soon as we lay hands on their armaments and that our best defense will be an increase of faith. I have faith, but I fear it may not be enough to keep me alive to see the lost city we are seeking.

Grace be. Yurril T'nak

November 26 – Day 95

I've made another discovery! I know which way to go now!

I set out this morning from the lighthouse in a roughly southeasterly direction. I was climbing the low dunes beyond the beach when I started seeing these peculiar stones lying around. They looked oddly smooth and flat, and after a while I realized that I'd found an ancient road. It terminates into a scattering of rocks at the sand's edge.

I'm not sure why the road ends there. Maybe it used to end in a dock for the ships that were led into the bay by the lighthouse. Either way, I now have a direction to follow. It's not much of a road anymore, but I can certainly follow the trail of cut stones to wherever it leads.

The road has led me straight inland all day, though I can still smell the salty breeze tonight as I make camp. The terrain is mostly open plains with lots of long grass and modest bushes. Dinner tonight is leftover fish, though I really wish I had some veggies to eat. My teeth and mouth hurt, and I worry I may be getting scurvy. I'll have to keep my eyes open for any plants that look palatable.

* * *

I thought that tonight I'd take some time to inventory all of my gear. It's been a while since I've taken stock. Here's what I have.

First, my clothes. I have two t-shirts, Dave's jacket, my windbreaker jacket, the poncho, and two pairs of jeans. Most of my clothes are in pretty good shape, though my socks are practically rags. In the last three months both pairs have worn away so badly that they seem to be more hole than sock. I may even try sewing them together to make a single pair. My shoes are doing much better, as I have good solid hiking shoes and Dave's sneakers in case I need them. All that, including two belts and Dave's ball cap makes up my entire wardrobe.

As for items from Earth, I have my writing bag, spiral notebook, pens (two full, three empty), two seatbelts, two oars, the flare gun kit, a half-full box of matches, the mess kit, plastic food containers, the signaling mirror, the first aid kit, my utility pocketknife, half a roll of duct tape, the plane hook and the fire extinguisher.

My items from Other World include the hammer and chisel rocks, a pile of unused forest behemoth hair, a short rope of behemoth hair, my fishing rod, four leviathan teeth, some fishbone needles, and my driftwood spear.

That's pretty much it. Not bad for someone who wasn't much of a camper growing up. I wonder what all those frustrated merit badge counselors would say if they saw me now. "Take a bath" probably, but soap isn't in big supply these days. I bet I'd smell even worse to myself if I hadn't already gotten used to it.

November 27 – Day 96

I think that I've discovered a whole new side of Other World. There's open grasslands as far as I can see ahead of me. The grass is long and a vivid bluish-green that flows in the wind like waves. Several small shrubs and bushes dot the landscape like islands. I'm calling one variety a whistler bush. This bush's branches grow out and then harden, becoming hollow as their inner core disappears. What makes the whistling sound is the fact that each branch has many small holes that allows the breeze to pass through them like a natural flute. It's a pleasant enough sound, but more practically I've found that whistler branches make the best fuel for my fires, since there aren't very many trees out here.

There's only one type of tree among the grass and bushes. I've decided to call them banza trees as they remind me of my grandfather's bonsais from a distance. Each tree reaches a height of about fifteen to twenty feet and is completely covered in thorny spines. Trunks, branches, even the tiny maroon leaves are festooned with inch-long spines. They're certainly not the kind of bonsai that you'd want to keep in your office.

Although the thorns are nasty, the banza trees have one redeeming quality: berries. Hundreds of small orange balls growing in bunches all along their branches. I'm operating on the assumption that if a plant is going to defend itself with such an extensive profusion of thorns that it wouldn't bother making its berries poisonous. I think that makes sense. I've already eaten a small handful, and twenty minutes later, I feel fine. More than fine.

I'm happy to have found this sea of grass. I love watching the aquamarine waves moving in the wind. The weather's warm enough now that I can go back to single layers. The breeze feels good against my skin and smells like soil after a hard rain. The sky looks so big and close. I feel like I could grab a handful of pink-ribbed clouds and make myself a bed out of them.

I'm sitting here watching the sunset, and I can't get over the colors painted in the sky. The beauty of it all is almost painful, I don't know why.

The stars are coming out now. I should get something to eat. I think those banza berries are safe. Goodnight.

November 28 – Day 97

I woke up this morning to find myself completely surrounded! A massive herd -I'd almost call it a swarm- of a new species of herbivores had managed to move so softly that they were nearly on top of my little camp next to the ancient road.

I was still trying to wake up when I saw them. At first I thought they were antelope. Of course, after my head cleared a little I realized that these Other World creatures are VERY different from Earthen antelope. Oh sure, they're mammals (at least I think so) with slender bodies and long elegant horns, but that's where all similarities end. This may be difficult to explain, but while they do have four legs these creatures do not have hips. Each creature's fore and back limbs are attached to its shoulders so that from the side they look like an open pair of scissors balanced on its tips. Between these muscular shoulders hangs what I can only describe as a kind of sack or long hump, which I assume, contains all the creature's internal organs.

Despite its awkward appearance, the scissor legs move with surprising grace and agility, though I still can't tell exactly how they keep from falling over. Somehow, they extend and contract their legs in a spring-like motion, propelling them at great speeds across the Sea of Grass. I've already decided that I have no hope of bringing one of these graceful creatures down using only my driftwood spear. It's too bad. I haven't had red meat since the meal pigs of Misty Falls. Oh well, I probably need the nutrients in the banza berries more anyway.

What I'm really concerned about right now is finding fresh water. I'm drinking some of the last of it right now. The banza berries do have some juice in them, but I'm going to need more than that. It's too bad that the scissor legs are so skittish. I'm sure that they would lead me to water if I could only follow them, but I'd never be able to keep up. I'll just have to keep an eye on animal movements as I travel along the ancient road. Perhaps the road itself will lead me to some fresh water. I hope so.

Expedition Log
14th of Spurr, in the 2nd year of The Return
Yurril T'nak, field scout

We have won, but at what cost? Treiipe is dead and Sasha has been gravely injured. Flain claims he is fine, but his body is covered in injuries. I myself am not able to use my right arm as it is too heavily bandaged to move much. Brendell too is hurt, but he spends all his time caring for the rest of us as if he were newly risen in the morning. Truly, he is a Divant of Shaelon.

All of our rebellious companions are dead, except for Huntil and two others who disappeared into the jungle at the end of the fighting. Flain swears he struck at Huntil just as he passed into the brush, so it may be that he has already joined his compatriots in death. It is a terrible temptation to wish him an end appropriate for the pain and death that his dissention has caused. I cannot say I have not dwelt on it.

It is a miracle that so few of us could survive against such overwhelming odds. I know that we are held in the hands of Shaelon during this darkest of times. Even as we sit in the library of the lost city, alone in this hostile world and wounded in heart and soul by the betrayal of our brethren, we take comfort in knowing that our journey may still continue.

Today -being the first day that any of us could be spared to look- I have spent the day's whole light searching for the ancestor's box containing the Records and Tokens. It is not here. Brendell says there are but two more places in this world where they might be. We are in luck that we will not have to travel on foot to our next destination. The river that runs through this city flows to the ocean and can be used to take us to the next place we shall search. Flain and those others who are not badly wounded have already begun work on two sturdy dugouts to carry what remains of our party and provisions. Brendell says this will be a blessing, as those of us who are more heavily injured may ride in comfort until we reach the sea. From there we hope to follow the coast to the old lighthouse of

Tethritan. We will pray it is still standing.
Grace be to you. Yurril T'nak.

November 29 – Day 98

Good morning. The scissor legs have moved on, but I can still see them in the distance. Hopefully they stay close enough for me to keep an eye on them throughout the day.

Just a random thought, but it's funny how I can wake up at dawn and still feel totally rested. I could never get up early back on Earth. Maybe the air here is cleaner and more rejuvenating. Maybe the nights on Other World are actually longer. Maybe it's just the fact that I'm going to sleep just an hour or two after sunset.

Well, I better grab some breakfast and get the day started.

* * *

Looks like I'm not the only one keeping an eye on the scissor legs. I've been observing the first major predator I've seen on the Sea of Grass. For once, I think I'm in luck, I don't think she'll pose any danger to me personally.

Actually, she's a very elegant creature. Picture a cross between a greyhound and a ferret and you'll get a rough idea of her general features. The only part of her that's not streamlined is a ponderous bulge at her stomach, which strongly suggests to me that she's pregnant. Judging from how large she is, I'd guess that she must be close, which would explain why she seems to be causally wandering along after the herd as opposed to actively hunting. I wonder if she'll stay with the herd long enough for me to see her babies when they come. I hope so.

* * *

Still no water, but I saw a... a something that I just had to write about. This thing was bizarre, even for Other World.

I was taking my afternoon siesta while having a light lunch of banza berries. The scissor legs were resting in what shade they could find and I figured I could afford a little nap. I was just about to close my eyes when I noticed something stirring in the grass. A flower blossom of white and violet was swaying slightly without a breeze. I wondered if some small creature was brushing against the flower and got up to investigate. But there was no creature under the flower. The creature was the flower!

At least I think so. I really don't know. I couldn't tell if this strange hybrid was a mobile plant or a photosynthetic animal. The blossom's stem gradually elongated out to a limbless, undulating body like that of a snake. The blossom seemed genuine as each little bloom had a pestle with what looked like pollen inside. The body moved swiftly, especially when I stepped too close to it. I wish I could have studied the thing more closely. How would it get necessary nutrients without a visible mouth or roots to plant in the earth?

Anyway, the scissor legs are moving on and I don't want to lose sight of them. I have to go.

* * *

I've lost the scissor legs. They've moved away from the road to the point where I can't see them anymore. I'm not sure what I should do. I'm out of water and following the herd may still be my best chance of finding more, but I don't want to have to leave the road. What should I do?

I don't know. My head hurts. I really need a drink. I'll just eat some more berries. Maybe I'll follow the direction that the scissor legs went in for a little while in the morning. Following this road won't do me any good if I die of thirst along the way.

November 30 – Day 99

I've found the scissor legs, and that's not all. Water! There's a small watering hole surrounded by grass that's been trampled flat by the numerous herds using this spot.

There's quite a variety of animals here. I'll have to dedicate some time later to describing each one, but at the moment I'm more concerned about how to get past them to the water.

I'm going to have to be very careful. There are a lot of big animals down there and I'm not sure how favorably they'd feel about sharing their drinking space. Even if I can get past all the large creatures around the water, I wouldn't necessarily be out of danger. I can't help remembering all those nature specials I've seen filmed in Africa where some poor wildebeest comes up to a perfectly still pool, then SPLASH! ...and Mr. Wildebeest is crocodile food. Who knows what kind of crocodile-equivalent Other World might have hiding in there?

Well, I guess there's nothing to do but try it. I've dealt with a bigmouth and a petal bear already. I'm not going to let the fear of an unseen predator stop me now. I'll carry a leviathan tooth for protection since it's sharper and sturdier than my driftwood spear. I should be fine as long as I keep my tooth aimed at the water and my eye on the surrounding animals. I'll be ok. I just hope this won't be my last entry.

* * *

Well, I made it to the water without any problems, though I did get some dirty looks from a few of the larger creatures. Most importantly, nothing came up out of the water… except for mud. This is some of the dirtiest water I've ever seen in my life. I'll probably have to strain it twice before boiling it. Maybe three times. Perhaps I should try a different method of purifying this water.

Ever since I was stranded on the ocean, I've been wondering about the feasibility of purifying my water by steaming it. I had an idea to put a pot of water over a fire in a semi-enclosed space and then collect the purified droplets as they condense on a non-porous surface. The downside to this process would be the additional time it would take, not to mention the complexity of the process, but in exchange, my water would always be as clean and pure as rainwater. Of course, I couldn't try this out while I was on the ocean, but maybe now would be a good time to try it.

I've sketched out a rough schematic of the contraption's set-up. I plan to build a fire with my pot over the flames, and then I'll suspend my space-blanket over the pot to catch the condensing steam. I'll also place a rock In the middle of the blanket so that its surface comes to a point that will feed the pure water into another pan. I know it sounds complicated, but it should work. At least I think so. We'll see.

* * *

Well that was useless. I didn't realize how long it would take to set up my contraption, and most of the steam from the boiling water was lost due to wind and not placing everything correctly. After a full afternoon of work, I've only got a mouthful or so of clean water. I'll just have to go back to straining and boiling it. Hopefully I don't get sick.

I'll probably spend most of my time tomorrow filling the rest of my containers with fresh water and using my off time to describe some of the creatures around here. I may even try to add a new item to tomorrow's menu. We'll have to see.

December 1 – Day 100

Happy day 100. It feels like a lifetime has gone by since Dave and I crashed on Other World.

Dave… I haven't thought about him for a while. I don't think too much about people anymore. The memories are too painful.

I find myself thinking about random things throughout the day. Thoughts that have no bearing on anything will pop into my mind. A few days ago, I couldn't get a bathroom cleaner jingle out of my head. And then I kept remembering how I'd cheated on a book report in seventh grade.

I wish I had someone to talk to.

I was thinking about trying to celebrate somehow for my hundredth day on Other World, but I just don't feel like it. Besides, I need to purify some more water. I'll write again later.

* * *

Hello again. I'm sorry I was so depressed this morning. I was just a little melancholy, that's all. I've already got a pot of water on to boil. I suppose I could take some time to describe some of the wildlife in the area.

First, I'll describe the setting a little more. Surrounding me on all sides are open fields of aquamarine sea grass and scattered banza trees. The area around the water hole is dominated by various small herds of creatures jockeying for position around the vital, life-sustaining water. The water hole itself seems surprisingly deep. Maybe it has an underground source.

I've already mentioned the scissor legs, but there are several other large creatures here as well. One species has six legs and what look like three sails of stretched yellow flesh extending form its narrow, maroon body. Each one is about the size of a deer and makes a call that sounds like a cross between a penguin and a pennywhistle. Watching those yellow sails moving through the sea grass I'm reminded of a small fleet of yachts coasting around a tranquil bay.

Another species is a hefty quadruped with legs like marble pillars and feet shaped like the blade of a shovel. Each of these creatures stands about five feet tall at the shoulder and is a drab green and grey color. A large hump stands out just behind its shoulders and resembles an oversized, hairy coconut. The creatures' heads are large and heavy, with floppy hound dog ears hanging along their necks. I'll call these creatures marmeldons for no reason other than the fact that I feel like the name fits.

There's also a cat-sized, two-legged species here. They have scaly, reptilian bodies but heads that look like they belong to tiny wild boars. Each creature has what I think are two thin tails protruding from the middle of its back. Of all the creatures here, I think these little beasts are probably the noisiest. They're always barking at each other, sounding like schizophrenic Chihuahuas. They're colorful though. Each one is covered with stripes of blue, green, and red. The banded runners are certainly pretty to watch, if not to listen to.

There's also a small variety of flying creatures around here, but to be honest I'm getting tired of writing. I'll stop after describing one more new species. It's large, about the same size as a sail beast but less ostentatious. This creature has the general shape of a large bluish-green bird with strong legs and long wings. What's strange is that while this creature may technically be a biped, the bird moves by crawling on its belly, using its folded wings like a second pair of legs, similar to the way a bat would move on the ground. I'm not sure how fast the crawler can move in this way, as I've only seen it walking slowly. I suspect that these creatures are carnivores judging by their large, predatory beaks. Perhaps the crawler rises up onto its legs to chase down its prey. Or perhaps it's a scavenger and primarily feeds on carrion. Either way, the crawlers definitely look to be the most dangerous creatures in the area and everything else is giving them a wide berth. I think it'd be wise for me to do the same. Luckily, there are only a couple of them around here.

I think that's enough writing for now.

* * *

Good evening. Well, I've got all the fresh water I can store. Now I'm just trying to decide what I can eat with it. There's a variety of possible game around the water hole, but I'm not sure what would be the best way to try to catch something. I could try pit traps again by digging a few by the water's edge, but I'm not sure how effective they'd be. The ground here is hard and full of roots from the sea grass. It might be easier to trying hunting instead of trapping in this open area.

With that in mind, I have a couple of ideas. First, I could try catching one of the banded runners with some kind of net made out of what's left of the seatbelts. If I can get close enough to a group of runners to throw the net, I should be able to tangle one of them long enough to rush in and finish the job with my spear. My other idea is looking for eggs. I haven't had eggs in so long… There must be some kind of creature out here that lays them.

Well, I think I've decided. I'll make that seatbelt net first thing tomorrow morning and divide my time between hunting with the net and searching for eggs. I'm hoping for eggs, but either way, I'm determined to get myself off this straight banza berry diet.

December 2 – Day 101

Morning. I've finished my seatbelt net. It's kind of a convoluted mess, but if it confuses a banded runner as much as it confuses me, it should work wonders. I'm off to try it out. Wish me luck.

* * *

Fire up the barbecue, we're having banded runner for dinner! Actually, the whole process was surprisingly easy.

I found a small group of banded runners sitting in the shade of a banza tree. I wondered at first if I'd wasted my time by making my net, since it seemed that all I had to do was walk up and pick up whichever one I wanted. It wasn't until I got within twenty paces that one runner (the lookout, I guess) began barking its head off. The whole troop came awake and began skittering away at high speed. I sprinted forward and flung my net into the thick of the runners. As soon as the net hit the ground they scattered away from it, but the damage was done with one of the critters snarling itself in the strongly tied bands. I finished the creature off with my spear and was able to carry my prize back to camp.

Well, my lunch looks just about done. It's surprising how appetizing this odd little creature looks roasting over my fire. I hope it tastes all right.

* * *

Yuck. This is gross. Some of the worst tasting meat I've ever had. It tastes like... mud. Bleh! I wonder if their banded coloring is a warning sign to all predators that they taste horrible.

Well, at least it's food. But if I can avoid eating it again, I will. I'll try to look for eggs before dinner tonight.

* * *

Hmm... Well, I'm not having egg for dinner. I'm having banza berries and disgusting leftover banded runner. But I think I know where I can get an amazing breakfast. A crawler egg. I mean, the bird itself is about the size of a full-grown human, so think of the size of the eggs that it would have. Think of the omelet I could make with one of those! Of course, it could be dangerous. The crawlers are big, and although I've never seen one of them move faster than I could on my hands and knees, that isn't saying they couldn't go faster. Still...

It's funny to think that only three short months ago I wouldn't even consider trying this. Maybe that's the real reason why I still want to try despite the possible danger. I'm not the same person I was then. I'm not afraid like I used to be, and my priorities have changed. I'm not in this just to survive anymore. I'm here to thrive. I'm not sure if what I'm feeling is courage or foolhardiness. Maybe they're more closely related than I had ever thought.

I'm gonna try it. Call me crazy, but I refuse to let myself not try. I know when to pull back if things get too crazy. I should be ok.

I'm gonna get some sleep. You wouldn't believe how many stars are in the sky. Even camping on Earth I could never have seen this many. Lying here on the Sea of Grass, listening to the crackling fire and watching the sparks fly up to join the shimmering stars... I don't think I've ever felt this alive. This is my world, and my home.

December 3 – Day 102

Good morning. And what a morning. I got up with the sunrise and I don't know if I've ever seen the sun look so big and full. It's like a great, orange ball rising up over the horizon. Wow.

I'm going to go for the crawler's egg now, before the day warms up. I'm taking my hunting spear, along with a tooth spike in case things get dicey. Wish me luck.

* * *

[unreadable]

* * *

Stupid. That was so, so stupid. I'm lucky to be alive. What an idiot!

I'm ok, I'm all right. Well, mostly. My legs are throbbing, but I think the bleeding has stopped... mostly. Now they just hurt. Oh, they hurt. My stomach's all in knots again. Ugh. I want to throw up.

This is what happened. After finishing this morning's entry, I went out looking for the crawler's nest. I found it out in the open, a large pile of dried grass maybe a foot deep. The crawler was lying nearby on her stomach, apparently asleep. My plan at that point was simple. I'd force the crawler away from the nest, slip the egg into my backpack, and then carefully leave. I figured the bird would give up once it realized it wouldn't be getting its egg back. In a best-case scenario, I'd never have to get close enough to even need my spear.

I got as close as I dared, picked up a rock, and threw it as hard as I could at the crawler. True to form, I missed badly. I tried twice more and missed again, though I think the crawler was probably waking up by then. Finally a large stone landed hard on its back. The crawler came awake with an angry noise that sounded like the muted buzzing of a table saw.

What happened next was so fast I can barely remember how it went. I thought the crawler would try standing its ground, maybe circle around me looking for an opening. It didn't. It charged straight at me without hesitation. I barely had time to get the point of my spear between us before it was on me. The spear's point bit deeply into its shoulder and it leapt back with another shriek. But it didn't back down. It crouched menacingly, buzzing madly as it watched me with those terrible black eyes.

I know I probably should have pressed my advantage, leaping forward and thrusting my spear into the large bird. But by that point, I was shaking so bad I could barely hold my spear. Somehow, I had become the prey of this formidable hunter. All I could think of was getting away. I took a step back. The crawler leapt toward me again.

This time it took the end of my spear in its beak. The crawler wrenched the wooden shaft in my hands, sending painful vibrations up my arms to rattle my whole body. With a twist of its head, it snapped off the spear's sharpened tip. I stumbled backward, trying to pull my ruined spear away from its grip. That's when my foot caught a raised stoned and I sprawled backward.

The crawler was instantly on top of me. I think there were two things that kept me alive at that point. One was how surprisingly light the crawler was, so that I was still able to move underneath it. The other thing was the fact that I still had a hold of the broken spear and used it to block the crawler's deadly beak. The crawler thrashed angrily trying to get at my throat. It kept kicking me with its clawed feet, raking them painfully along my thighs and legs. I screamed, and the giant bird attacked with increased ferocity.

All this time I'd been trying to get my tooth spike out from where I'd slid it into my belt. I couldn't get it out! In desperation, I twisted it upwards -still in my belt- and dropped my legs, letting the crawler fall down onto the point. Lucky for me the point hit home and stayed there.

I rolled out and away from the horribly screeching and thrashing crawler. I scrambled several yards away from it, still afraid that it might charge me again. But it didn't, and I watched until it finally stopped thrashing. I stared at its dead body for a long time before I realized I was bleeding.

My jeans had several tears, revealing long, shallow cuts on my thighs and calves where I was trying to block it from clawing at my torso. I wasn't bleeding very much, but I started to cry. It hurt to stand and walk but I was able to do it. I almost left before remembering the reason I'd done such a stupid thing in the first place. I quickly examined the dead crawler's nest and found a single, coconut-sized egg lying in the dried grass.

So now I'm back here in camp. I'm so glad I had the small guide in the first-aid kit to tell me what to do about my legs. I've cleaned the cuts with hot, clean water and bound them up using gauze from the first-aid kit and duct tape. The cuts weren't deep enough to get to the muscles of my legs, so I shouldn't have any permanent damage, according to the guide.

So, was it worth it? I've got the egg now, and I dragged the crawler carcass back to camp as well, so I've got plenty of food. I may have some uses for what's left over, particularly the giant eggshell and the crawler's beak. I've got more food now than I've had since the morning on the beach after the hurricane. Yet I'm sitting here, washing my own blood off my hands and desperately hoping my legs don't get infected.

Was it worth it? I don't think I'll ever try it again. Is that answer enough?

December 4 – Day 103

Mmm… Good morning. Well, I'm more sore and stiff than I can ever remember, but there's no discoloration around the cuts, so I don't think I've got an infection. I've changed the dressings already for today. I'm not sure what I'll do when my first-aid kit finally runs out.

I used a rock and a tooth spike to break open the top of the egg shell. Right now, I'm making scrambled crawler egg. There's too much to eat this morning, but I figure I'll cook all of it and eat my fill over the next couple days. I also need to butcher the crawler. I'll get to work on that after breakfast. I wish I had some way to store all this food. I'm worried it's gonna go bad before I can eat it all. Wouldn't that be a pleasant problem?

* * *

Eggs never tasted so good. It was a surprisingly filling meal, but I still managed to devastate half of the food I made this morning. It's so nice to have a big, hot, filling meal. I can only hope the bird itself tastes this good.

Speaking of which, I better get to work on that crawler carcass.

* * *

Whew! Can you imagine how many feathers a five-foot chicken would have? A lot! My fingers are aching from all the plucking I've done. Still, I think I can get some long-term benefits from all this work. I couldn't help but notice how soft the smaller feathers are, and I remembered my old feather pillow at home. Why couldn't I have that? I'd need some kind of container for a pillow, and I can't sacrifice any of my clothes for that. Maybe I could try using the paper sack that Dave had his lunch in. I still have it. I could duct tape it shut if I really wanted a pillow.

Well, we'll see. I'll hold on to the feathers until I figure out exactly what I want to do with them. In the meantime, sleeping on piles of fresh-picked grass isn't all that uncomfortable. It's like what I imagine sleeping in a hayloft would be like.

Anyway, butchering the rest of the bird didn't prove to be any easier than de-feathering it was. I finally had to settle with taking one of the legs to roast over the fire. The rest of it is kind of a mess. But the drumstick looks pretty good, especially since it's the size of my forearm.

Speaking of which, I better check how it's cooking.

* * *

Oh my gosh! You would not believe how good this tastes. It almost makes up for how sore I am.

At least I know I can stand and walk, though I'm trying to stay off my feet for a few days. I wonder if I'll have some nasty scars when they've healed. Oh well. At least it makes for a better story than telling how I got my appendectomy scar.

I was thinking about home again today. It's getting closer to Christmas. I wonder if Mom and Dad will have their Christmas lights up already. Maybe Bryant and Hannah will bring Amy up for a week with Grandma and Grandpa for the holidays. Amy was born around Christmas time. Poor kid will probably get birthday presents in Santa Claus paper for the rest of her life.

I guess I still can't let go of home, no matter how many times I tell myself that I have to. Then again, maybe that's not such a bad thing. I'd hate to completely lose any connection with the people that I love. I just wish it didn't hurt so much whenever I let myself think about it. Maybe with time it won't be so bad. I hope so. I'd like to remember home with a smile, not tears.

December 5 – Day 104

Had a little bit of a scare this morning. I woke up to the sound of a creature breathing very close to me. I froze, remembering the episode with the petal bear and its cub. I slowly took hold of a nearby tooth spike and cautiously raised my head. Turns out, I needn't have bothered being so on-edge. It was only the ferret hound I'd seen earlier eating off my crawler carcass. An angry shout and a few tossed rocks was all it took to drive it off. I noticed as it was running off that it looked much slimmer and streamlined than last week. I wonder if she's had her babies. Maybe I'll go out and take a look after breakfast. It'd give me a chance to exercise my aching legs a little.

Breakfast first though. Luckily, there's still plenty of meat on the crawler carcass that hasn't been chewed on by the ferret hound.

* * *

I guess I can't be too mad at that ferret hound. She's got a lot of mouths to feed nowadays. I found them playing around a shallow den dug into the side of a banza tree. They were cute, all the little critters scampering over each other, frolicking and playing like any bunch of puppies. Their mother kept a wary eye on me until I left.

I need to start thinking how I'll score my next big meal. I think it's been established that tangling with a crawler is just too dangerous, and I'm positive that the banded runners' taste hasn't improved. I guess I'll just have to try my pit traps again, though it'll be more difficult in this open plain than it was up north. In the forest, there were animal trails that I could use to maximize my traps' effectiveness. I guess I'm just going to have to think some more about it.

Well, it's sunset now and I'm sitting here listening to the calls of the animals blending with the growling of my stomach. Maybe I'll come up with something in a dream.

December 6 – Day 105

This is very, very bad. I really shouldn't be writing right now, but I can't help myself. I'll do this entry real fast and then get out of here.

I woke up this morning to a sound that seemed more like a quivering in the air than an actual noise. My first thought was that it sounded similar to the glowing leviathan I saw out at sea. But this sound was softer, more subtle, like an ominous breeze through the sea grass. I got up to look for its source and found what I had wished I would never see again: a bigamouth. But not just one. It's a herd. Or a pack. Maybe twenty of them, and they're big. Some of them look like they're twice the size of the one that was hunting me up north, though I'm too far away to tell for sure. I really don't want to get any closer to find out.

I'm hiding under the lowest hanging banza tree I could find. I'm watching them. I don't think they can see me. I wonder how good their sense of smell is.

All the herds are nervous. You can feel it in the air. The scissor legs are the most ill at ease. Every time one of the resting bigamouths stirs, a whole section of the herd instantly sprints a dozen yards further away. I think they may have the right idea. I definitely do not want to hang around until the bigamouths realize that I'm not as fast as the scissor legs. There's no way I could hope to stand up to a whole pack of these monsters.

I saw just them take down a sail beast. They surrounded it, cutting it off from its herd and then moved in. One of the big ones wrapped its massive jaws around the beast's neck and bit down. The poor creature went limp in less than a heartbeat. I think its spine was broken. That could have been me.

I'm not going to wait any longer. I was going to try to risk one more foray for water, but I'm leaving now. Better to get out of here while I can. The ancient road leads east and away from the bigamouths. I'll follow it.

* * *

I've managed to put the water hole and the pack of bigamouths far behind me. Well, far for me and my stiff legs anyway. I doubt they'll follow me with all that food and water back there. I hope I'm right.

There sure isn't much out here. I'm glad that I packed along all the berries from the banza tree I was hiding under. There aren't many of the trees out here.

I think I'm at a point where I can describe the bigamouths from this morning a little more. Each one was a mix of white and dark brown with black and white tiger stripes on their hindquarters. Their eyes were much smaller than those of their northern cousins, which suggests to me that they do more of their hunting during the day. They have the same big mouths though, with heads at least half again as big as those of the northern bigamouth. I saw one of them yawn as I was leaving. I swear you could fit an entire watermelon down one of these things' throats. I'm very glad I've got some distance between me and them.

Well, I'm curling up for a night's sleep now. No need for a fire. It's a warm night and I'm pretty alone out here on the plains.

The sky sure is big out here. The stars are crammed on the surface of the sky. It's really amazing. Part of me wishes I was up there somewhere. Up above and far away from being hungry and afraid.

Anyway, I better try to get some rest. Goodnight.

December 7 – Day 106

I'm never going without a fire again. I don't care if it is getting warmer. I do not want a repeat of last night.

I was sound asleep when I woke up to hear the snuffling of a creature right next to my leg. I opened my eyes and leapt for my tooth spike. I turned over and saw... a weird looking little creature. It was round with poufy blue feathers and huge eyes that shone duly in the double moonlight. It had a small beak and stood on two knobby little legs. I haven't come up with a name for it yet... besides "breakfast." It tastes pretty good.

I don't want to get caught unaware that way again though. Next time it could be a bigamouth. Still, I did find a new source of food. Maybe if I spend some time hunting before bed tonight I can find another of these meal birds. They're very tasty and pretty easy to kill. I wonder what it was looking for in my camp. Maybe some kind of snack? Perhaps it was looking for my store of berries. It might be a good idea to try making a couple traps using the berries as bait. I'd be willing to sacrifice some berries in exchange for a whole meal.

I better keep going. My water supplies are at about half of what they could be, so I should be good for a while. I just hope that waterhole I was camping at isn't the only one around here.

* * *

Man, am I stiff. My legs still ache from the fight with the crawler. I took the bandages off, but it will probably still be a while before they've completely healed.

The weather's been nice and warm lately. I've shed all of my long sleeve shirts in favor of my t-shirt, or what's left of it anyway. It's amazing how much wear and tear you can get from just three months of wearing the same thing. It's got little holes all through it. I should really get around to sewing it back together.

You know, having eaten so well this morning, I was able to enjoy the scenery much more as I made my way across the plain. It's almost like going for a walk on top of the sea as the wind sends rippling waves through the long grass. The only downside is that I worry that something could be stalking me through the tall grass. I always keep a tooth spike in my hand now as I travel, even while pulling my sled.

Anyway, I've decided how I'll try to get breakfast in the morning. Instead of staying up all night waiting for a meal bird to come along, I'll go back to my old friend the pit trap and use a bunch of pulled up grass to cover the hole. I'll put a fat pile of berries on top and the tooth spikes down inside it. It'll have to be a big hole, but I've still got an hour before the sun completely disappears. Cross your fingers.

December 8 – Day 107

Ha ha ha! Good morning! Good breakfast! You know how it feels to wake up and find a fat meal bird already dead in your pit trap? It feels great, that's how it feels! Tastes really good too. How could nature ever have evolved such a perfect animal to be consumed? I wonder if this is the way early man felt when he first discovered the chicken. "What's this fat, dumb bird? I wonder how it tastes…"

Anyway, it's not meat I'm concerned about now. It's water. I know, I sound like a scratched CD saying that over and over, but it's true. I almost wonder if I should have risked staying back at the water hole. Almost. Those bigmouths are enough to convince anyone to move on. Not to mention the crawlers possibly wanting revenge. Or a marmeldon accidently stepping on me. Or the banded runners turning carnivorous. Yeah, I definitely think it's just better that I keep moving on.

The landscape is still open plains for as far as I can see. Just gently sloping hills and spotty green meadows amidst the weaving plain grass. It's beautiful, but it's also relatively dry. I'll keep going and following the ancient roadway. Maybe if I don't find water within the next few days I can try digging in one of the meadows. If it's greener, then maybe there's some water under the surface. Still, I'd prefer finding some water rather than having to dig for it.

* * *

Good evening. I just had to write a little tonight and describe a new creature I saw on the plains. It was another gigantic creature like the forest behemoth, though this one wasn't nearly so stocky. It had three legs, two thin front ones and a single shorter back one. It's head and mouth were circular, and when it fed it twisted it's head to tear out perfect circles of long grass. He was much taller than he was long, maybe three stories tall. It looked kinda funny when he would bend down to eat, as his front legs bent outward from his body like the doubled-up legs of a grasshopper. The grass chomper is a big benevolent creature, and just another of the wonders that you get on a world like Other World. This is such an amazing place! If only I could share it with someone.

December 9 – Day 108

Well, water is starting to run low, so I better find something soon. I was thinking that maybe I could try collecting dew. Every morning I wake up soggy and wet and you can see it rising and steaming all morning. Who's to say I can't just rig something together for catching the moisture? It could work. If things get bad I'll have to look through my stuff and see what I could use.

I've discovered what is probably the largest herding creature I've seen yet here on the plains. It's a fleshy pink, with spotted tufts of hair and weird rounded eyes. Each one stands at least eight feet at the shoulder. They have crested horns and bony plates all over their bodies, with occasional large, elongated horns that spring up from seemingly random points on their bodies. One has a horn four feet long sticking out of its left hindquarters, while another has a two foot long one thrusting from just below its throat. Very bizarre, and surprisingly asymmetrical. I don't know if I've ever seen a more random creature. I'll call them "spikers" for obvious reasons.

For the time being, the small herd of spikers seems to be moving in a direction that is roughly parallel to the ancient road, so it looks like I'll have traveling companions for a while. Who knows? They may even lead me to water.

* * *

It looks like I'm not the only one traveling alongside the spikers. There's a pair of crawlers out here following them as well. I'm leery of them to say the least. Actually, I don't think the crawlers are going to be a danger to the spikers, except for maybe the babies. There's two of them, and their spikes are still milky white compared to the yellowed looking ones on the adults. Ever since I noticed the crawlers I've observed the spikers keeping a loose circle around their little ones. I wish I had some tank-sized spiky creatures circled around me right now.

* * *

All right, I think the spikers are done traveling for today and so am I… and so are the crawlers. I'm keeping the fire burning high, or as high as I can using chopped-up chunks of whistler bushes. Actually I had a little good news regarding the whistlers. While I was getting fuel for my fire tonight I noticed a fat bug of some kind hiding in the bush. Since I figured I probably wouldn't get any meal birds tonight with the crawlers around, I threw my jacket over the bush and caught it.

It looked somewhat like a two headed centipede, though I couldn't tell if one of the heads was a fake. But he was pretty big, and since I didn't have enough water to waste boiling it, I skewered it on a stick and roasted it. Tasted terrible. At least I know I've had some protein. Maybe I can find some more bugs before going to bed.

The night sky is flooded with stars. I'm just sitting here, listening to the whistler bushes and the spikers' low moaning and grunting, staring up into the black and violet sky. I wonder if this is similar to what they say it looks like in the Australian Outback at night. It's just gorgeous. With so many stars and the two nearly full moons, it's a wonder it's even dark enough to sleep. I'm definitely tired enough though. I'm gonna call it a night.

December 10 – Day 109

I hate waking up that way. Ugh, my stomach is all in knots. Stupid crawler.

I guess I better explain. When I woke up this morning I sat up to see one of the crawlers coiled up in the grass nearby, watching me. It didn't move. It just sat there making that strange buzzing sound the other crawler had made during our fight. I got up slowly, still trying to wake up and more than a little stiff. I grabbed two tooth spikes, one in each hand, and aimed them right at the creature. Nothing happened for what seemed a very long time. We just stared at each other. I yelled at it.

"What?! What do you want? You want a piece of me? I've eaten your kind before. You wanna start something? Come on!"

I pretended to charge towards it, taking a few aggressive steps forward. That was when the thing finally reacted. It hissed at me and leapt forward like a coiled spring. Luckily for me, my tooth spikes were between us. One point missed its head, but the other caught the crawler just under its beak. The creature turned its head and grabbed the spike in its mouth, trying to break it or throw it away. But these spikes aren't wooden spears, and while it was distracted with one spike I used the other to stab it again. It tried to jerk away but I kept my spike in place.

I was about to try driving the spike in deeper when I heard a rustle on my right side. I looked over my shoulder and saw a second crawler rushing towards me. I pulled back, letting the first crawler leap away as I charged the second one, screaming at the top of my lungs. This one stopped and hissed, but didn't come close enough for me to attack it. I quickly stepped backward to keep both of them in front of me. My heart was slamming against my chest. I thought I was about to die.

Well, obviously I survived, otherwise I couldn't be writing this. But it looked really close there for a while. The three of us stood there for what seemed like an eternity but was probably only a few seconds. There was no sound except for the low buzzing noise of the crawlers. After a few moments I decided to try going on the offensive again before they could circle around me.

I turned and charged the one that was already wounded, this time saying nothing as I ran at it with my spikes out front. The crawler launched itself forward to meet me and ran directly into my spikes, lodging both the points deep in its chest. This time I threw myself forward and heaved with all the strength in my shoulders to drive the points in. The wounded crawler tried to back away as I pushed forward. It stumbled, trying to get away from me and my deadly spikes. I just kept pushing the points in. I wanted it to die.

I only stopped when I again heard the movement of the other crawler. I yanked both spikes free, leapt back, and screamed a primal challenge at the top of my lungs at the other crawler. It stopped and looked at me with my two bloody spikes raised and ready to drive into it as well. It buzzed angrily but it didn't move. I took a couple of steps towards it and it shuffled backward. The wounded crawler was bleeding very badly now as it slowly slunk off into the grass nearby. I let it go, keeping my eye on the other, healthier one until it finally left as well. I had won.

I've calmed down now. I want to follow the tracks of blood and try to find that wounded crawler. I'll leave my camp stuff here and just take the sled to carry it on. I better get moving. I'm hungry.

* * *

I'm too tired to write very much right now. Suffice it to say I got that crawler. It was lying down, dying in the thick grass. The other one was nearby, but it didn't try to stop me as I killed the wounded one and carted off the body. I spent the rest of the day slaughtering the bird and trying to continue traveling, but I just had to stop. I'm so tired.

I'm cooking some of the crawler for dinner. I'm also drinking the last of my water tonight. I know from experience now that after keeping very hydrated and not rationing I can go on for a good day or two without water. After that... well, let's just hope I find something by then. In the meantime though, I may have an idea of something I can do.

I'm thinking I'll try collecting dew in the morning. I'm not sure how well it will work, but I'll give it a shot. If I rig my poncho in such a way as to drip down into a bottle, I could potentially get the same kind of moisture condensation as I got with the water purifier. Should work pretty well.

I better get it rigged before I go to sleep.

December 11 – Day 110

The dew trap didn't work too bad. A third of a bottle is enough to quench my thirst anyway. I'll need more than this to keep me going though.

I can't write much. I need to keep traveling. The spikers are still moving parallel to the ancient roadway, so I'll keep following it. Please God, let it lead to water soon.

* * *

Well it's not water, but it looks promising. There's a distinct change in the landscape... could mean water. I'm too tired to write about it right now though. I gotta get some sleep.

December 12 – Day 111

My head aches. Not much success with the dew-catcher this morning. I guess I better keep moving.

* * *

Don't worry. Things are much better now. Really. I've found water, more than I could ever drink, and I'm in the process of purifying my second batch.

This morning I found an area where the sea grass gives way to a short, coarse grass growing among a collection of rocky outcroppings that looked like a giant had littered the area with boulders and smaller rocks. There's a stand of trees nearby. I've never seen their type before, but I was far more excited at the possibility of finding water nearby... and I found it. A lake. A great, glorious lake. There's a large river feeding into it from the north, and a much smaller river trickling away to the southeast. I'll never run out of water here.

There's such a variety of creatures around here. The spikers I'd been following are here, as well as a group of marmeldons and a bunch of sail beasts and scissorlegs. There's even a few grass chompers munching the tree tops. There are more edible things here as well. The trees here bear some new kind of fruit. I'll have to try some later on. And I saw a couple meal birds among the bushes. I think I'm gonna like this place.

Right now I'm camped out among the scattered boulders and large rocks. I just feel a little safer here than among the trees. It's easier to see what's coming. I've already drunk half of the first batch of purified water and I've got the second batch cooking away right now. I've got some crawler roasting near the fire. That's gonna be good. Actually I think it's done. I'll be back.

* * *

That was so good. It's always nice to be able to eat my fill and drink until I'm not thirsty anymore. So nice.

I'm feeling tired. Not sleepy... just tired. It's nice out here in the boulder field. Watching the moonlight on the rocky outcroppings... I feel like I'm a part of something so much bigger than just myself. I wish I could share all this with someone.

It's been a long time since the plane crash. A long time since I've been home. That world seems so far away now. Refrigerators, toilets, beds, air conditioning and heating, friends, family. People. I wonder what day Thanksgiving fell on this year. I never could keep those dates straight. Maybe Mom and Dad invited some of their friends over this year along with the rest of the family. That way they'd have more than usual. That way there wouldn't be a missing space. An empty chair.

Do you think they're over me? Have they already moved on? Did they already say their goodbyes and I'm the only one still hanging on? I know my friends have probably all moved on long ago. Sarah would definitely be dating by now. I miss them. I'm sorry, I should be happy that I've had a good meal and...

Sorry, I'm crying.

I'm ok now. Just had to get myself together. I miss my Mom. I don't think I told her I loved her nearly enough. Or Dad for that matter. I know that I gave my brothers a lot of flak they probably didn't deserve. It's just a shame I can't make it up to anyone now. I can't say I'm sorry. I can't change what I'm doing to make things better for them.

It's like I'm dead, only I can't stop worrying about them.

I'm gonna eat some more. Then get a good long sleep. I'm sure I'll feel better after that.

December 13 – Day 112

Good morning. Sorry about last night. I don't know what came over me. I'm better now though. Everything's good. I've got food, water, and everything is good. I want to go down today and check out the fruit trees I noticed yesterday. See what they're like.

* * *

This is odd. This fruit looks more like garlic than regular fruit, with papery compartments in an ugly, bulb shape that reminds me of a small wasp's nest. Inside I've found some thumbnail-sized things inside. Fruit maybe? They kinda look like cashews. I wonder what they taste like. I'll try one, but I better make sure it's a small bite. If it's anything like garlic, I don't want to taste it in my mouth for the rest of the day.

Mmm! This is good! Yum! It's like a chewy, sweet nut. Like a macadamia gummy fruit nut. That's so good! I've found a new favorite food around here. It's so good to eat something other than meat and berries. And the best part is that there are plenty of these things, and I suspect they'll last longer in my supplies than either the berries or the meat.

I'm gonna get some more.

* * *

I've got a whole backpack load now. I figure I'll leave them inside their shell/peelings until I want to eat them. They'll probably last longer that way.

I also noticed another new tree today. It looks like the coin leaf trees up north, only these trees have leafs that look kinda like fried eggs, and their wood is patterned like cinnamon streaks through pale dough. I tried climbing one of these trees to get at some sweet nuts on a nearby branch and discovered that this new kind of tree is as hard as stone. Each one of these species is like a living, petrified plant. It got me thinking. Wouldn't it be cool to have a spear made of stonewood? I mean, it'd be just as durable as a tooth spike, only it would be much more functional for hunting.

I'm going to try and see if I can make a spear this evening. I'll probably have to use my hammer and chisel rocks to get a branch off, and I'm not sure how I'm going to sharpen the end. I'll try to figure that out.

* * *

Well I didn't end up making a spear, but I did manage to get something pretty cool anyway. I found a branch that was fairly thick and straight, but had already broken off from its tree. It's about as tall as I am, and I think it will make for a great walking stick once I chisel the smaller branches off. I'll figure out a sharpened tip later.

I guess I'm going to hit the hay. Have a good night.

December 14 – Day 113

It's mid-morning and for the first time in I can't remember how long, I have some actual free time. I mean, I've got plenty of water and food. I don't have a canoe or a sled or a hut to build. I'm not sure what to do with myself. I suppose I could do some exploring. Just for the fun of it. I mean, the rocks and boulders to the south look pretty interesting. Maybe I'll spend some time trying to sketch them. Right now though I just want to walk around and take a look at them. Let's see what's out here.

* * *

This is awesome. This must be one of the best days I've had since coming to the Sea of Grass. I'm writing this inside what is definitely the most comfortable dwelling I've had in the last three months. I'm inside a cave. I found several, but this is the best one. Nice and big and spacious. It's so nice to be able to lie down and not worry about being wet in the morning. I've gotten a pile of sea grass and made myself a nice bed against the wall. It's not that deep of a cave. It's probably the size of a walk-in closet and just about as roomy, but it's home and I like it.

The rest of the crawler isn't any good anymore. Too bad. Anyway, I made a pit trap back among the trees by the lake. I wasn't able to find too many banza berries, so I mixed in some shelled sweet nuts as the bait. Hopefully I can catch one of the meal birds for tomorrow.

Goodnight.

December 15 – Day 114

Good morning! I had a great sleep last night. I really think I'm going to like living here. Time for me to go and check my pit trap. Cross your fingers and maybe we'll have a grand feast tonight!

* * *

Hmm, well the feast tonight may or may not be postponed. I didn't catch any meal birds last night. Oh, the trap was sprung, but nothing was in it. I think I didn't dig the hole large enough. I suspected that, but it's just so hard to dig a hole with the torn up end of an old paddle.

Anyway, all is not lost. I still have my fishing pole. I was thinking maybe I'll take it down to the lake and try my hand at catching some fish. Might be worth a shot. I can also fix up my trap and try again during the day. You never know. I may get several things for dinner. Better get a move on then. Wish me luck.

* * *

Wow, what a day I've had.

Things started off pretty casually though. As I said this morning, I went to the lake to see if I could use my fishing pole and try to get some dinner, just to see if I still had the same touch with the old rod and reel. Or just the rod and twine, as the case may be.

I turned over a few stones and was able to find several creepy crawlers to use as bait, including one of those two headed centipedes again. I'm still not sure whether or not it's got two real heads or if one of them is fake. Maybe both of them are fake. I was just glad I didn't have to be the one eating it this time.

The lake looked beautiful today and the sun was shining bright. The clouds looked like little clumps of cottony, peppermint candy scattered all over the sky. There was a small herd of marmeldons down by the water drinking. There was also the constant annoying twitter of banded runners and my old friends the spikers were there getting their fill of the crystal clear water as well. I found a nice spot where one of the sweet nut trees had a low hanging branch extended out over the water. I climbed out onto the branch, set myself up, dropped my line, and sat back to enjoy a lazy day of fishing.

The first part of the day passed by peacefully. I enjoyed being able to actually take a rest after days of walking and searching for water. It feels so good to be fully fed and fully hydrated at the same time.

I knew that there were creatures in the lake. I could see some of them swimming under the surface of the water. I don't know what they all are.

Some of them look pretty interesting. One of them had legs instead of fins and was swimming in a sort of undulating movement, kind of like the whale fish I saw up north.

The best part about fishing here is that the water is so clear that I could actually see the fish as they came up to my hook. That was a good thing, because there were times today that I wouldn't have even known that there was something checking out my bait. As it was, I was able to watch, wait, and catch my first lake creature. It was a skinny little thing with no fins but a very big mouth, which was good, since I don't think he could have swallowed my hook otherwise. He's about a foot long and put up a good struggle. Hope he tastes good.

I was looking for more to eat when something amazing happened in the afternoon. I was sitting there calmly fishing when I heard, or rather sensed, a disturbance. I looked up, trying to figure out what was wrong. I realized after a moment that the marmeldons seemed restless. They were snuffling and shuffling about, calling to each other. The banded runners were gone. The spikers had drawn up into a protective circle around their young on the banks of the water and in the shallows. I was wondering if I was safe out on my branch. My first thought was bigamouths, and I was wondering if maybe I could jump off the branch and swim away if one of them came. But it wasn't bigamouths. It was something much, much bigger.

It came through the trees quietly and slowly. The thing was massive, about the size of a cement truck. It looked kind of like a gigantic grey lizard with a bizarre, double-jawed head that had one set of jaws stacked on top of the second. The creature had three eyes, one in each of its cheeks and a third placed on a raised ridge on the top of its head. It had six legs and a long, skinny tail.

It slinked into the small clearing around the lake as I watched it nervously. It was too close for comfort on the other side of the water, but it seemed docile enough, as if it had just come down to get a drink. The spikers were still on the alert, but the marmeldons seemed a little more relaxed as they went back to their drinking. The doublejaw bent down to drink, its lower eyes looking at the water, but I was watching the thing's third eye, and it was on the marmeldons.

Suddenly, it lunged across the lakeshore towards the marmeldons. They bellowed in terror, scrambling to get away. In a moment the nearest marmeldon was snatched up in the top jaws, while the second mouth stretched around until it was oddly disjointed from the top one, so that the creature was biting its prey in two different places at the same time. I could see now that the top jaws had large, jagged teeth while the bottom jaws had teeth so small I could barely see them at all. The mouth with shorter teeth seemed to chew its prey as the other mouth held it tightly. Eventually, the marmeldon's frenzied thrashing became only feeble struggling. With its prey subdued, the doublejaw dragged the marmeldon out of the water and began to feed. I noticed that as the doublejaw ate it kept the lower set of jaws closed, using only the top jaws to eat.

I stayed in the tree a long time, even after the doublejaw left. I managed to catch one more thing before calling it a day. It looks a little like something you'd find in a dentist's aquarium. It has kind of a rounded triangular shape with no body, just a head. I just hope that there's some edible meat on him somewhere. I'd rather not have to gnaw on a skull for dinner.

That was my day. I'm cooking the fish now, they should be just about done. I was able to get two nice long fillets from the eel fish. I think it's going to be good. As for the skull fish, I haven't messed with it yet. I'm gonna try right now. I'll let you know how dinner is.

* * *

Well the skull fish was useless. Nothing but bone. The eel fish on the other hand was delicious. Very succulent meat, very tasty. The two fillets filled me right up, and with the sweet nuts for dessert it made for a very satisfying dinner.

You know, I'm very proud to be alive. I don't think there are many people who could have done it. I just can't help but wish that Mom and Dad knew that I am alive and doing well. Even if I couldn't see them again, I'd like for them to know that I am surviving. I am living. I'm moving on. I'm still sad that I'll never see them again. Still, it feels good to know that I'm able to survive, and I'm able to live. I'm proud of myself. And I'm happy. I really am.

Well, It's been a long night and I'm gonna get some sleep. Actually, I think I'm gonna sleep in. I've had a good long meal. I even have some leftovers for breakfast tomorrow along with more sweet nuts. Maybe I'll try and find some food in the afternoon. I've set the trap again. Who knows? Maybe I'll get another meal bird in the morning. Alright, goodnight.

December 16 – Day 115

Good morning. These sweet nuts sure are good. I'm just hanging out right now in the cave. I figure it's a nice safe place to be, especially considering that the doublejaw might be out there. Hopefully he's fully fed and not all that hungry right now.

Anyway, I think I'll do some exploring today among the other rock formations. Maybe I'll find some caves. I might even find one I like better than my current home. We'll see how I do.

* * *

I've just made another discovery. There's more evidence of intelligent life here! I found it in another cave... pictographs. Pictures drawn on the rocks. They're simple and stylized, but they look like photographs for someone like me who hasn't seen a printed image in months. I can see a couple of spikers, and a crawler. A herd of stylized scissorlegs are gathered around a lake and an enormously tall thing that I think is supposed to be a grass chomper. Most importantly, there's an additional creature depicted on my cave wall that I have yet to see on Other World. There are three of them, just to the bottom right of the lake. They look humanoid.

Two of them are holding spears and the third seems to have some kind of club or cudgel. There's not much detail. While some of the other creatures have tones of red in them, these three hunters are black stick figures. They're each made basically with three lines, one for the body, one for the arms and one for the legs. I keep studying and scrutinizing them, hoping that I could find some additional clue to the previous inhabitants of this land.

I wish I could tell how recently these pictures had been made. Are they ancient, or are they recent? These drawings are definitely too primitive to have been done by the same civilization that built the lighthouse and the road, but who's to say that these people didn't come through here after the more advanced culture was gone?

Well, I do know one thing. I want to search the rest of the rock field. Maybe there are more caves, with more pictures. Maybe there is even some evidence of recent inhabitants. Wouldn't that be incredible?

I just remembered. I forgot to check my pit trap this morning. I'll have to go do that first. Amazing discoveries or not, a guy still has to eat. I'll be back.

* * *

Well I did get something in the pit trap. It's a meal bird, a nice big one. By the time I got there the banded runners were already snooping around, but I got rid of them pretty easily. I brought the bird back and I'm cooking it right now. Should be ready in a little while. Maybe after I've eaten my fill I'll go around and look for more caves. I'll be sure to take two tooth spikes with me, just in case.

OK, I'm gonna work some more on my sketches of the pictographs while lunch cooks.

* * *

Not much luck in finding any more caves. I only found two more, and only the second one had anything that looked like a picture, though I think it may have just been some kind of water damage in the rock. But that's ok, I still have plenty to explore in the rock field. I definitely want to go out in the morning to do some more looking.

December 17 – Day 116

Good morning. Today is a big day. I'm gonna go out and check the rest of the rock field for any more caves. I hope I find some more pictographs. I'll carry my writing satchel and my tooth spikes and leave the rest of my stuff here. It's nice to have a place where I know my things are safe. Ok, I'm off.

* * *

I've hit the jackpot! I've found a huge cave, much bigger than my own. It's the size of a small warehouse with a single, rounded room. There are pictures here. A lot of them. It's going to take some time to examine them all . They're everywhere in here. This must have been a place of congregation for these people.

It stinks in here though. I can't really identify the smell, but it seems familiar for some reason. The only evidence of habitation are what look like sheets of a weird fabric which may be the remnants of some kind of ancient bedding. I'll have to check those out later. Right now though, I'm really eager to examine these pictures. Give me a minute.

* * *

Oh my gosh. I think I've found out what happened to the people around here. This is incredible. And terrifying. What could it mean for me? Am I still in danger from these things?

I found a picture that looks to be depicting what may have been…

* * *

I… I… [unreadable]

* * *

I'm ok now. I think. I'm safe inside my own cave. I don't think anything will get me here. There's solid rock all around me. I should be totally protected and safe in here. I should be.

That was close. That was so close. Why was I so stupid? Why was I so careless? Letting myself get so caught up in finding evidence of lost cultures that I didn't recognize an animal's den when I first saw it! And not just any animal, of course. It was the den of the doublejaw.

I was just about to seriously begin describing the pictographs when I heard a strange sound from the cave mouth. It was a kind of a muffled thump with an odd clicking sound. I looked up and suddenly the cave went dark. The sunlight was blocked out as the doublejaw entered into its lair, its long claws clacking on the smoothed rock. My heart seemed to stop. I was trapped inside a stone prison with the largest land predator I've ever seen.

I leapt up and ran to the back of the cave, desperately trying to find somewhere to hide. Maybe I had missed a small passageway, a crevice, anything to get out of the beast's way. But I couldn't find anything. In moments the giant creature was in the cave with me. The best I could do was to crouch down in a corner, trying very hard not to be seen.

The cave seemed full of the sounds of the beast reverberating off the walls. I could see it in the muffled light as it rolled around in the center of the room, curling up to finally let itself down with a loud "Huff." The smell was strong, so strong I almost gagged. It reeked of old dead skin, saliva, and blood.

I held my tooth spikes out, wondering just how useless they would be against a monster that size in the dark of the cave. I waited, my nerves tense, until I was aching with the anticipation of it stirring and moving towards me. But it didn't. It just laid there. I sat in the dark, trying very hard to convince myself that it was asleep and not hungry any more, but I couldn't get up the courage to move. Making myself known in its den could very likely make it defensive and territorial. All it had to do was shift its weight and break my body against the wall of the cave. I stayed there for what must have been hours, or at least felt like it.

I was getting so sore and stiff from crouching that I began to worry I wouldn't be able to move even if the doublejaw did finally leave. I shifted to a new position on the floor as quietly as I could. There was no stir from the creature, and I rose up onto shaky legs. I began edging my way around the cave wall to the entrance. I moved slowly, focusing all my attention on not doing anything to make any kind of noise. At one point I had a random memory of trying to sneak downstairs as a kid late at night to watch late night cartoons. Dad usually caught me.

At last I made it to the entrance and sprinted outside. I've never run so fast. I came straight here, and I've been huddled up against the far wall ever since. It's a good thing I already cooked the meal bird from yesterday, because there's no way I'd go outside to light another fire right now.

I just had a thought. What if the thing wakes up and smells my trail? What if it follows me to my cave?

OK, I need to calm down. I'm safe now. I'm really tired. I need to get some rest. I'll tell you about what I found in the cave tomorrow morning. I really need some sleep.

December 18 – Day 117

Hi. I feel a little better this morning. A little. My stomach really hurts. I feel kind of sick. I think I've been having way too many shocks to my system lately. I just wasn't made to live in a hostile environment. I mean I can survive, but can I live comfortably? Is that even possible out here? I wish so badly I wasn't in this by myself. If I could just talk with someone, figure things out together with someone. Even if they disagreed with everything I said, at least I'd be getting some input. I just can't tell which ideas are bad ones until I do it. What's gonna keep me from one day making a fatal mistake? Who's going to stop me?

Sorry. I'm just freaking out I guess. Yesterday was hard, that's all. It's always hard to calm down after a life or death situation. Anything anybody says about it being exciting and scintillating is a lie. It's scary and it makes you sick to your stomach and you hate it. I do.

Anyway, I was going to describe what I saw in the pictographs yesterday. The walls of the cave were filled with pictures, which makes me wonder if it used to be an ancient gathering place. A lot of them were variations of the same creatures and landmarks that I saw in the pictographs on the other cave's walls. There were a number of scissorlegs and sail beasts, as well as some ferret hounds and a few creatures I didn't recognize but I'm very interested to see. I've done sketches of all of them.

There were also more of the humanoid figures on the walls. There were groups of them hunting, dancing, and gathering together. Each figure of a person was drawn in the same simplistic representation of three lines making up body/head, arms, and legs.

The one picture that didn't fit in with the others was the one I got really excited about. It was strange, weirdly out of place with the other pictures. It seemed to have been done in a more erratic, ugly way that the other pictures. It contained two different types of figures. One was the familiar humanoids, but the other was something… unsettling. Drawn like a humanoid, these figures are much taller and have a fourth line at the top of their heads which seems to signify a great gapping maw or terrible jaws. These jawed figures are drawn attacking the humanoids. It's a grisly depiction. It seemed that the humanoids had tried to battle them with spears and clubs, but a great mound of dead bodies shows that they were not successful. Each body on the pile is broken. Bit in two. I haven't seen anything that even vaguely resembles these jawed beasts, and I hope that I don't.

Anyway, those pictures were made a long time ago, so there's probably nothing to worry about. The inhabitants of these caves have long since departed. There were water stains in the rocks over many of the pictures, which suggests to me that it's been centuries since they were drawn. No danger there. Just from giant two-mouthed lizards.

Well, giant carnivores or not, I'm running low on drinking water again. I'm going to have to go out and get some more. I should also check my pit trap. I'll just have to put all these other things out of my mind for now. I still have to survive, even if I am scared. It's just something I have to do.

I'm still going to survive this place. Just watch me.

* * *

There was nothing in the trap today. I ended up just collecting a bunch of sweet nuts to munch as I purified more water. Time has kind of slipped away from me today and I'll have to finish purifying in the morning. It's just as well. It gives me some more time to study the sketches I made of the pictographs.

I wonder what medium they used to make the pictures. Banza berries for the red maybe? Charcoal for the blacks, most likely. It almost makes me wonder if I should make a mark somewhere around here. You know, kind of a memorial stone. No, not a memorial stone, that sounds too morbid. A message, maybe? Perhaps to anyone else who might find themselves stranded on Other World later on. Then again, maybe other people have already been stranded here. What if the pictographs are from a group of people that were originally from Earth? Of course, there's no way to know. All I can do is wonder.

Anyway, I'll think about the possibility of leaving a message somewhere. Would it be appropriate to write it on my cave wall? Should I try carving it? I'll think about it. I guess I better get some rest.

December 19 – Day 118

Good morning. Well it'll probably be a day of water purifying and fishing since it's easier than hunting, and as good as sweet nuts are, I always need some variety. See you this afternoon.

* * *

I can't stay here. I can't. It's just not safe. This is nothing like Misty Falls up north. This place is too wild, too dangerous.

I was coming back from fishing. I'd gotten a pair of eel fish and was looking forward to a leisurely afternoon of purifying water and cooking the fish. But when I got back to the cave I found the doublejaw sniffing around. It was pawing at the entrance, trying to fit its head inside. Luckily, the space was too small for it to squeeze in. Very luckily, I wasn't trapped in there. I was able to just turn around, go back to the lake and eat sweet nuts until the doublejaw finally decided to leave.

When I got back to my cave the entrance was dug out and scraped up by the doublejaw's claws. It stinks in here now. It smells like that monster. I'm just glad it didn't get to any of my gear piled up against the far wall.

I can't stay here. I've got to move on. I wish I didn't have to, but it's become a necessity. The doublejaw could come back at any time now that it knows I'm here.

I think I'll camp out on the other side of the lake tonight. There are enough overhanging branches at the narrow, feeding river that I should be able to ferry all my stuff across in it a few trips. I'll spend the night on the other side of the water. Hopefully the doublejaw can't track me down. Tomorrow I'll leave for good. I think I'll continue to follow the ancient roadway. It looks like it follows the river that feeds into the lake, so I'll have water as I travel. Ok, I better get moving.

* * *

I'm across the river. It took some work, but I managed to get everything onto this side. I'm cooking the eel fish now, looking forward to a good meal. I'm tired. I'm sorry to have to leave, but I have to.

OK, I'm really tired. I'm gonna eat and sleep. 'Night.

December 20 – Day 119

Morning. I'm tired and sore. It's rough how quickly you can get used to sleeping in a nice, warm, dry cave. I hate that doublejaw. Why couldn't he just leave me alone? Well, it's no good getting angry. I'm just going to have to move on.

Like I said yesterday, I'll be continuing to follow the ancient road as it runs alongside this river. It may still lead me to some remnant of a civilization, and besides, the farther upstream I go the fresher the water will probably be.

There's nothing keeping me here. I'll fill up my bag with sweet nuts and head out.

*   *   *

I've found something again, and this time it's another structure. Well, sort of a structure. It's a canal, an artificial waterway branching off from the river. There's some kind of clay in the bottom. It's cracked and broken up, but it must have been originally laid down to help the water flow more freely. The ancient road leaves the river and follows the canal, so I'll follow it too.

OK, I have to keep going. I'm just too excited to keep writing.

*   *   *

I've found it! Structures! Homes! Houses! I'm not alone! I'm not! I'm shaking all over. I'm excited and scared all at the same time. I've got to get out there. I'll write again once I'm there. This is incredible! I'm not alone!

*   *   *

Distances sure are deceiving out here. The sun is setting and the structures are still off in the distance. I've got to rest, I've been traveling all day. I'm sure I'll reach the settlement in the morning. Maybe it's for the best. Resting for the night gives me a chance to get my head together. Figure out what I'm doing. If living on this world has taught me anything in the last four months, it's that recklessly running into things is rarely a good idea. I need to think and plan this out.

Ok, first, I need to list the things I know. What I could see in the daylight was about a dozen structures, all looking fairly small and box-like. They were surrounded by four small squares which looked to be outlined by walls. A fortress? Does that mean they could be at war with someone? Sorry, jumping to conclusions.

Another thing that I do know is that the waterway is definitely in a state of severe disrepair. The water is still flowing, but the cracks in the clay and the amount of debris that's fallen into the canal is really hampering its progress. I keep passing little ponds where the water has backed up before finally flowing on towards the structures. Whoever made this waterway obviously isn't working very hard to keep it up. Could the structures be abandoned?

I think the biggest issue is how to make peaceful contact with whoever built those structures. What if they don't understand what I'm trying to say? How will I communicate with them? Anything could be taken the wrong way. Waving and smiling could be taken as acts of aggression. An offering of sweet nuts could prove to be poisonous to them. What should I do?

I know one thing I need to do: calm down! I need to get my head together. There's nothing saying I have to run up and ring the doorbell right away. I can be cool about it. There are still a fair number of hills around here. I could probably stay out of sight fairly easily while I scope out the situation. Tempting as it is to run down there and throw myself at their doorstep, I think it will just be smarter to err on the side of caution.

Glad I got that worked out. Now I can try and get some sleep. Yeah, right.

BIGAMOUTHS

December 21 – Day 120

Good morning. Well, this is the big day. I didn't get a lot of sleep last night. Don't worry, I'm still planning on just spying on the buildings to start. I'm just excited to see people. Or even something vaguely people-like.

Sorry, I just can't write right now. I can hardly eat. I've got to get down there. I'll write once I know more.

* * *

I'm trying hard not to be disappointed. There's so much for me to write and be excited about, but I can't help but be sad. I'm still alone. For all the great things I may have found, I'm still alone.

* * *

Sorry about earlier. I really need to keep things in perspective, and things are actually probably much better than they have been since coming to Other World.

First though, let me report that no one lives in these buildings. No one's lived here for a very, very long time. It's plain enough just looking at these buildings. This level of disintegration doesn't happen after just a few years, or even a few decades. It's probably hundreds of years. This is an archeological site.

There are nine mud brick structures here. They vary in size, from some that are barely the size of an SUV to others that are bigger than trailer homes. One of them looks about the size of a small house. Most of them have lost their roofs, each looking like they've caved in many, many years ago. Three of them retain their roofs though, and the longhouse, as I'm calling it, has part of its roof still on one side.

Surrounding the compound of houses is a very tall wall which also looks to be made of some kind of adobe. It's sturdy, with a large gate in the southern side. It may or may not be against invaders, but I would guess it was probably more useful as a protection against predatory animals. Outside the walled compound are four smaller squared off sections of ground surrounded by lower walls. Each square looks like it may have originally been home to either an orchard or garden, though I don't know much about agriculture. Of course, it doesn't look like any of it has been tended for many years.

Most interesting though, is the fact that the aqueduct, for all its cracks and natural dams, is still working to some degree. The water flows into the compound, then feeds out into the four fields surrounding the structures, with a fifth channel running the majority of the water on and out of the compound to the east to disappear into a strange looking dirt field. I can't get over the amount of planning and coordination it would have taken to make this water flow everywhere that the original inhabitants wanted, and it's all done with nothing but gravity. It definitely speaks to the advanced nature of their society. It also explains -at least in part- why they made the waterway in the first place. To irrigate their crops.

So really, things are looking up more than they ever have before. The water flowing in from the aqueduct has kept a number of plants and trees alive in the compound's fields. I wonder if any of the plants that are growing out there now are edible. Do you realize how long it's been since I've had real fruits and vegetables? It'd be so great to get some healthy food. I've been really worried lately about getting scurvy. My teeth have already been hurting.

Anyway, it's getting late and I should be thinking about where I'm going to put myself up for the night. I figure I'll use one of the more intact buildings. It should be nice to finally sleep under a roof again, even if it is a mud brick one.

* * *

Well, I found a house that works for me. At least, I think it was a house at one time. Little still remains that isn't in a shambles. The building I'm in is square and made of the same mud bricks as the rest of the compound. There's a large window framed with wood, and the roof is supported by similar wooden beams. The wood seems to be very old. I'm surprised it's lasted this long.

It's getting dark and too hard to see any more. I'll describe this place more in the morning. At least I can sleep well tonight. I closed the gates to the wall surrounding the compound. The doors and the latch are both made of stonewood, so I'm sure they'll be more than sturdy against anything trying to get in. It'll be nice to sleep without being worried about something creeping up on me. It will be nice to relax.

December 22 – Day 121

Good morning. It's funny, but I couldn't help but enjoy waking up this morning. Watching the sunlight slowly work its way across the roof with the dawn, it just felt so right to be inside again. And not in some dirty, rocky cave or hut, but in a structure that was built to last. That's obvious enough now that I can recognize the kind of wood they used for the supports. It's stonewood, still stained black in most places with some kind of pitch or tar. No wonder the roofs have lasted as long as they have. I wonder how in the world the original architects were able to fell entire stonewood trees. Hammer and chisel? Some kind of firing process?

Anyway, the day looks to be another bright and sunny one. The whistler bushes are singing and sunlight is glistening off the water in the aqueduct. It really looks like it'll be a nice day. Smells nice too. It smells really, really nice out here. Sweet, and very fragrant. The orchards and fields maybe? Could it be that they are still producing edible foods? I sure hope so. I'm going to take a look today. We'll see what I can 'turnip.' Ha ha ha.

* * *

Wow, what a variety of plants are out here. And not just little ones. There are at least four varieties of trees scattered around, along with a bevy of other smaller shrubs and succulent plants, mostly closer to the places where the water is distributed to them. It's very clever the way the water system was worked out. It flows into the complex, then branches into two smaller channels that run under two different buildings before branching again to move outward to the four squares of plant growth. It must have been incredibly efficient when it was all kept up and new. A lot of it is still working even after all this time.

Of course, the fields and orchards have suffered a great deal of neglect. It's next to impossible trying to tell the good plants from weeds. They all grow together in clumps and seemingly random groups. It's easier to tell with the trees, but there are fewer of them. One orchard is almost totally devoid of trees, with only three sad little stunted things. The southeastern field looks fairly good though. And the southwestern field has a very impressive array of smaller plants. If it weren't for the bugs this place would be perfect.

The bugs are everywhere among the plants. There are sweet smelling flowers and blossoms all over, and the bugs are thick in them. Buzzing, humming, twittering, you'd think they own this place. I guess they do. At least the low walls around the four squares have kept out any plant-eating creatures. That would explain why the plants look so much more abundant here than at other places. The only way into these fields is by going over a low point in each wall facing the complex. It's all very ingenious.

I have to admit, I'm too excited about exploring the rest of this place to take the time and seriously collect any plants and study them right now. I'll have to do that later. First, I want to take a look at some more of these buildings, particularly the ones that have water running through them and the longhouse.

* * *

More and more ingenious all the time. The buildings with water running through them are incredible examples of complex structures made with simple principles. One of them looks to be a kind of bathhouse, with a large pool made of some kind of clay and several holes over an otherwise covered channel farther down that must have been some kind of crude toilet. Would you believe it? Toilets! Finally! I almost can't wait.

I'm guessing that the bathhouse resembles its former self only vaguely. Right now it looks more like a swamp, and the pool in the center of the building seems to be the primary location for bug love-making in the complex. I couldn't even stay in there with all the bugs that came flying up at me when I tried to get close. I was bitten several times and I already have red bumps forming on my arms and hands. If I want to use the tub, I'll definitely have to clean it out first.

The other building with flowing water was probably the kitchen, but there's not much left to work with. There is a large object in the corner that looks like the hollowed out stump of a stone wood tree. Could it be an oven? Wouldn't the wooden stove burn up? Does stone wood burn? Maybe it was specially treated. The rest of the floor is scattered with random bits of debris from the fallen roof. I'll have to clean it out to try to find anything more in there.

Well, as thrilling as all this is, I still need to eat. I'm running low on sweet nuts, so I'll have to collect some specimens to experiment on in the fields and orchards. I suspect it will be easier to recognize the fruit than the vegetables. I hope I can figure out which parts of the plants are the edible parts. I can just imagine myself trying to eat the greenery off the equivalent of a carrot. Well, experimentation is the only way to find out. At least I have less fear of finding something poisonous. They wouldn't have raised poisons here. Would they?

* * *

Well, I got one night's reprieve from eating anything totally new. There was one sweet nut tree in the southeast orchard, so I'll be able to have one more night of nuts before trying any of these other things. Tomorrow morning will be a big day for experimentation. I'll boil up some water and try a little bit of everything. I'm nervous, but excited too. Wouldn't it be nice to find the equivalent of an apple, or an orange? Cross your fingers.

December 23 – Day 122

Good morning. Well I've got the water on to boil in the courtyard and I'm going out to collect some test subjects. Hopefully nothing kills me. I'll take notes of which ones I find, and what each is like. Better get started.

* * *

Ok, here's the first subject. It's got long green leaves that grow straight up from the ground all from a central ring of green. Once you dig it up though it's got a funny surprise. The root system is almost entirely this single, narrow taproot that winds all around in the dirt. I accidently broke it twice before I had the thing totally dug up. All along this taproot, which is maybe five feet long, there are these half-dozen bulging lumps that look like ugly potatoes. Maybe they are. I'm boiling a lump and some of the greens as well. I don't think the taproot would be any good, it's fibrous and just doesn't look very appetizing. OK, I'm gonna try this thing.

Gak. The skin of the lump is bitter. But the inside tastes pretty good. Meaning that it tastes like bland food, nothing distinct one way or the other. The greens are inedible. I think I'll cook up some more of the lumps while I try out this funny fruit I found on a tree in the southeast orchard. It's odd, looks kinda like a cross between a pineapple and an acorn. I washed the outside, but I think it needs to be cut open. I'll give it a good whack with my hammer and chisel rocks.

Wow, it's a bright red inside. Red as Kool-Aid, with a bunch of little seeds grouped in the center of it. Let me try a little of the fruit. Mmm! It's sweet! Really sweet and juicy. Like a cherry-flavored orange. Very good. I hope this one is good for me, because I'm really tempted to try some more. I'll wait though.

I suppose I can spend a little time while I'm waiting for the lumps to cook and describe a little more of what it's like here. This compound has a great view of a far off mountain range to the east, where the mountains raise up in dark masses devoid of snow. It's beautiful in a very stark kind of way. Like the mountains are silent sentinels watching down on me. The surrounding area is hilly with long sea grass, much the same as it has been since I left the waterhole over two weeks ago. It's nice, but I kind of miss the trees from the north. I mean sure, I can see things a little better, but not by much. The hills could hide a lot. I sometimes wonder if something is out there watching me. Sometimes it feels… I don't know. Like I'm not as alone as I think I am.

Sorry, I guess I was just a little spooked there. Maybe it's being in this compound. All these empty buildings. I mean, being alone in the forest or the grassy plains, even being alone in the desert can be soothing and peaceful. Being alone in structures made by people? That just creeps me out. I really shouldn't be ungrateful, but I just don't like feeling so alone. I almost want to leave here.

There's another thing that's odd about this place. No artifacts. None. I don't know much about archeology or ancient sites, but you'd think there'd be some broken pottery or something. But there's nothing. It's as if someone came along and cleaned house. All the debris that is collected in the structures has come from the structures themselves as they have slowly disintegrated. Where's all the stuff?

Anyway, I still feel fine, so I'm going to eat the rest of the rope potatoes and then go out shopping again this afternoon.

* * *

I'm not alone any more. I wish I were. Bigamouths. Are they the same ones that were at the waterhole? Did they follow me?

I was out in the field, digging up a tuber the size of my leg. It was a real handful, like a potato had forgotten to stop growing. Anyway, I was out there sweating and struggling, when I happened to glance up at the hills to the west. They were all there. The whole pack. It was too far away for me to count them, but there looked to be around a dozen individuals or so.

As long as they stay out of the compound I figure I should be ok. I mean, I've got the compound wall, and it's solid. I'm sure not even a bigamouth can climb ten feet of flat brick wall. And those gates made of stonewood will last longer than the bricks will, I'm sure. I should be safe. As long as they don't dig under it. Or maybe they can climb over it. Or they could come after me while I'm out in the fields.

There I go, just making myself scared. I'll be ok. I'm sure they'll move on. They probably don't even know I'm here. Besides, with the size of this tuber I should be able to stay comfortably inside the compound for days, provided it's actually edible. I don't enjoy thinking about having to go out into the fields, even with a tooth spike in each hand. Besides, I'd have to put them down long enough to get something to eat. Well, at least I'll have water no matter what. I can wait them out.

* * *

There. I knew there was nothing to worry about. I can't even see those bigamouths anymore. Like always, I got all worked up over nothing. Well, almost nothing. Anyway, I just wanted to report that the giant tuber is very good. It's a vibrant purple inside. Very strange, but it tasted good, even slightly sweet. It almost reminds me of Mom's sweet potatoes.

Christmas. Sweet potatoes at Christmas. I'd tried to put it out of my mind. Of course I saw the dates getting closer and closer, but I didn't want to say anything. I didn't want to admit that I'll be stuck out here all alone on Christmas.

Maybe I should try to do something special for it. Would that help, or just make it worse? What would I do? Give myself a gift? Make a big dinner? What would be the point?

* * *

Starting tomorrow I'm going to work on cleaning out the kitchen, and then if I'm brave enough I'll start on the bathhouse. Maybe if I wear my poncho I won't get as many bug bites. I hope so, because the ones I got yesterday are still itching.

OK, I've got a plan for tomorrow. Makes me feel like I have something to accomplish. I think that's the best thing I can do with Christmas coming up. Just let it pass and stay busy. I'll try.

December 24 – Day 123

Good morning. Well, the bigamouths are back, but I'm not going to worry about them. There's not much I can do about it, and as long as I stay behind the gate and wall they can't do anything to me. I'm just not going to think about them. I'll focus on more enjoyable things. Or, relatively more enjoyable. Cleaning out the kitchen house shouldn't be all that hard, but cleaning the bathhouse is going to be a major ordeal. It'd be so much easier if I had a rake and a shovel. Well, I can use my oars, but I'll have to figure out something else to clean out all the additional sludge. I'll think about it while I get the kitchen cleared out.

* * *

Well, I got the kitchen cleaned up and it looks really nice. Granted, it doesn't have a roof, but I'm just calling that my extreme sky light. I've already put all my food into it, and I'm excited to use the fire pit in there from now on. It will be so nice to be able to light fires without having to deal with the wind. Of course, I still have to get outside to get to any fuel for my fires, but I'll worry about that later. I've got enough fuel for the rest of the day anyway.

My next big project is going to be the bathhouse. Hopefully I come out alive.

* * *

I found something in the pond of the bathhouse, and I think it may explain quite a lot. I was scraping up all the sludge in the bottom, trying to get it all into the open sunlight. My main hope was to kill any of the water dwelling larvae that may still be in there, not to mention get rid of what must have been several centuries worth of crud at the bottom. Anyway, I was getting in there pretty good when I hit something hard down under the water with my oar. I thought it was a rock or part of the crumbled structure, but it felt too light to be a rock. I finally got it up and out of the water. It was a skull. I almost dropped it. As soon as I turned it around it was obvious what the skull had belonged to. It was a bigamouth skull. Not a large one, maybe a juvenile. When I searched again I found more bones scattered in the muck. It looks like the bigamouth fell into the pool and died somehow.

Finding the bigamouth remains got me thinking. At first, I thought that the rubble in this compound was scattered randomly, but now that I think back about it, it did look like someone, or something, had been rearranging it. There are scattered remains of dead animals and old piles of dung that suggest I'm not the only thing that has come through the front gates in the recent past. This compound may very well be the permanent residence of that pack right outside my door. It would definitely explain a lot, like why the bigamouths have stayed outside and keep coming back. This is their home. Maybe for decades. Those gates out front could have been left open for centuries.

I'm almost wishing now I could respectfully bow out. Just let those uglies outside have their stupid little fort back and let me get out of here. But it's too late for that now. I suppose I could try escaping in the night, but who's to say that these things aren't primarily nocturnal? Their northern cousins certainly are. No, I'm not running. I'm going to stick it out. They can just find a new home. This place is mine now. I'm not going to give up a good thing, food and shelter and running water just because there's danger. There's danger everywhere. In fact, I'm going to finish cleaning out that bathhouse in the morning. By tomorrow night, I plan on taking my first real bath in months. Those uglies outside are not going to scare me away. I'm here, and I'm staying.

December 25 – Day 124

Merry Christmas. I... I love my family and wish them the best Christmas they could ever have. Please God, give them a merry Christmas.

Not much more to say. I'm going to work on clearing out the bathhouse. I'm not going to worry about trying to get more food this morning. That's for this afternoon. Hopefully the bigamouths will be having their siesta about that time. Anyway, I better get to work.

* * *

Well it's all cleared out, but it doesn't look all that appealing right now. I'm going to let the flow of the water clear out the rest of the light muck towards the fields and orchards. Hopefully now that the water is less hampered it can flow much more quickly through there and clean out the rest of the basin. Hopefully the bugs will finish leaving too, because I really enjoy using the stone toilets in there, and it'd be nice to be able to use them without getting bitten.

So now it's the lazy heat of the afternoon. I think if there's any time to go out into the field for more food, it's now. The bigamouths are all lying down to the northwest. I've been keeping an eye all around, but I don't see any of them circling around to the south where the gate is. I figure my best bet is to crack the gate open, go to the southeast orchard, pick as many cherrapples as possible, maybe grab some promising looking plants and hurry back inside. I figure I won't try to get another purple giant or any rope potatoes since that would require time to dig them up, although I may grab some sticks and such for firewood. Shouldn't be too hard to find any of that, since everything is dried-out in the greater portion of the orchard where the water doesn't reach.

I'll only be taking one tooth spike, since I'll need a free hand to pick and grab, and I'll use my backpack to carry stuff in. OK, I need to go. Wish me luck.

* * *

Whew! OK! I'm alive! Barely. Ick. I hate that. At least this time I was half-way expecting it.

Everything went exactly according to my plan… up to a point. I got to the trees without problems. I managed to fill my bag full of fruit and even a few random plants, even though some of them are probably just weeds. I looked around and didn't see any bigamouths, so I figured I was safe enough to move a few yards farther out and get some firewood.

I smashed a few whistler bushes and picked up the woody pieces, tucking some of them into my bag and clutching the rest to my chest. Feeling confidant, I even took the time to pick up a large fallen branch from one of the fruit trees that I could use as a broom as I tidy up the compound. But when I turned around I saw a bigamouth had come around the southwestern corner of the wall. It froze when it saw me, but luckily I had already thought through what I would do in that situation.

I walked -quickly and confidently- back towards the gate. When the bigamouth launched itself forward, I was already close enough to the door that I could sprint inside and latch it before I even heard the sound of it running. I heard a nasty, thrumming growl like the muted rumblings of a motorcycle on the other side of the gate as I made triply sure the latch was in place. The sound it made was like a combination of a motor starting and someone swearing. I would have yelled something snide through the door at it, but I couldn't breathe all that well just then. I'm just glad I had the presence of mind to pull the gate almost totally closed while I was outside, otherwise I'd be up all night wondering if something had gotten in while my back was turned.

As it is, I've got enough food for a couple of days, and enough wood to purify a new batch of water. You know, I think I deserve a reward. I'm going to take a bath. A nice, long, relaxing bath. That'd be a nice Christmas treat. The basin looks pretty cleared out now, and there are hardly any bugs. I really could use some relaxation. I'm going to spoil myself a little, starting right now.

* * *

I needed that. I can't remember how long it's been since I had a nice, long bath, but I know it was too long. Being in the cool water after the hot sun and then back into the hot sun to dry off was so nice. Now I'm watching the sun set into the hills to the west. The sky is painted in reds and golds with a little green tinged in here or there. Far off I can hear the low cries of the bigamouths mixed with the gurgling of the water in the aqueduct. There's a fragrance of flowers on the cool evening breeze coming from the fields outside the walls. It's such a nice night.

You know, I had so much fun clearing out the bathhouse and kitchen, I think I'll do the same for the rest of the compound. I think next I'll work on the longhouse. That will be quite the project, since half of the roof has come down on one side. But it gives me something to do and it only seems right that I should be working to make my new home as habitable as possible.

I wonder why anyone would decide to build their community here. Why go through all the trouble of making the aqueduct? Why not just build your structures closer to the water? Maybe I'll find something under the rubble in the longhouse to give me some clues about this civilization that doesn't leave any artifacts. We'll see.

December 26 – Day 125

Good morning. Well, I got up with the sun this morning and climbed up onto the wall to observe the bigamouths. I wanted to see if they seemed less active in the morning than in the afternoon. Turns out I climbed up onto the wall above where one was walking! I definitely think they're patrolling out there. This one looked a little smaller, about the size of a Great Dane. There it was, walking around, just waiting for me.

I guess I was feeling a little impish, because I got a little idea. I went back to the pile of rubble I had cleared out of the kitchen. I found a nice, big chunk of brick, carried it back to the wall, and lobbed it at that ugly thing's head. I missed his head but did manage to hit him square in the back. He yelped and leapt away from the wall, looking around and trying to figure out where the hit had come from.

"How did you like that, Stone Head?!" I yelled at it before ducking down quickly and having a good laugh. It may have been stupid and childish, but it still felt good. Maybe I'll do it again, later, when he's gotten cocky again. Maybe I can convince the whole pack that this property just isn't available anymore. Maybe.

At any rate, I'll be spending some time clearing out the longhouse today. Hopefully I'll find some kind of clue as to why the original inhabitants left this place. Maybe I'll even find something I can use. We'll just have to see.

* * *

There's a lot of junk in there. I'm beat. I need to take a rest. It's going well though. I've been dividing my time between cleaning out the longhouse and purifying another batch of water.

I can tell you one thing. I feel much, much better since being able to eat some more fruits and vegetables. I realized today that when I grabbed a handful of plants yesterday I managed to get something else that's edible. It's a funny looking, nearly cylindrical stalked thing with long dangly fronds coming out of the top which culminate in small seed pods. I thought maybe the pods would be edible, a variation of the pod rice up north, but no such luck. The cylinder stalk on the other hand, is very tasty with a bright green color and a juicy, bland flavor. I'm having it for lunch along with a nice, ripe cherrapple. The two of them together are so juicy I barely need to take a drink. Why couldn't I have found things like this when I first made it onto this world? If you don't count the nasty beasties trying to kill me outside, this place is paradise!

I should probably get back to work.

* * *

I've got the longhouse cleared out. Well, mostly. Except for that huge pile of dirt right in the middle of it. It's a mound of earth at least as tall as me. I wonder what in the world it's doing there? Could it have been something that the bigamouths did while they were living here? That seems unlikely, because all the rubble was on top of it, not under any of it. That suggests to me that it was there before the roof came in. Maybe the original inhabitants made it. But for what purpose?

I'm trying to come up with things that it could possibly be. The best guess I think I have is a burial mound. I'm not sure why they'd have a building over it, unless it was something like a chief's burial and this is his tomb. If that's the case, I wonder whether I'd be justified in digging it up. I mean, is that grave robbing? Or would it be an archeological dig? What's the difference? How long does someone have to be dead before digging up their remains is a scientific adventure instead of an illegal, immoral practice?

Well, there's probably plenty of other things that I've done on Other World that wouldn't be acceptable in polite society. But then, I'm not in polite society. I'm going to dig it up. What's the worst that could happen? A terrible curse? What could be worse than being stranded on an another world stuck in a brick compound surrounded by creatures that want to eat me? Anyway, I might find something useful inside the tomb. Or at least some kind of clue as to who these people were. Maybe they were humans who also got stuck here. I just need to know.

It's too late to start digging out the mound today, but I'll start on it first thing tomorrow. It feels good to have something to do. It's kind of exciting to be delving into something new and mysterious. Everything has taken on a kind of mystical feeling as the sun sinks into the hills and the whistler bushes cry sadly into the wind. It's easy to imagine a people living here, full of ancient wisdom and mysterious secrets. It's very exciting. I hope I can get to sleep tonight.

December 27 – Day 126

It's so nice to have fruit for breakfast. By tomorrow I'll have to make another run for food, but I should be good for today as I start work on the earth mound in the longhouse. The earth seems packed in pretty hard, but I should be able to dig it up. I won't be carrying the dirt very far, just to other end of the longhouse. I can get it out of the building later. Right now I just want to see what's under the mound, if anything.

I better get to work.

* * *

I'm halfway there, but it's hard work. I'm glad the longhouse is adobe and not metal, otherwise I'm sure it'd be an oven in there by now.

OK, enough wasting time. Back to work.

* * *

I'm done. The whole pile is on the other side of the room. And there was something under the mound after all.

It's a door of some kind built into the floor. It's square, and made with planks of stonewood fastened together with metal bindings. It's the first metal I've seen since coming to this world that didn't come with me. I wish I could tell what kind of metal it is. It's fairly free of any corrosion, but that's probably because it's been covered by the mound for all this time.

But the metal isn't the most interesting thing I found on the door.

Right in the middle of it is a large symbol carved deeply into the stonewood planks. It's nothing like the pictographs I've found. This looks much more advanced, like it had been cut out using very precise tools. It's a stylized symbol, looking a little like a star with twelve points. I'm not really sure what it is. I've made a simple sketch of it, though I'm unsure if I have it right-side up. If nothing else, it gives me an idea of what to call the people who carved it... the Star People.

I'm exhausted. I've dug all around the door and found all the edges. It doesn't look like there are any hinges. It's just resting over a hole in the ground. I know there's a hole because I used my stonewood staff to pry up one edge. Underneath the door was a black hole, stretching off into I have no idea what. The tomb itself? A burial chamber for a whole line of chiefs perhaps? If so, the mound would mean that this place has not been touched since the Star People left.

I'm so excited that I wish I could go down there right now. But it's late and as I said, I'm exhausted. Not to mention it's getting dark, and I can barely see to write this. In the morning I'll start a fire so I can make myself a torch of some kind. Then I'm heading down. I wonder what I'll find. Maybe nothing, but then again, it may be something very, very worth finding.

December 28 – Day 127

This is the day. I'm very excited. I know I need to get some food at some point today, but I'm just too eager to see what's down that hole. I've made myself a torch by hacking up one end of the branch I took for a broom the other day so that it has a lot of exposed fibers and will burn more easily. It should work, but I'll need to get more branches later today along with more food.

Ok, I'm going down there. I can't wait to see what I'll find.

* * *

Well, I didn't find a tomb. I found a cave system, a long, running labyrinth stretching off into what seems like eternity. And it's all sloping down. There's one central tunnel at first which then splits into three different passages. I wasn't able to go down all of them. I went down the left tunnel and didn't get to the end of it. There were several short branches off it, but I tried to keep to what I thought was the central passage until my torch started to die and I had to hurry back. I'll have to work on my design for the next torch.

What is that place for? Again, I couldn't find any artifacts down there. Not a single thing. All the tunnels just seemed to be carved rock and earth with stonewood supports. I did notice that the work on the tunnels is exceptional. I mean, it's held up incredibly well for however long it's been down there. I don't have to worry about tripping over any roughly cut floors, although I do need to be careful of the few places where walls or ceilings have come down. I saw at least one side-tunnel that was completely gone after just a few feet. I wonder if this may have been a place of dwelling for the Star People, or a secret hideaway. Honestly, I have no idea.

Well, as much of a mystery as it is, my stomach is really empty right now. I have to get something to eat. I'll check to see whether or not there's another bigamouth before I go outside. If there is, maybe I can give him another flying rock present before going out there.

* * *

I made it. Barely… again. I wish so badly someone else was here. Just to have a lookout. It's so stressful to be looking over my shoulder ever five seconds expecting some large creature with a mouth big enough to swallow my head to be right there, drooling. That didn't happen, but I did see the bigamouth in the field with me. It wasn't the same one that I clobbered with the rock the other day. This one was much bigger with a long, pink scar running across the stripes of its right flank. Even at a distance I could tell that this one was nearly half-again as big as any of the other pack members. Could it be the dominant male or female? I wouldn't be surprised. I wouldn't challenge the authority of something the size of a horse.

The really scary part was that he didn't come after me. He just stood there at the edge of the field, watching me. Never moving, just watching me. That's why I kept looking around. I thought for sure he was trying to keep me distracted while one of his buddies snuck up behind me. But that didn't happen, and I was able to get a bag full of cherrapples and juicy tubes, along with some more firewood and dead branches for torches.

I don't know why the bigamouth leader didn't attack me. Respect? I doubt it. It almost felt like he was studying me, peering deep inside of me, learning everything about me. I almost feel drained, like he took something from me, just by staring at me. I don't feel as afraid as I feel… hopeless?

I'm sure it's just the stress. I shouldn't worry. I've got a solid wall between me and old Scar. I don't have anything to worry about. I'm fine. Really. But next time I'm going to have to take a chance at staying out there longer. I picked the last of the cherrapples today and the only remaining juicy tubes are looking very scrawny. So I'll have to be out there a little longer as I dig up some of the potatoes to eat. Maybe I'll try going even earlier in the morning than last time. Maybe I'll catch one of the bigamouths napping. But I don't have to worry about that for a couple more days.

I'll be going down into the caves again tomorrow. I want to try to discover what purpose they served at one time. I think that if I can entwine the top of a torch with some twigs and forest behemoth hair it may burn longer. It's worth a try.

I'm tired. It's been a long day. I'll write again tomorrow once I have something new to report on the caves.

December 29 – Day 128

I've made it through the entire left and middle branches of the tunnel now. The left one was actually collapsed after a few dozen feet, but the center one stretches off for what seems like forever. Luckily I brought my box of matches, so I could re-light my torch when part of it started to look like it was going out. By doing that and keeping my torch alive I was able to go all the way to the furthest extent of three different branches from the central passage. In fact, I think I've discovered the purpose for these tunnels. It's a mine.

These are mining shafts. While I didn't find anything in the first and third tunnels, the second one had veins of a strange, silvery metal streaked all through the solid rock walls. It may be silver, I don't know. I do know it's not the same metal as the stuff which makes up the fasteners keeping the stone wood supports in place. I wonder what they used this metal for? If it's anything like silver, then they probably wouldn't use it for building things. Maybe they used it for decoration? I haven't seen any evidence of it. Could they have taken it all with them when they left? What if they were wiped out and the invaders took everything of value? That would explain why they left the big pile of earth over the mine entrance. Maybe they were trying to hide it from the invaders. It's possible.

Still, I don't think this could have been a very big operation. It's just a hunch, but I don't think that your typical mine is this small. I remember watching shows on TV where some mines would stretch on for miles underground. Of course, if this mine were all dug and carved by hand it would make sense that it wouldn't be as big. Yet, the fact that there is still plenty of the metal down here suggests that it might have been a new mine that had to be closed up before the miners were finished.

Once again, a little information doesn't do anything but make me more curious. Why did they leave such a nice mine with such plentiful deposits of the metal they were obviously looking for? Was there perhaps a city somewhere nearby that they were mining this metal for? If there was a city, would the ruins still be in existence? I would think that would be fairly likely, considering the condition of the buildings in the compound.

So where does that leave me? Should I try to leave the compound to look for a mystery city that may or may not exist? Even if I could get past the bigamouths, which I'm unsure about already, who's to say I'll find anything out there besides more rolling hills? It could be that this mine is here simply because the deposits of the metal are here, and that it had to be shipped long distances before it could be used. That would certainly explain why they had their own fields and orchards, not to mention a road leading to the sea.

I don't know. I'm not sure what I should do. I'm gonna sketch a while and think some. Maybe something will come to me.

* * *

Nothing came to me. How am I supposed to think with all this silence all around me? All these empty buildings, the moaning of the wind, the stale hot air… I can't concentrate. I feel like I'm being spied on by ghosts. It's so lonely and sad here, like an abandoned cemetery. And those bigamouths. I can't forget them anymore. I keep remembering the way the big one was watching me. I'm shaking a little just thinking about it.

I'm going to take another bath and then go to bed early. I have to figure out what I'm going to do.

What am I going to do?

December 30 – Day 129

I need to leave. I need to get out of here. This place must be haunted or something. I feel wrong just being here. I've been in dangerous situations before, but never something so maddening as being trapped. Now I know why putting someone in prison can seem worse than death. I can eat and drink all I want, but I can't leave. I'm stuck in here. I hate it. I hate it! I want out!

I'm leaving today. I'll travel light, and take only what I can carry in a backpack. That way I can move quickly, maybe even be gone before the bigamouths know about it. I have to try. I can't stay here any longer. I'll find the city and live there. There has to be a city. I'm going, I'm leaving right now. Wish me luck.

* * *

I'm back. I didn't get very far. I tried to. I really did. I was all packed up to go. I checked the grounds outside the wall, and right there was a bigamouth waiting for me. I don't know what's wrong with me. My first thought was that I could kill it and then move on without any concerns. I got out two tooth spikes and started to go out the doors at the gate. I just wanted to fight. I wanted to stand up to the terror that was outside. But I couldn't. Even though this particular bigamouth wasn't Scar, he acted just like him. He didn't rush me like the younger one had the other day. He stood out there watching me. Just stood there.

I was so angry I dropped my backpack and charged at him, both tooth spikes held high and screaming in what sounded to me like a crazy man's voice. The bigamouth watched me as I came, and then retreated, pulling back to the edge of the southwestern orchard wall. I stopped, for a moment elated it had run, but then instantly paranoid that another one was sneaking up behind me. I kept turning around, convinced that I was being stalked. I couldn't see anything. The bigamouth at the edge of the orchard just kept watching the whole time. I screamed at it.

"What are you staring at?!"

It just stood there. I couldn't handle it anymore. I ran back inside.

I want to go home. I want to worry about what classes I'm going to take in the spring. I want to stress over whether or not a pretty girl likes me, or trying to handle a lame part-time job. I'm tired of making life-or-death decisions. I don't know what I'm doing! I hate this! I want to go home!

I'm crying.

* * *

Have the bigamouths cast a spell on me? I'm not acting like myself. I need to get a grip. I've looked death in the face multiple times in the last four months. This isn't any different. I can stand up to this. I can, and I will!

I need plans. Plans and things to do. I have to figure this out. I know now I can't stay here forever. Eventually the food in the southeast orchard and southwest field will run out. I don't know the first thing about gardening, and I don't have time to wait for things to grow back anyway. I'm guessing that I have about two weeks' worth of food that's still growing out in the fields. I don't know if that's longer than the bigamouths can hold

174

out. I haven't seen them do any hunting, mainly just sitting around. If that's the case, I shouldn't have to worry about them much longer.

Of course, if they're doing their hunting at night, I'll have to think of something else. A diversion? Could I do something to distract the bigamouths as I run out the back door, so to speak? Maybe lighting a brush fire. I know that it's destructive to the environment, but I'd rather kill a bunch of sea grass than end up dead myself. It's been so dry lately, the grass would probably go up like tinder. It's not that bad of an idea.

Ok, so now I have the seeds of a plan. I'm already feeling much, much better. I'll have to refine it all in my head, but I have the time. That's the one thing I have plenty of... time. One thing I should do before I go is make sure to explore the rest of the tunnels. I may still find something useful down there, and besides, I just wouldn't forgive myself if I didn't check that last tunnel off to the right. Maybe I'll do that this afternoon or evening, just to get it out of my system. I think I will. I'll write again once I've finished.

* * *

There's something down there. Oh, nothing scary, nothing bad. Something... I don't know. I walk in there and I feel... peace? Calm? Even... happy? How is that possible?

I went down the right-hand tunnel. I didn't find much of anything as I went down the side passage, just more earth and stone. Finally I came to the end of the main tunnel, and that's where I found something. I didn't notice anything at first... other than the strange feelings of being very comfortable all of a sudden.

I almost missed it. I was just turning to go when I realized that something was out of place. All the other natural endings to a passage, the ones that weren't blocked off by cave-ins, were flat walls with no irregularities in their surface. This wall was different. It looked like a shelf, with a large rectangular piece sticking out like a large single step. I examined it, and realized it wasn't connected to the wall, but sitting next to it. I looked closer and found that there were hair-line partitions along the edges of the top of the stone rectangle. It's a box with a lid! It's large, about the size of a very big trunk or suitcase. There are artifacts down there after all!

I tried to get it open but there's no way I can move that giant slab of stone with only my bare hands. I'll have to try again tomorrow and use my stonewood staff as a lever. I'd do it now, but I'm so sleepy I can barely write, let alone crawl down there and lift a huge slab of rock. I'll just have to wait until the morning.

You know, it's funny. I feel better right now than I have in a while, and waiting for the morning to open a mysterious box... it's like some bizarre archeological Christmas!

Expedition Log
5th of Taik, in the 2nd year of The Return
Yurril T'nak, field scout

Sasha has made a most intriguing discovery today. While the rest of us searched the remains of the lighthouse he explored the shore-line below the sea cliff. It was there he discovered the remains of a great beast of the sea, a monster of impressive size. The carcass has been on land for some time, as it is stripped of all but the most inedible bits of flesh and the bones lay bleaching in the sweltering sun. After examining the remains closely, Sasha has found that several of the beast's teeth seem to have been forcibly removed. Could this be evidence of the native inhabitants of this land? Let us pray that they are friendly if we should find them.

Brendell told the rest of us that neither the Records nor the Artifacts will be found here. He is heartened though, with the knowledge that there is but one place left where they may be: the nyrium mine in the eastern plains. The Divant says we should not despair now. He says that this journey has been a purification of our hearts and a test of our faith. We believe him, and we are ready to follow the Divant to the ends of this world if necessary. We mourn the loss of those who came with us, but we have hope in Shaelon and we take solace in the calmness that His aura brings.

We leave in the morning for the mine. May we go with the grace of Shaelon, and may our journey's desire be our waiting goal.

Grace be. Yurril T'nak

December 31 – Day 129

I woke up this morning to a pounding sensation in my temples and a strange pressure in my ears. I instantly came awake, recognizing the bizarre "call" of the bigamouths. I rushed out of the structure that I've taken for a home. I didn't see anything immediately, so I climbed up the wall to get a better look. The bigamouths were there. They'd made a kill in the night. The entire pack was surrounding a marmeldon carcass in the early morning sun. They were all calling to each other, as if arguing over the order in which they would eat. I recognized Scar as he settled down next to the kill, eating peacefully as the others squabbled over the rest of the meal.

I wonder how the bigamouths make that low thrumming that almost doesn't seem to be a sound. It was almost like I could always feel it, rather than hear it exactly. I wonder how they do it, and why?

Whatever the reason, I wasn't going to let an opportunity like this get by me. I quickly ran out to the fields and grabbed more food, even taking the chance to dig up another giant purple potato. My gamble worked. There wasn't a bigamouth in sight. I'd lucked out considerably. I've got plenty of food now, and things are definitely looking up. I was also thinking, and I realized I'd forgotten I could use the flare gun as a defensive weapon as well. I'll have to take it with me next time, just to be safe. Shooting off a blindingly bright flare might even be enough to scare them away permanently. You never know.

Well, now that the morning's excitement has died down, I can finally find out what was in the stone box down in the tunnel. I'll write again when I find out what's inside.

* * *

Wow, what a find. The first real artifacts I've found since coming to this world. And not just any artifacts. I think I may have found an ancient time capsule, something left purposely for some future generation to find.

Inside the box I found another small box made from stonewood and covered in carvings of strange looking birds and animals. Inside are a number of small discs made from what I think is the same metal that's in the mine veins. Each disc is about the size of a nickel and is carved with the now-familiar emblem of the star on both sides. Perhaps they're some kind of money? They're not completely round, there's a small flattened end at one point on each of them. Also in the stonewood box and mixed in with the coins are what look like a bunch of small beads, again made of the same shiny metal. I have no idea what purpose they serve.

The other thing I found in the box was much more exciting. Books! Well, of a sort. Each one is a perfect circle, with writing spiraling around from the outside edge of each page and working its way in towards the center of the circle. The pages are very thinly hammered sheets of the same shiny metal. Each page is so thin that I was so worried I was going to rip them. But the condition of all the metal is actually pretty amazing. No rust or corrosion. That's probably why they chose it, especially if the Star People intended for these things to be found and read again someday.

Unfortunately, the writing in the books is totally indecipherable. It's not like any language I've ever seen. Instead of individual characters, the writing on each page is a single, squiggly line in a long spiral. I'm pretty sure the spiral is some kind of writing, because the line has plenty of dips, peaks, swirls, loops, and other distinct characteristics. The writing looks like it was scratched into the surface of the page with some kind of stylus. I wish I could read it.

I debated for a while whether I should bring everything up into the sunlight to get a better look at it. I decided against it though, mainly because I was worried that if I took any of the artifacts out of the atmosphere and conditions they had been stored in, it might permanently damage them. I'm not sure what I'm going to do with what I've found, but I at least want to keep it in good condition until I decide.

Well, I've got to think. And eat, I'm starving. Maybe I'll write more today. We'll see.

* * *

Just a quick thing I wanted to mention this evening that was kind of strange. I was sitting by the campfire when I heard something strange outside the compound wall. It was similar to the noises the bigamouths were making this morning, only this time it was much closer. I climbed up onto the wall and saw by the light of Mike and Ike that there were two bigamouths standing together in the northwest field. I got down low, hoping they wouldn't see me, but I don't think they would have noticed. They were much too interested in trying to kill each other. That's what it looked like anyway.

One of them was definitely Scar, but I had a harder time trying to identify the other one. He was much smaller than Scar. It wasn't until I saw the smaller one take a few steps that I recognized a distinct limp in its left hind leg. It was Stone Head, the one I'd caught by the wall with a lump of rock several days ago.

It looked like Scar and Stone Head were definitely angry at one another. They were making noises that sounded like a dog's snarl at the far end of a metal storm drain. The air practically rippled with their strange thrumming sounds as they faced off against each other.

Stone Head made the first move. He darted forward, hardly slowed by his limp, looking like he was going for Scar's throat. Scar jumped forward as well, but slightly to the side, so the two ended up passing each other, but not before Scar's back leg kicked out and gave a solid hit to Stone Head's shoulder. It must have been a hard kick, because Stone Head actually stumbled and fell over for a moment before rising again and immediately throwing himself back at Scar. This time, Scar planted his feet, allowed his smaller opponent to get close, then sprinted forward. He bowled over Stone Head, knocking the other bigamouth onto his back. Scar bent his massive head down and opened his gapping jaws, encircling his opponent's entire head in his fearsome mouth. I waited to hear the crunch of Stone Head being decapitated, but it didn't come. Scar just held his position, poised to bite down and sever Stone Head's neck. Eventually Stone Head stopped trying to kick and struggle. The two of them stayed that way for a while, thrumming loudly in the balmy night air.

Eventually, Scar released Stone Head and allowed him to get back up on his feet. Then a strange thing happened. Stone Head moved forward meekly and began to nuzzle and rub his large head against Scar's chest and flanks. Scar stood very still as this continued, allowing himself to be groomed and rubbed by the same creature which had been attacking him only moments ago. I watched this fascinating behavior until it was over and Scar turned without looking back, disappearing into the northwestern hills and assumedly returning to the rest of the pack. Stone Head turned and moved to the northeast to be lost among the shadows of the orchard trees.

I haven't studied very much biology, and I really don't know much about the pack behavior of big carnivores. But there was definitely something subtle in the way Scar and Stone Head established dominance without actually hurting each other. It makes me wonder again… just how smart are the bigamouths? Could it be that they are the dominant life forms on this world, both in predation and brain power? Have I ruined my possible relations with the dominant species? I keep thinking of those cave drawings in the doublejaw's den. Could those strange, large-mouthed creatures preying on the humanoids be the ancestors of the bigamouths?

I'm not sure. The drawn figures were bipeds, while the bigamouths are quadrupeds. Could they have evolved this way? And who built this compound and the mine underneath it? The bigamouths couldn't be responsible for the delicate metal books I found in the stone box, could they? Could they be the Star People's descendants? Could those horrible drawn figures actually be the Star People?

I wish I could read the writing on those spirals. I wish I could understand.

January 1 – Day 130

Well, I realized that I was a little short-sighted yesterday morning. I spent so much time getting the giant purple potato that I forgot to gather more firewood. My fresh water is low, so I'll have to go out and get some more whistler bush wood if I want to have any pure water to drink this evening. I shouldn't have to worry too much about it. Even though it is mildly dangerous, I think I have this situation pretty well under control now. I'll just check to make sure the coast is clear up on the wall, dash out, and smash a few bushes to bring back inside. If anything goes wrong, I'll have my trusty tooth spike and the flare gun just in case. But I'm not worried. I'm finally starting to feel really in control again.

* * *

Stupid! Stupid, stupid! Why wasn't I careful? Why didn't I check more thoroughly? Make sure the coast was clear? Now I'm in more trouble than ever, and there's no way out. I want to go home! I want home!

* * *

This morning was very, very bad.

I'd gone out to try and get some more firewood. I thought I had checked the fields thoroughly from up on the wall to see if it was safe to leave the compound. It seemed safe enough. Obviously it wasn't.

I was out in the southwest field, smashing the bushes to make kindling. I was nearly done when I realized something was wrong. It was just like before. I could feel the growl more than I could hear it. I looked up, and there was Stone Head, staring at me, his jaw hanging open and quivering. He was much closer than I'd ever been to a member of his pack, just a stone's throw away in the direction of the southeastern orchard, and he looked angry. There was no watching, no staring me down. As soon as I knew he was there he was charging at me.

I had no time to think and barely time to react. My mind said raise up my tooth spike to catch his charge as I'd done before with the crawlers, but my hand raised my flare gun instead. I didn't even know if it would work when I pulled the trigger. It did. Stone Head was within ten feet of me when there was a blinding flash of red that burned away my vision for a moment. I fell to the ground, fumbling for my tooth spike even as I heard Stone Head's howl of terror. It was a horrible sound, like metal being torn in two.

I swear the ground was shaking as I fumbled around until I found my tooth spike. All the world seemed stained green and red from the flash of the flare. Tears were streaming down my face, but I found Stone Head. He had been hit in the eye with the flare. His head was smoking horribly. I coughed and choked as I rammed my tooth spike into him, driven completely by adrenaline. I turned and ran as best I could, not stopping until I got inside the compound and had slammed the door shut behind me. Then I threw up.

Eventually my eyes refocused, and I was able to climb up onto the wall to see what had happened to Stone Head. He was dying, that was plain to see. His body was twisted up horribly, contorting and spasming from the pain in his head. All the fear and anger had gone from me. I felt nothing but a strange kind of pity for the poor creature. He'd only wanted his home back.

After a few moments several of the other bigamouths began to arrive. Scar was among them. They cautiously approached Stone Head, still writhing and smoking terribly. Eventually Scar stood over the dying bigamouth. He was thrumming, a peeling wail echoing softly from somewhere inside his mighty frame. I thought I heard Stone Head whimper in response. Then, with a quick and merciful bite, Scar ended the life of the suffering bigamouth. Instantly the peeling sound from Scar was echoed by the other bigamouths who had gathered. They all came close to the body of Stone Head, the air vibrating with their unhearable tones. I was captivated by fear and fascination. Were they mourning? It certainly looked like they were expressing grief. I felt waves of guilt rush through me. It was my fault.

I think Scar had the same thought. He looked towards the compound, and realized I was watching him. What he did next will haunt me forever. He opened his great jaws. They stretched open, wider than I'd even seen before, wider than I thought physically possible. The scream he gave stopped my heart. It was full of rage and grief and hatred. The others turned and joined his horrible choir. It scared me so badly I actually ran and hid in the longhouse until the thrumming finally died down.

I'm so scared. It was bad enough when they were angry with me for stealing their home, but now I've killed one of their own. There's no chance of their not coming after me now. And I know it won't be just a staring contest next time. That Scar. He'll kill me. He'll use those jaws, those awful jaws…

I can't write. I'm shaking.

January 2 – Day 131

I barely slept last night. It was so hard to close my eyes. I kept seeing the mouth of Scar stretching open for me. The night was filled with the sounds of the bigamouths wailing just outside the front gates. I slept in the longhouse, trying to be as far away from the walls as possible. I almost slept down inside the mine, but the reverberations from the bigamouth's strange calls were even louder down there.

I looked over the wall this morning and found that the bigamouths must have dragged Stone Head's body away some time in the night, as it was nowhere to be seen. But the sentries outside were very plain to see. Two of them, lying just outside of throwing distance in the southern field, facing the gates. They saw me almost as quickly as I saw them, and I ducked out of sight immediately.

What am I going to do? I can't stay here, that much is obvious. It's also obvious that I can't get out. I can't even get to the fields or orchards without getting torn to shreds. What am I going to do?

I have one idea. The mine. Maybe I can find another way out through the tunnels. If not through one of the cleared passages, maybe through one of the ones that's had a cave-in. I don't know much about mining, but it makes sense that there could be another opening somewhere. Or does it make sense? I don't know. I can barely think with that low rumbling. I hear it all the time now, or rather feel it. Or sense it. I don't know, all I know is that I wish it would go away so I could concentrate!

Sorry. Anyway, I'm going to go down in the tunnels for a while and take one of my oars for digging. Maybe I can find some way out of this death trap without the bigamouths even knowing I'm gone. I hope so.

* * *

No luck. It's so hot up here. I'm sweating like a pig. All I can hear is the thrumming of the bigamouths and the whistler bushes. I've got such a headache. Just get a big drink of water and then go back down. I've got to find something.

* * *

I've found something that might work. I wasn't having any luck with the left or middle branches, so I went down the right branch more to look at the stone box than anything else. But while I was down there I realized that there was a shaft leading upwards at a steep angle just a few yards back up the tunnel. It's narrow, about two feet-square, and begins towards the top of a passageway wall. It's not a tunnel, but I think it could have been an air shaft. Makes sense, you'd need to be able to breath down there. I'm not sure where the shaft will lead to. It's so easy to get turned around when you're underground. But I'm going to dig it out. I have to. I have no other chance of getting out of here alive.

I just checked, and there are still two bigamouths watching the gates. They're different from those who were out there this morning. They're taking turns. I have to clear that shaft.

* * *

I couldn't get it done today, I'm just too tired. I have to sleep. I'll get it tomorrow, and then I'll escape. I'm getting out of here. I'm not going to die trapped in here. I'm not.

January 3 – Day 132

Not much time to write. I've got to get that shaft open. It shouldn't take much longer. There are just some loose rocks and dirt. I'm using my hammer and chisel rocks along with my oars to clear it out ahead of me as I crawl. I should be writing my next entry in the free air outside this death trap. Wish me luck, I'll write again soon.

* * *

It's so unfair. Everything. All of it. I hate this world, and I hate everything in it. I can't get out. I'm going to die here.

I was so close. I was climbing up that narrow shaft, clearing dirt and rocks and letting them fall down into the passage behind me. I came to a large clump of dirt blocking the entire shaft. I broke it up, sent it all showering down the shaft. When it finally cleared, and I could open my eyes again, I looked up and saw sunlight! I was thrilled. I thought I was getting out. But there's no getting out for me. I'm not even close to the surface yet, and the light was coming through a hole that would be barely big enough to fit my head through. The entire shaft reduces in size as it goes up. I'd have to dig and widen the entire passage to get out. It's hopeless.

I won't give up. If I have to, I will dig out the entire shaft. I don't care if it is thirty more feet to the surface. I wouldn't care if it were a hundred more feet. I will get out.

I'm hungry. I'm tired of eating purple potato, which is fine, because it's almost gone. I miss being able to eat meat. Even bugs. I wish the climate were wetter so I could find some nice beetles or grubs. I'd even eat banded runner right now. There are still two bigamouths watching the front of this place. Maybe I can watch them. Maybe there's a moment when it would be clear for me to go out and get something to eat as they "change the guard." I'll watch them for a little while. Besides, they aren't the only ones who can play the staring game. I've still got one more flare. They give me a dirty look, they'll end up like Stone Head. I will not be intimidated.

* * *

No hope in sneaking out there. It wasn't ten seconds that I was sitting up on top of the wall before they noticed me. Instantly, both the bigamouths in the southwest field began thrumming. They wouldn't stop. I even thought I'd try to do some sketching up there on the wall, trying to lull them into a false sense of security. It didn't work. The entire time they kept thrumming and staring. I wasn't able to do any sketching. It got so maddening, I started to yell at the bigamouths. At first it was just screaming, but then I started talking to them. I just kept talking and calling out to them, as if they could understand me.

"I'm sorry! I didn't mean to kill Stone Head! He attacked me. Was he just a child to you? Tell Scar I'm sorry! Was Stone Head his son? I'm really very sorry, so stop trying to kill me!"

They didn't seem to care. They just kept staring and thrumming. I'm going back to work on the shaft now. I'll eat the last of the potato for dinner, and then I'll just make do. I remember hearing that you could survive for weeks without food as long as you have water. Well, I have water, and I have enough wood to purifying probably one more batch on the stove in the kitchen. If I stretch it, that's enough for about a week. I could be out of here within that amount of time. I don't have to worry. I have a week. Lots can get done in a week. I'll definitely have that shaft dug up by then.

* * *

Progress is slow. I'm trying to dig out along the bottom part of the shaft to keep from bringing anything more down on me. But it's slow going when I'm lying on my stomach trying to dig above my head. I think I only made about six inches of progress today. But maybe by tomorrow I'll get a rhythm down and I'll go much faster. I hope so. I really hope so.

As a little side note, I noticed that the light coming down the shaft this afternoon manages to bath the stone box in light. I wonder if this branch of the tunnel was set up that way, or if the box was put here after the mine was already dug out. I wish I had the time to study and figure it out, but I'm just too exhausted. Maybe I'll come back some day to look further into it.

I wish I could go home. I don't want to be alone anymore.

January 4 – Day 133

I won't spend too much time writing. I'm going straight down into the tunnels to work on the shaft. With any luck, I can get several feet done by lunch. Or, at least, what would be lunch if I had anything to eat. No matter. I'll get it done anyway.

* * *

This is harder than it looks. It's not possible to do all my digging at the bottom of the shaft, mainly because of the angle that I'm at on my stomach. I have to dig into the sides some as well so I can actually fit through, and then I have these issues of stuff falling into the main shaft where I just dug. I have no idea how the Star People dug this originally. Were they just skinnier than me, or did they use some kind of technique that I'm not thinking of? Either one is possible I suppose. But neither really helps me now.

I'm hungry. I didn't think I would get so hungry so quickly. I only skipped breakfast and lunch. But I'm already turning in knots with hunger. I think it's the fact that I was eating so well and suddenly not at all. My body's just going to have to get used to fasting for a while. As long as I keep myself hydrated I think I should be ok. Worst case scenario, I can just drink the water from the canal without purifying it. I know that has the potential to make me sick, but it's better than dying of dehydration.

Anyway, better get back to work.

* * *

I'm starving. I'm so hungry I can barely work. I thought I was stronger, but apparently I'm not. I don't think it's all my fault. I think I can sense the bigamouths' thrumming even as I'm digging. I'm sure that isn't helping anything. But this hunger... I can't stand it. I can't work so hard on an empty stomach. I feel sick, and I know from experience I can't get very much done this way. I'll have to risk it. I'll have to try going out to the field to get something to eat.

I'll go in the morning. A night's sleep will help me get a little strength. I'll take the flare gun and another tooth spike. I'll be ready this time. I know I can kill them, and I will if I have to. I'm sorry to Scar for killing what may have been his child, but I have to survive too. If they can't let me live with them, then they will have to fight me. And I will fight. But first I need sleep. I want to just sleep.

January 5 – Day 134

I'm going out today. I feel like I'm going to war. I don't want to go out, but I have to. I have to eat. I can't work without food. I have to do it.

I've got the flare gun ready and the tooth spike, along with an oar to dig up some tubers. I'll save the flare until something gets too close. About the distance that Stone Head was at when I shot him. It's no good to try aiming for the eyes, that was a lucky shot. But just hitting one with the flare should be enough to shock and hurt it, I'm sure. Maybe it will kill it. I wouldn't mind. They're trying to kill me.

I didn't want this. They are the ones who brought this on. If I kill more of them, it's their fault. I don't care how intelligent they may be. I have a right to live too. I have a right to fight for life.

OK, no more stalling. I'm going now. God go with me.

* * *

It's here. I can't stop shaking. I know it's in here somewhere. I'm down in the tunnel, by the air shaft, so I think I'm safe. But I'm not sure. Can it move the door? I hope this isn't my last entry.

I went out into the southeast orchard. I didn't have to take my oar because I realized from the wall that some more cherrapples had blossomed since I'd last collected them. I was ready for the bigamouths to attack. My flare gun was ready, my sharpest tooth spike was out in my hand. But they didn't come. Just like Scar had done before, they just watched me, thrumming. Why do they do that?

I kept looking over my shoulder. I could just feel an attack was going to come. But it didn't. I got my cherrapples into my backpack and turned to run back to the gates. I didn't realize at first what was so wrong.

The gates were wide open. Something had gotten in while I was in the orchard. Something is still up there.

I don't know what to do. I closed and barred the gates, so it's only me and whatever got inside. The last thing I need is any more bigamouths getting in here with me. Maybe I'll be lucky and there will only be one of them in the compound, if you can call that lucky. At least it would mean that I have a chance of defeating it. Who knows? If I kill it, maybe I can eat it. Wouldn't that be something? Then I could take my precious time in digging the shaft. It could be my first lucky break in a long time.

Well, I don't have to do it today. I've got all my gear down in the right-hand passage with me. I'll just spend the rest of the daylight working on the shaft, and then in the morning I can go hunting for the bigamouth.

Provided there is just one of them. If not, I'll just go back down into my safe little hole and keep working on this shaft. I have enough fruit to last me two days. It's juicy enough I probably won't need to use as much of my fresh water. Everything's going to work out fine. All I need is for this headache to go away, and I'll be fine.

* * *

The sunlight's dying so I don't have long to write. I don't want to waste my last few torches. Digging went well, I got another three or four feet today. A week's worth of work like that and I should be good and gone. Tomorrow I'll finish off that lone bigamouth, and have meat again for the first time in I don't remember how long. I'm going to be ok. I am going to survive.

January 6 – Day 135

I'm so scared. They're in. All of them. I went out this morning and the gate was open. Open! I know I locked it last night but whatever got in last night opened it. They let in all the rest of the pack. Even standing there in the middle of the compound, I could feel the thrumming all around me. Inside of me. They're here. They're close. I can't fight off all of them.

I'm back down in the tunnel. I hope I'm alone. I barely made it down here. As soon as I realized what had happened I turned and sprinted back to the longhouse. I was down the hole and pulling the door back over it even as I heard the pattering of footsteps behind me. I caught a glimpse of who it was that came into the longhouse as I struggled with the door. It was Scar. The door was barely in place before I heard the footsteps above me, and then a scraping on the stonewood door. I ran in the darkness all the way here to the light shaft. I want to at least see them coming.

They may already be down here. The door is definitely in place, but who's to say they can't open it? They opened the front gate. The lock was a simple mechanism, a stonewood plank placed on two carved brackets to hold it. The door to the tunnels is just a square made from planks of stonewood set into grooves cut into more stonewood in the floor. I'm not even sure how I moved it into place with just my hands. I guess adrenaline really does work, because I didn't even notice until the light was completely shut off from above me. But can the bigamouths open it? Will they come after me? They have their home back now, but has everything become personal?

Well, as long as they can't move the door I'm safe. I still have my water and a day's worth of food. I can work on my shaft. I can still get free. I can get out of here. Let them keep their stupid home. Just so I can live. Please let me live. I've worked so hard... only to die down here. Please... let me live.

I better get to work while I have the strength. Wish me luck. Please.

* * *

That thrumming. The thrumming. It's so loud. I can't think. Can barely work or write. So much worse than before. Can't make good progress. Trying! Try until I die. But hard, so hard. My head feels like it will explode. It hurts.

Made more progress. Don't know how much, but I am going to get through. I will!

Gotta eat, rest, then work some more. I don't need light to work. I can dig in the dark as the sun sets. I want out. Get me out!

Mom, Mom can you hear me? I love you. Please think about your little boy. Please love me. I miss you and Dad. Dad, take a turn at helping me dig? I'm tired. Bryant, Mark, go watch the door? Make sure nothing comes in. Sarah, don't worry, we'll be safe. I'll protect you. Kiss me in the dark and everything will be all right.

I have to keep going. Too dark to see. Must keep digging.

Expedition Log
3rd of Lark, in the 2nd year of The Return
Yurril T'nak, field scout

We have finally found the nyrium mine amid the endless grassy hills of this plain. We take courage that our goal is close in sight. But it seems we have a final trial before we can begin our search for the Records and Symbols. From a nearby hill we can see that a pack of the same jawed beasts which attacked us three days ago seems to have taken the remaining buildings above the mine as their own personal dwelling place. We do not know if they have found or are using the tunnels underneath the surface where the Records and Symbols were most likely kept. We are also unable to determine how many of the creatures there are, although Flain has supposed that there must be at least fourteen individuals, counting their young.

We are unsure of how we should proceed, whether we should move in to usurp these interlopers or wait in case they decide to move on and leave the mine site unmolested. Brendell is seeking Shaelon's guidance even now. If we are to attack it will be most dangerous, as our weapons are nearly spent and our numbers are few. Perhaps it would be best to wait.

In observing the jawed beasts' habits we have noticed that the majority of them seem to spend most of their time inside the structure which covers the mine's major entrance. Perhaps they prefer the larger building as a central commons for their den, or the entrance to the mine is open and they are using the tunnels as their underground warren. They seem distinctly agitated however, not at all like creatures which are comfortable with their surroundings. They make their strange calls incessantly to each other, and Brendell warns that we must guard our hearts against the maddening effect of their voices.

We will stand ready and follow Brendell's guidance. If he says we are to move in, then we shall invade these creatures' home to drive them out with all the fury we can muster. If not, then we shall wait to see what shall occur. We are but instruments in Shaelon's hands, and we wait upon His direction.

Grace be to you. Yurril T'nak

January 7 – Day 136

I'm not going to make it. I'm not digging fast enough. The thrumming keeps going, but I'm used to it, like a steady headache you just deal with. I'm still so far away from the surface. How will I ever get that far? I should give up, except I have nothing left to do. I can't just let myself die of dehydration. I have to try. I don't want to open the door to die at the hands of the bigmouths. But, maybe they'd be merciful and kill me with a single bite. That may not be so bad.

What am I saying!? I have to survive! I will survive! I'm digging some more.

* * *

Did I close the door to the mine? I know I said I did, but did I actually do it? The adrenaline was pumping so hard in my veins I didn't really know what was happening. Maybe I only thought I'd closed it, and then ran before I could really check. But do I want to risk going back there to check?

No, it's bad enough as it is. At least here I have light during the days. I can see a little of what's coming. In the tunnels I'd be totally in the dark. I'm out of torches. I'd have to crawl there. I'd be completely helpless. No, I'm going to stay here and dig. I've got to dig.

Oh my head hurts so much. I just want to get out of this shaft! I want the sunlight! I wish I were back at Misty Falls, or the Purple Desert, or a

Dairy Queen. I'd love to have some chicken tenders with gravy. Or a milkshake. Or see Sarah. Sarah please help me…

I have to dig. Dig. Goodbye.

* * *

God help me.

* * *

I'm so tired. I've got to sleep. I wanted to write more, but I'm so tired. Love.

January 8 – Day 137

I thought about it all night, and I know I didn't close that door. I thought I had, but I didn't. I have to do that. Just to buy myself some time. I can dig out, but I have to close that door first. Then the thrumming will stop. I'll be able to think again. My head will stop spinning. I'm hurting so bad. Everything hurts. Please, let me go close the door so I can get back to escaping. I'll go now. I have to close the door.

* * *

I didn't go. My head hurts too much. Try to dig a little more.

Ow… Please make it stop. Stop the thrumming, Scar. I didn't mean to kill Stone Head…

* * *

Now I'll go close the door. Then I can dig. Close the door, then dig. Ok, be right back. Ok.

* * *

It won't be long now. The door was open. Wide open. Light was pouring down. They must already be down here. They're probably starting at the left and working their way around. I'm ready. I have my gun and spikes and pocket knife. I will fight. I will stop the thrumming. I'll kill each one as it arrives. I'll kill all of them. I'm ready to fight. I'm ready to die.

* * *

The thrumming has stopped. It's so peaceful. Death is coming soon. I'll put my journal in the stone box so they won't get it. I want everyone to know. I want them to know that I survived. I survived! For one hundred and thirty-seven days, I survived. Pretty good I think. Could have been longer, but that shaft is too high.

* * *

Thought I'd heard something. It's black now, it's night. I can't see what I'm writing. I'll wait until I hear something, and then I'll shoot. I want to say goodbye to Mom, Dad, Bryant, Mark, and Sarah. I love you all. I did really good. I did my best. I'm ready to quit now. I'm tired.

But I will fight. I'm a survivor. Remember, I was a survivor.

Here they come. I'll see you soon.

THE STAR PEOPLE

Expedition Log
5th of Lark, in the 2nd year of The Return
Yurril T'nak, field scout

    At long last, our journey has ended. We have found the Records and the Symbols which we came seeking. Already Brendell has divined some of the Symbols' power, and with them we shall finally be able to return home. We have truly been blessed. We know Shaelon has carried us in the palm of His hand.

    It also gladdens me that the young stranger we found inside the tunnels woke briefly today. While the Symbols allowed us to communicate with him, he was not conscious long enough for us to learn anything of who he is or how he came to be here. We've yet to understand the simple message he gave us before passing out once more: "I'll have fries with that shake."

Grace be, Yurril T'nak

January 11 – Day 140

    I finally feel good enough to write a little. My head still hurts, and I feel weak all over, but I need to write.

    I'm safe now… I think. The bigamouths are gone, but I'm not alone any more.

    The last thing I remember was lying in the dark waiting for Scar and the rest. After I finished writing what I thought was my last entry I put my journal into the stone box and crouched behind it, listening. The thrumming had stopped, and I almost passed out from the relief, though the pain in my head continued. I listened there in the blackness, holding my flare gun and tooth spike.

There was a soft sound like a hand drawn across leather, and a click of something hard against the stone floor. The sounds grew louder but I waited. I only had one shot. I heard the sound of heavy breathing. It felt so close.

Suddenly there was a thrumming growl. I pointed the flare gun into the darkness and pulled the trigger. There was a brilliant flash and I was blind. I'd forgotten to close my eyes. Something howled nearby. I held up my tooth spike, but I couldn't see anything. I tried to crouch lower behind the stone box, thrusting the point of my tooth spike into the empty space around me.

There was a strange whimper from nearby, followed by a staccato, high-pitched call. The sound assaulted my ears and I felt as if my head would explode. My skull seemed too small to contain the echoes of the shrieking call and I felt my mind snap under the strain. That's the last thing I remember before waking up much later.

I remember having dreams that seemed to last for weeks. I attended my classes, went camping with my family, went on dates with Sarah. I talked and laughed with friends and family I hadn't seen in months. Slowly, their familiar voices became strange to me, more resonate and deep. There was a light, and finally I realized I wasn't dreaming. I was hearing voices. Real voices.

I have to go, someone's coming.

* * *

Ok, I'm back.

Like I said earlier, I'm not alone anymore. I think these are the Star People. The ones who originally built the lighthouse and this compound. They're not human, but they're close enough for me. Some of the differences are pretty obvious. The smallest of them is at least a head taller than me, and their skin seems to come in a variety of colors. There are other things that are different, but I'm getting tired of writing.

I will say that I'm very grateful that we can speak the same language. I think it has something to do with the tokens I found in the stone box down in the mines. These people have brought the box up into the compound and have been busily working, heating the small coin-like discs until they are able to punch a hole in the flattened end and then run a length of string through it. Each of them is wearing one of these small medallions. I'm wearing one too. They must have put it on me while I was unconscious.

I can't write anymore. My head is throbbing and I can barely hold my pen. I'll write again in the morning, if I can.

Expedition Log
6th of Lark, in the 2nd year of The Return
Yurril T'nak, field scout

The young man has awoken and seems to be recovering. He has kept to himself, writing much in a strange book he never allows far from him. We have given him food, which he accepts and eats, but there have been few words passed between us. He is still weak, and I marvel that such a small child of Shaelon could survive against the jawed beasts for so long.

And yet, it was a close thing. When Brendell said it was the will of Shaelon that we attack and drive the jawed beasts from the nyrium mine, we charged forward with the might and fervor of vengeful glories. Most of the beasts fled the outbuildings after we had fired several blasts into the air, but we soon discovered that some of them had managed to open the entrance to the mine and were scattered among the dark tunnels. These we were forced to fight in the terrifying darkness, the flash of our weapons like lightening strokes in the blackness of night. Three of the creatures fell before our might in the northeast and northern tunnels before we explored further into the eastern passage.

It was then we saw a brilliant flash of light down the corridor, followed by horrible screams. We flew down the passage just as a magnesium candle spent itself against the far wall. It was there we saw the young man crouched in a corner and a monstrous beast with a deep scar in its side before him. The creature charged us, but Flain, our ever-present guardian, faced the monster with naught but a small blade he keeps always on his belt. We emptied a dozen shots into the creature before it finally gave up its essence, though it did take Flain some twenty minutes to retrieve his blade from where he had wedged it into the joint of the beast's jaw.

The battle won, we turned our attention to the young man. We knew at once he was not Freiisianen, but could not discover among us who he was or where he had come from. Brendell bid that we see to his needs and carry him away from the darkness of the mines. In the light we saw that he was very thin and we feared he might not live. But through Brendell's tender ministrations he has recovered enough that now we must decide what is to be done with him.

Brendell has said he will speak to the man today if he is able, and discover what he may about the young man's past. How did he come to be here? What did he know of the Symbols and Records that we found him so close to? We share the hope that the Divant may discover these mysteries soon, that we may begin preparations for our return to Freiisian.

Grace be to you, Yurril T'nak

January 12 – Day 141

I've just had a very long talk with one of the Star Men. He called himself Brendell, and seems to be the leader of the group. He told me a little about them, and why they are here on Other World.

Apparently, they're some of the descendants of the original Star People that originally built this mine and the lighthouse. In the distant past the Star People were world travelers, but somehow the means of moving from world to world was lost. Brendell was unsure how it had happened, but he said he was a Divant, a kind of holy man, and that he'd received direction from his god that the time had come to rediscover the Star People's secrets. They found an ancient device on their world that would open what he called doorways between worlds, and used it to come to Other World. Unfortunately, it broke when they arrived, and they've been stuck here ever since, trying to find a way home.

He then asked me to explain how I had come to this world. I told him about the strange portal that seemed to open in the sky in front of Dave and I. As I spoke, the Divant's eyes went wide, and he suddenly dropped his head into his overlarge hands.

"So, arrogance has followed my people even since our fall," he muttered to himself. "To think that we deemed the risk too small to be concerned with. More lives on my hands for my foolish pride."

I didn't know what he was talking about until he explained that they were responsible for the portal we had passed through. Suddenly it all made sense. I wasn't sure how I should be feeling. Grateful for being saved from the bigamouths or furious that they were responsible for stranding me out here and for Dave's death. Maybe I was feeling some of both.

Brendell seemed to realize at least some of what was going on inside of me, because he looked at me and apologized for all the hell I'd been put through because of their actions. I had wanted to make some angry retort, but I just couldn't. He seemed so sincere. And he hadn't intended for any of this to happen. Besides, I'd been alone too long to throw away someone, anyone, trying to reach out to me. I accepted his apology.

Brendell says that he will do everything he can to make it up to me. With the medallion that he's wearing he says he can read the strange metal books from the stone box, and that he thinks he'll soon understand the process of traveling from world to world. Once that happens, he says that he and his companions will take me home.

Home. I'd given up on ever going back. It's been almost four months since I left it. Can I really just go back? What will I say when people ask me where I've been? What am I going to do?

Expedition Log
7th of Lark, in the 2nd year of The Return
Yurril T'nak, field scout

Brendell has told us of Richard's story, and it grieves me to know that we have been unknowingly responsible for his long suffering on this world. However, all is in Shaelon's hands, and perhaps we will one day discover a great purpose for his sufferings.

Brendell's study of the Records has at last revealed how we may return home, and we make our final preparations for the journey. Our task has been achieved, but the cost was dear. The deaths of our rebellious brethren and Richard's companion weigh heavily on our minds. The sacrifice that they have made must not be forgotten. We shall press on.

Now that we have the Records and Symbols, we can at last begin restoring the glorious work that the ancestors began so long ago. It will begin with exploration. Perhaps we will soon return to this world to discover its secrets, but whether we return or not, we will follow the will of Shaelon. May we prove worthy to continue this great work.

Grace be to you. Yurril T'nak

January 13 – Day 142

I've had another talk with Brendell. He told me that he now understands how to take me home, and that they're preparing to leave soon. I'm nervous, but I've been thinking it over and I think I have a plan for what to do when I get home.

I won't tell anyone about Other World. How could they believe me? I'll have no proof about where I've been since Brendell says that his group isn't ready to make contact with Earth yet. My plan is to say that Dave's plane crashed into the ocean around the San Juan Islands, and I've been surviving on a small uninhabited island since that time. I'll have to make a raft or something to get me to civilization, which will give me time to make up the story of my survival on a small island. Hopefully Brendell can find an island to suite my purposes to drop me off on. I thought about asking his group for help in making my raft and gathering supplies, but I don't think I'll need it. After four months on Other World, another week on an island back on Earth will seem like a vacation.

So, tonight's my last night on Other World. Looking up at the violet-blue sky and the two moons, I feel excited, melancholy, and afraid. This place has been terrible at times, but it's also been wonderful at times. Catching moths at Misty Falls, watching the giant, luminescent creature swim under my dugout, watching the wind move through the sea grass like waves on the ocean… There's a part of me that will miss this place. Miss it terribly. Earth is going to seem very ordinary after all of this.

I've been thinking about what I'll do once I start my life again. Maybe I'll try to get work as a writer for one of those magazines that sends its people into the Amazon or the Sahara. If nothing else, I think I've developed more skills in the art of survival and writing about my experiences than they could ever hope for. I think it's a great idea, and as always, it feels good to have a plan. Yes, I'm looking forward to this next adventure. I'm going home.

Finally, I'm going home.

ABOUT THE AUTHOR

Lindsay Schopfer is the author of two novels, the sci-fi survivalist *Lost Under Two Moons* and the steampunk adventure *The Beast Hunter*, as well as the fantasy short story collection *Magic, Mystery and Mirth*. When he isn't writing, Lindsay is a writing coach and instructor for Adventures In Writing, where he helps writers learn about and improve their craft. His workshops and panels have been featured in a variety of Cons and writing conferences across the Pacific Northwest, and he is a member of the Northwest Independent Editors Guild. He is also a mentor for Educurious, a Gates Foundation-funded program designed to connect high school students with professional writers.

Made in the USA
Monee, IL
10 March 2024

54298315R00125